The Marginalised

TERESA DEVEREUX

Matador
9 Priory Business Park,
Wistow Road, Kibworth Beauchamp,
Leicestershire, LE8 0RX
Tel: 0116 279 2299
Email: books@troubador.co.uk
Web: www.troubador.co.uk/matador
Twitter: @matadorbooks

ISBN 978 1800464 117

British Library Cataloguing in Publication Data.
A catalogue record for this book is available from the British Library.

Printed and bound in Great Britain by 4edge Limited
Typeset in 11pt Garamond by Troubador Publishing Ltd, Leicester, UK

Matador is an imprint of Troubador Publishing Ltd

To my husband Grahame and daughter Louise for their patience and support. To my granddaughter Iola for her talented photography, which produced the book cover, and my other two grandchildren Amelie and Sabastian for posing so beautifully in the photograph. I would also like to say thank you to my good friend Amanda, a hardworking and dedicated social worker who played an important role in forming the final draft of 'The Marginalised'.

Tves- Devereux

1

SAMANTHA

After the final hearing, social worker April Gardiner watched from the first-floor window of the courtroom as the lone figure of Samantha Bushell walked away from the building. Hands in pockets and shoulders hunched against the cold, her thin nylon jacket thrashed about her in the wind.

It was the 21st December and just after 5pm when she walked along the high street on her route back to her flat. The shop windows were ablaze with fairy lights of all shapes and colours. 'Away in a Manger' played softly from a stationary fire engine in the pedestrianised area, and one of the firemen held out a helmet in front of her as she walked by, asking for a donation for Save the Children. She walked blindly past. The festive jollity intensified her sense of loneliness.

She crossed Princess Park. There had been a market earlier, and a few stallholders were packing up the last of their goods and throwing them into the backs of their vans. The festive atmosphere behind her, Samantha crossed the road into Coronation Estate and then around the corner to Elder Road and her flat. She unlocked the communal front door, and as she walked in, the damp coldness of the building struck her like a slap in the face. With a very heavy heart, she continued up the stairs to the small landing and, with the door to her flat facing her, stood for a moment looking at it, reluctant to confront the emptiness inside.

This was the first time she had come home to her flat knowing that her girls would never return there. She hadn't believed this could be possible. She'd always believed they would come back. It seemed impossible that children could be taken away from their mother and be adopted. She felt she had been a good mother. She had done her best and loved them to bits. Somewhere though, deep within, there was an awareness that she hadn't been coping, and knowing that her girls now had a nice home to live in, and two parents who could give them everything they needed, made the burden of grief a bit easier to bear.

It was just as cold inside the flat as it had been in the corridor, and her whole body shivered as she walked inside. Keeping her jacket on, she went to the meter and fed it some coins. The old central heating boiler groaned into action. There wasn't much food in the kitchen, but there was a stock of strong cider and, taking one of the bottles she sat down on the settee, intending to drink herself into oblivion. What did it matter now? She had lost everything. There was a screwed-up letter in the bin telling her that she had fourteen days to leave the flat. She had only read it once but the words were imprinted on her memory. If she didn't leave within that time, she would be taken to court. The letter went on to say that, if it became necessary to apply to the court, she would be likely to incur court costs which could amount to over a thousand pounds. Samantha was seething about this. She'd known it was coming but it felt so unfair. She had got into rent arrears because her benefits hadn't been paid. Somebody – she never had found out who – had reported to the Social that she had someone living with her, which had led to her benefits being stopped. Although it was true that Curtis had stayed with her sometimes, he hadn't been living with her and he certainly hadn't given her any money. By the time the benefits were reinstated she had accrued substantial rent arrears which she'd struggled to pay off. She'd barely had enough to get by from week to week, let alone extra for rent. That said, she had managed to pay off small bits here and there, but, to add insult to injury, after Tayla and Lily Grace were taken into foster care, her benefits stopped again, and the rent arrears escalated.

As if it wasn't bad enough to lose her children, now she was going to lose her flat as well. She didn't like April Gardiner but at least she had tried to help her keep the flat. The landlord had let her stay a bit longer since April's intervention, but the shorthold tenancy had ended and she still hadn't managed to catch up with the rent. The letter had arrived the day before the final hearing.

Sam hated the flat, and since Tayla and Lily Grace had been taken from her she hated it even more. She wanted to move, and had planned to ask the council to find her somewhere else. She had been helped before when Tayla was a baby. They had put her in a hostel for young mothers. She hadn't liked it, but it was somewhere to live, somewhere to come back to.

With each bottle of cider, her optimism grew. Feeling confident that she would be helped, she stretched out on the settee and spent the rest of the evening floating in a drunken haze of illusory happiness.

She woke early in the morning with a thumping headache and feeling sick. The money in the meter had run out and she was shivering with the cold. She took three paracetamol, gulped down with black coffee. She didn't want any breakfast. There wasn't much in the cupboard anyway, apart from a few tins of beans (which she really didn't fancy) and some dried pasta. She turned on the television, sat back down on the settee and snuggled beneath a faded tartan blanket. After a bit, the pain in her head seemed to lift and she decided to get herself ready and go to the council offices to find out where she was going to live. She pulled on a pair of black jeans which she had purchased in the children's department in Primark, and topped them off with a colourful jumper which hung loosely around her small frame. She tipped her head upside down and brushed her hair vigorously before pulling it together with an elastic band. If it hadn't been for the crow's feet and the dark shadows around her eyes, she could easily have been mistaken for an adolescent girl.

It was after 11.30 when she arrived at the council offices. The large double doors swung open as she approached and she found herself at the start of a wide, high-ceilinged corridor. Following the signs, she came to the customer service area, went immediately to the counter, gave her name and a brief summary of why she was there.

'Take a seat, please,' the woman said sharply. 'There's a queue but someone will call you shortly.'

Samantha looked around to see, sitting in rows on tubular steel chairs, a number of other people with solemn faces, waiting patiently.

After a long tiresome wait, she was finally called into a small side room. The woman (who she guessed was probably younger than she was, with long, shiny black hair, a heavily made-up face and fancy nails) looked at her coldly and, in a tone that resonated boredom, asked her why she was there. After finishing her story about losing her children, her benefits being stopped, and how she had already been in rent arrears due to her benefits being stopped once before, Sam took a deep breath and sat back in the chair, waiting for the woman to end her troubles.

The woman did not hesitate. In the tone of a recorded message, she said, 'I'm sorry but we can't help you. From what you have told me, you have made yourself intentionally homeless. You have no children with you; therefore the council has no obligation to house you.' The response was cold, unsympathetic and devoid of any compassion.

Samantha just stared at her, speechless. She hadn't expected this. Then, struggling to hold back the tears, she managed to ask, 'What am I supposed to do then? I can't get private rented. I haven't got a deposit and no one will have me anyway. Where will I go? I've only got just over a week' She held out her hands in despair.

The woman shrugged her shoulders. 'I'm sorry. Why don't you go home to your family?'

Once again, Samantha found herself almost speechless. The girl had no idea about anything. She didn't say any more; she just stood up and, with her head spinning in disbelief, walked out of the building.

By the time the eviction period was up, Samantha had left the flat. She had taken a few of her possessions with her. Not much. A few photos of the children, some clothes, a hairbrush, and bits and pieces from the bathroom. There wasn't much in the flat that belonged to her anyway.

Her mum had said she could sleep on their settee as long as she got herself sorted out quickly. To Sam's surprise, Wayne had agreed to the plan. Unfortunately, it wasn't long before things went pear-shaped. Three days, to be exact. Sam had been trying hard not to cause any problems, treading on eggshells. She knew what would happen if she upset Wayne: he would have her out on the streets with no second thoughts. She hadn't been sleeping very well on the settee. It was plenty long enough for her small body, but it was hard. Instead of springs there were planks of wood holding it together, topped by a long, thin cushion and covered by an old candlewick bedspread which stank of dog and stale sweat. On the third morning she woke in the early hours. The dawn was just starting to break. Her body ached and she knew there would be no more sleep for her now, so she got up and switched on the television. She made a cup of tea before making herself as comfortable as possible back on the settee. The programme she was watching was something about a sheep farmer, which she had no interest in, but the mindless viewing settled her down and she started to drift towards sleep.

All of a sudden a loud thump from upstairs startled her into wakefulness and, sitting bolt upright, she held her breath. The thump was followed by footsteps stomping down the stairs. Her pulse began to race; she knew it was Wayne, and that she was in trouble.

'What the fuck do you think you're doing in my house? Look at you, you fucking waster, lying there like Lady Muck watching my telly and drinking my tea. You haven't given your mum a penny towards your keep. What do you think this is, a charity?' He was standing over her intimidatingly, arms flailing.

Samantha couldn't speak. She didn't know how to respond. She knew Wayne well enough to know that whatever she said would only make things worse. The tirade of verbal abuse continued until the lounge door flew open and she could see her mum standing in the doorway, her faded blue dressing gown over her nightie and her grey-brown hair in tangles.

'What's going on here?' she asked, looking from Wayne to Samantha and back again.

'It's your daughter, little shit that she is. Look!' he said, thrusting his forefinger violently towards the clock on the mantlepiece. 'Four o' fucking clock. We're all awake now. She sleeps on our settee, eats our food – don't give us any money though does she?'

'She hasn't been here long, though, she—'

For a brief moment Samantha thought her mum was going to take her side.

'Oh, is that right? She hasn't been here long,' he repeated sarcastically. 'Well, she's been here long enough. I want her out.'

Samantha looked towards her mother, hoping for support, but instead her mother turned around and walked back up the stairs, submitting as usual to the man in her life rather than standing up for her offspring.

'I want you out by the time I get up,' Wayne snarled, sprays of saliva flying from his mouth. With his wild, contorted face and his thick neck, he reminded Samantha of a rabid bull mastiff, like the one that Tayla's dad used to own.

She was petrified. She knew he meant it. She had not expected it to last, knowing what her mother's partner was like, but she had thought that, if she trod carefully, she might be able to stay until she had something else sorted. As it was, she had no idea what she could do or where she could go, but she had to be out of the house before Wayne got up again, otherwise all hell would break loose. She didn't dare make any breakfast, so just gathered her few belongings, threw them into her rucksack and walked out of the house, slamming the door hard behind her. She was seething with anger and hurt – not towards Wayne, that's what she expected from him, but towards her mother. She would never forget watching her mother as she turned around and walked back up those stairs, leaving her to her fate.

As she made her way across Princess Park, tears began to flow. She looked across at the bench where she used to meet her drinking pals. They didn't come any more; she wasn't sure why. It was still very early in the morning but the rising sun was reflecting off the frost-covered ground. It was too cold to sit so she just kept walking; she didn't know where to. Her flat had not been the most comfortable home but it had been somewhere to go, to sit, to eat, to sleep and to belong. It was home, and home draws you back like an umbilical cord, however humble. She could never have imagined how dreadful it would feel to have nowhere to go. Helpless, frightened, cold, detached from anything, disconnected, alone.

2

APRIL

April was woken by the sound of Demelza's endearing chatter as she moved around in her cot. She lay there, enjoying listening to her daughter from the adjacent room. Jed, who was lying beside her, continued to sleep. The bedroom doors were ajar and April could see a streak of sunlight beaming across the baby's room, and within that, the silhouette of her child as she tried to find a comfortable spot under her duvet to put her teddy to bed. Since Demelza seemed perfectly happy, April decided to leave her to play for a while and enjoy a few minutes' relaxation whilst she had the chance. After all, it was only 6am and in a few days' time everything would change as April's maternity leave came to an end.

Whilst she lay in bed, April's thoughts returned to the awful days when she and Jed had thought they would never have their own child. She had vivid memories of how it had felt to want something so desperately and fail to achieve it. It had been particularly harsh because every woman around her of childbearing age had seemed to get pregnant with ease. She remembered the deep feeling of failure eating away at her sense of identity; wondering why she could not do what almost every other woman could. She remembered the combination of pain and compassion in Jed's warm brown eyes as he tried to console her by pretending it didn't matter. And now here they were, parents to the most adorable little girl. April still had to pinch herself sometimes when she thought about how things had turned out.

Jed turned over onto his side and, still half asleep, placed his arm over her and drew her towards him. She allowed herself to be moved across, and nestled into his warm body. *I have everything I have ever wanted*, she thought as Jed continued in his state of half-slumber. She couldn't help wondering what it would have been like if things had not turned out the way they had. They had given up on having their own child and had been planning to adopt. Would they have had the same pride and unconditional love for an adopted child that they felt for Demelza? She would like to think so, but who knows?

Demelza was now calling her. 'Mummummum.'

April could see that she had pulled herself up and was moving her little body back and forwards against the railings as she called out. She pushed the duvet aside, swung her legs over the side of the bed and walked across the small space between her bedroom and Demelza's. The child beamed with happiness as her mum appeared before her, arms already outstretched, ready to be picked up.

'Hello, my little angel, what a good girl you've been for Mummy and Daddy. Shall we go and wake Daddy up?'

Demelza chuckled as April bounced her up and down whilst heading back to her bedroom. She placed Demelza on top of Jed and climbed in beside him, watching as Demelza leant over him and tried to prise open his eyes with her tiny fingers. April watched Jed emerge into full consciousness, and the look of delight appear on his face as his eyes were prodded and Demelza's incomprehensible but earnest chattering reached his ears. He suddenly grabbed her by the waist and lifted her high in the air, and she squealed as she went up, legs and arms thrashing around helplessly.

'What shall we do today, then? It's all change on Monday,' April remarked.

Jed yawned. 'I might just stay here.'

April became thoughtful. She sat up in bed and wrapped her arms around her folded knees. 'I'm not sure about going back to work now. I might change my mind and stay at home. I hate the thought of leaving Demelza. What if she misses me?'

'You've been spoilt, April. Too accustomed to lazing around and doing nothing, strolling off to mother-and-toddler groups, chatting, drinking coffee, daytime television, afternoon naps.'

April poked him in the stomach. This was Jed's wicked sense of humour, although she wondered how much he really understood about the amount of work involved in keeping a house *and* looking after a toddler. Saying that, Jed had said all along that she didn't have to go back to work if she didn't want to. His salary was easily enough to provide them with a comfortable lifestyle. April had considered staying at home, but worried that she would find herself getting bored just being a mother. She loved her job, and missed the frenetic adrenaline rush of the social work team. Going back had seemed like a good idea, but now the time had come, all she could think about was parting from Demelza for two-and-a-half days a week; going out in the morning and not seeing her again until bedtime. April's mum was going to babysit for the first few days, but after that Demelza would have to go to nursery. April was dreading that.

'Right, I know what we should do today. We should take Demelza to the swimming pool; she loves being in the water. You can go down the slides with her. We could go to the seafront afterwards and put her on some of those little rides. It looks like it's going to be a nice day. We could take a picnic,' April said, slapping Jed's arm to get him moving.

'OK, I suppose we should get up, then. You make breakfast and I'll do the egg sandwiches to take with us.'

The kitchen soon became a hive of activity. Jed was working on one side, next to the cooker, as steam from the boiling eggs billowed up towards the extractor fan. He hummed an unrecognisable tune as he buttered slices of multi-seed bread. Demelza was sitting on a soft woolly rug in the dining area, both legs beneath her, chatting away to her teddy as she pushed it head first into its pushchair. At the same time, April put containers of muesli, Weetabix and yoghurt on the table, alongside a jug of milk. Just as she finished placing the spoons beside the floral table mats, the phone started to ring.

'Morning, Diana… yes, we're fine, thanks. Just getting breakfast,' April heard Jed say. 'It's your mum.' He held out the phone in front of him and handed it to April, who couldn't hear a thing with all the noise going on around her.

'Hello, Mum; I'm just going out of the kitchen where it's quiet. Yes, we're looking forward to seeing you tomorrow. I'll be at the station to pick you up at 10.45. Yes, Demelza slept really well. She rarely wakes up in the night now. OK, I'll put her on. Demelza, it's Nanny on the phone; say hello to Nanny.'

April pressed the loudspeaker button before bending down to hold the phone against Demelza's ear. Demelza, not happy about her mum having control of the phone, pushed her head backwards and tried to pull it out of April's hand. April tried to keep hold of it but Demelza became quite determined and, with both hands around it, pulled with all her might, saying, 'Mine!' April gave in, and Demelza held the phone upside down against her cheek and babbled in response to Diana's questions.

'How is my little darling today?' Diana asked.

In less than a minute Demelza grew bored. She placed the phone carefully on the floor beside her and turned her attention back to her teddy, which was upside down in the pushchair, completely covered by a blanket.

April was, as always, looking forward to seeing her mum, but due to recent events concerning her father there had been a bit of a strained atmosphere between them. They had been a close-knit family – April, her mum and her twin brother Max – especially as there had only been the three of them. That was, until circumstances occurred which brought their father, Diana's ex-husband, back into their lives. This had had a huge impact on the family dynamics. Diana had always been a loving, forgiving mother who lived for her children, but overshadowing this was the unspoken mystery of her husband, who had supposedly walked out of their lives when April and Max were babies, never to be heard of again, or mentioned, until April turned their lives upside down by finding him.

Jed sat in the driving seat as April strapped Demelza into her seat in the back. The warm wind blew her dark curls across her face as she struggled to find the clasp. To make it even more difficult, Demelza wriggled and twisted her body in her attempt to assist with the task.

'Sit still for Mummy please, Demelza, I can't do it if you keep moving.'

She finally heard the sharp click, slammed the door shut, and was just about to climb in beside Jed when she remembered the bag with Demelza's armbands in it which she'd left lying in the hallway. 'I won't be a minute,' she shouted as she ran back up the short path to the house.

Jed rolled his eyes. He had made a point of asking her if she was sure she had picked everything up before slamming the front door shut. This wasn't like April; she used to be so organised. He couldn't help feeling a bit concerned about how she was going to manage her job, which was all-consuming, as well as being a mother, which had been her total focus for over a year now, notwithstanding the pregnancy, which had been tense from beginning to end.

As they drove away, April gloried in the array of colourful hanging baskets that were beginning to appear on people's walls. It was early May, and the rows of identical Edwardian houses with their bay windows and black-and-white facades were lit up by a range of spring flowers in assorted colours illuminated by the sun. She was reminded of when they'd first moved to this area just over two years before. It had been May then, too, and just as colourful. April had fallen in love with the house, the street and the area, with its closeness to the sea, and its location which, although it appeared rural, was on the outskirts of town. Still, it was a double-edged sword because, for all her delight in their new home, the tragic circumstances which had led them to move cast a dark shadow which refused to disperse. Even though they now had Demelza, the painful memories from years of IVF and April's miscarriage had left their scars.

At the pool, Jed sat Demelza on his knee while he slid down the water slide. Demelza screeched with delight, squeezing her eyes closed as they hit the water. She was confident enough to swim off, held up by her armbands; she had no fear of the water. April watched from the side, laughing. Afterwards, leaving the car in the pool car park, they put Demelza in her buggy, which Jed pushed as they walked to the beach. April laid out the picnic blanket on the grass overlooking the bay and started to open the wrappers containing the sandwiches. Demelza was enthralled by the seagulls, which flew at them brazenly, trying to snatch their picnic, whilst Jed and April waved their arms frantically in an attempt to ward them off.

They were all tired on the way home but Demelza was asleep within minutes. April watched as her eyes slowly closed, opened for a second in her fight to stay awake, then closed again, her dark lashes motionless against her cheeks.

'How nice is that?' April commented. 'To just sleep when you feel like it, without a care in the world?'

'We haven't got too much to worry about, really, have we, April?'

'No. You're absolutely right. We haven't, and I will never fail to remember that.' April detected a hint of mild criticism in Jed's comment, but nevertheless, it started her thinking about some of the families she had come across in the course of her work, and the sadness and hopelessness of their situations. She had never forgotten Samantha Bushell, and watching her walk away from the court that day. That was nearly two years ago now, and how ironic it was that the day Samantha's children had been officially removed from her care had also been the day that April felt the first flutter from the baby inside her.

3

ISOBEL

Isobel sat on her bed, gazing out of the window, watching the stream of fluffy white clouds moving swiftly across the dull grey sky. Her eyes appeared focused but were oblivious to the outside world. Her thoughts came from deep within. She wanted to get up and do something but had no motivation to move. When she'd lived at home, she had been allowed to go out with her mates. They would hang around the park, smoke, chat. She used to get bored at times, but never as bored as she felt now. She had been excluded from school for two weeks, and since being in foster care she was too far away from her mates to meet with them.

There was a mirror opposite her bed, and she turned from the window and moved her head to the side so that she could see her reflection. To herself, she looked scrawny, baggy-eyed and ugly, whereas anyone else would have seen a pretty, petite young girl with lovely long, rich brown curls, large green eyes fringed with thick dark lashes, and skin the colour of caramel. Isobel saw beneath the skin. She saw the pain and despair, the delicate contours of her face distorted by the anger in her soul.

Isobel had no recollection of feeling joy or happiness. She had been the victim of her father's perverted behaviour since as far back as she could remember, and this blighted her every living moment. At such times as birthdays and other family occasions, when everyone else was having a nice time, she had learned to go with the flow. Nobody would ever have guessed that she wasn't having a good time. Behind the smiles, though, she wore a heavy cloak of shame, guilt and confusion. Any possibility of joy was smothered by this cloak, like the flicker of light from a candle starved of oxygen.

This had inevitably caused severe problems for her in trying to manage her life. Striving hard to be like everyone else, to fit in, whilst at the same time knowing she was different. The other girls became giggly and stupid when they discovered new information about sex. Isobel couldn't understand what was funny. Her concentration at school was intermittent, depending on what had happened to her the evening before. She was always being told that she could do better and needed to apply herself more. Her mum used to get really frustrated with her: 'Why don't you just try, Isobel? You used to be one of the cleverest children in primary school. What's the matter; why are you throwing it all away?'

So many times, she had wanted to scream at her mother, tell her what her dad was doing, but the words stuck in her throat. It was all so confusing. She couldn't be sure whether her mum already knew about it. And what would happen then? Her dad would deny it. She hated hearing other girls talking fondly about their dads, or, even worse, complaining about them for some pathetic reason. This made her angry. In fact, she felt angry most of the time.

When the truth came out, it was just as much a surprise to Isobel as it was to Mrs Oliver. They were in a small meeting room behind reception, Mrs Oliver telling Isobel off for skipping science. She was being really kind – too kind. Isobel wasn't used to it. Mrs Oliver asked her a number of times if she was worried about anything. Although Isobel just shrugged her shoulders, she persisted, as though she knew she was hiding something.

'Is there anything I can do to help you, Isobel? I can see

something isn't right, but if you don't say what's troubling you, no one can do anything.'

Isobel shrugged her shoulders again. She was trying hard to disguise her feelings, pretend she didn't care, but the tears were stinging her eyes. She fought them back for as long as she could, but the torrent came and soon they streamed uncontrollably down her face.

It was the kindness that did it. Mrs Oliver moved forward and covered Isobel's hand with her own. 'What is it, Isobel? Please let me help you.'

The words gushed out like water from a burst pipe. Things she had never contemplated saying to anyone; her darkest secrets. To Isobel's surprise, Mrs Oliver suddenly stood up and asked her to stop. This was extremely confusing.

'I am going to help you, Isobel, don't worry, but I have to pass this on. Please believe me, I'm going to do everything I can, but I have to follow child protection procedures. I'm so pleased that you've told me, but I need to report this to Social Services. What I would like you to do for me now is find a nice book and go to the library while I arrange for someone to come and talk to you. Are you OK with that?'

Isobel looked up at her through wet lashes. 'Will my mum need to know?'

'A social worker will come to see you and he or she will be the best person to tell you what will happen next.' Mrs Oliver hesitated. 'I would expect she will have to know, Isobel, but don't worry; everything will be all right, I'm sure.'

Isobel did as she was asked: she picked up a book and found a corner to sit in. She never even opened the book. There was a tornado whirling through her head, pieces of rubble thrashing around her brain, bashing themselves against her skull. Questions like *Why did I tell her? What have I done? What will Mum say when I get home? What about Dad? He might go to prison. Do I want him to go to prison? No… yes… perhaps… I don't really know. Child molesters get beaten up in prison. He deserves to be beaten up. No, I don't want him to be beaten up.*

Later that afternoon, two women turned up. One was a social worker called Lynda; the other one said she was a special police officer. It was confusing because she didn't have a uniform on; Isobel thought police officers wore uniforms. She seemed nice, though. She said her name was Fleur. They went back into the little room behind reception, where Isobel repeated some of the things she had told Mrs Oliver. It wasn't so difficult the second time. Both Lynda and Fleur sat quietly opposite her, listening intently. When she finished speaking there was an uncomfortable silence. Terror began to build; she thought she must be in trouble. For a brief moment she wanted to retract everything, tell them she had made it all up. But then Lynda spoke.

'You've been very brave, Isobel, and you are right to have told Mrs Oliver and us what has been happening to you. I'm going to find a safe place for you to stay tonight while we find out what needs to be done.' She stood up, walked towards Isobel and stroked her arm, trying to put her at ease.

Isobel was rendered speechless. Her head was all over the place. She must have misheard. Why would she not be allowed to go home? She needed to go home. She needed to see her mum to make sure she was still all right with her. At last she spoke. 'I don't want to go somewhere else, I want to go home.' She felt better for saying this. The social worker probably hadn't realised. She'd probably thought she wouldn't want to go home.

To her horror, though, Lynda persisted. 'I'm afraid you will need to stay somewhere else tonight whilst we make further enquiries. We need to be sure you will be safe at home before we can let you go back.'

Isobel was about to respond that of course she would be safe, before she realised the absurdity of that. She slumped back into the chair with an air of submission. 'Will it only be for tonight?'

'I can't say at the moment, Isobel. I'm sorry.'

It was quite late in the evening when Lynda returned to collect Isobel, to take her to her emergency foster placement. It was in a small village just outside town which Isobel had heard of but had never been to. It was where posh people lived. You had to be rich to have a house there. As they turned into Attlee Avenue, she spotted the most beautiful white-painted bungalow with a curved dormer in the shape of an eye, set within the thatched roof. She tried to imagine what it would be like if that window belonged to her bedroom. Disappointingly, the car went a bit further on before pulling up outside a quite plain-looking modern detached house.

The foster carer, Denise, was waiting by the open front door as they walked up the pathway, Lynda carrying Isobel's possessions in a holdall. Isobel was greeted warmly and, after Lynda had spoken briefly to her, Denise took Isobel around the house and showed her where her bedroom was. The rooms were quite small, apart from the kitchen-diner, which was huge and had a conservatory with open doors leading into the long, narrow garden. There was a little grey Scottish terrier called Suzie who jumped at Isobel's legs as she walked around, despite Denise telling her firmly not to.

After Lynda left, Isobel was given a meal of sausage and beans followed by a mug of drinking chocolate before being told it was time to go to her room. This seemed odd to Isobel because she was used to going to bed when she pleased, not when she was told to. She was also annoyed at being separated from her phone. What would she do in her room without her phone?

The next day, Lynda came and drove her to a house near the town. It was a modern semi in the middle of a housing estate, and Fleur was there waiting for them, still not wearing a uniform. She explained to Isobel that she would be interviewed and what she said would be recorded. She asked her to be as clear as she could about what had happened to her, and told her that if she felt uncomfortable or wanted a break she shouldn't be frightened to ask.

Isobel sat on a sofa which was covered with a lambswool blanket and bright pink scatter cushions with gold stars.

'Make yourself comfortable,' Fleur instructed from the chair opposite.

It surprised Isobel that she didn't find the experience too difficult. Everything was out in the open now, and despite all the worries around it, there was also a great sense of relief. At last she wasn't harbouring a huge, sordid secret from the rest of the world. She was no longer alone with her shame. She was going to be helped. Things were going to be better for her at last.

She spoke openly about the abuse, going back as far as she could recall. She detailed where it happened – she couldn't give specific dates, of course, but she was clear about the days of the week because it generally happened when her mum was out at aqua aerobics or shopping. It had also happened a couple of times when her mum was out with mates. She was asked to be as specific as she could about the abuse, which caused her insides to knot together, but she did the best she could.

When the interview was over, Lynda took Isobel back to her foster placement. She arranged for them to have some time on their own for a chat, and they were shown into the conservatory, where Denise left them, shutting the door behind her.

'I wanted to tell you that you will have a new social worker. She will arrange to meet you shortly. I can't be sure but I think she might be called April.'

Isobel took a deep breath. 'I'm not saying it all again. I just can't. Why can't you be my social worker?'

'Don't worry, Isobel, you won't need to tell her anything. She will know everything that I know. If it is April she's very experienced and has been a social worker for many other young people who have had similar experiences to you.'

'When will I meet her?'

'I can't say exactly but it will most likely be before the end of the week. She will also go to talk to your mum.'

Although Denise tried to be kind and welcoming, once Lynda had gone, Isobel was left feeling abandoned and alone. She was in a strange house which was nothing like the home she was used to, in a strange area where she had never been before, with people who were strangers. She stayed in her room as much as she could. She came downstairs for her meals but felt out of place and awkward, which wasn't helped by the stilted table conversation between Denise, her husband Harry, and a skinny, spotty teenage boy whose name Isobel couldn't remember.

4

BACK TO WORK

April sat in the car opposite the main exit from the station, waiting for her mum. She watched as a stream of people hurried through the doors and onto the pavement outside, then jumped into waiting taxis, stood still and looked around for someone who should be picking them up, or just crossed the road and disappeared into the melee. The stream became a trickle before April spotted the tall, attractive blonde woman, weighed down by a heavy-looking holdall and a large leather bag hanging from her shoulder. She dashed out of the car to help her mother with her bags.

'Hello, darling.' Diana put her bags down and hugged April, kissing her on the cheek and leaving a whiff of flowery perfume and a smudge of pink lipstick on the side of her face.

April took the holdall from her mother. 'How was the journey?'

'Very nice, thank you. I met a lovely young girl who was about to start her A Levels. She's hoping to go to Cambridge to do physics, or was it chemistry? Something like that, anyway. You should have done that, you know, April. You could have gone to Cambridge if you'd wanted to. Just think – if you were a scientist, it would have been so much nicer for you. I do worry about you having to see horrible people all the time, all those drug takers. I wish you didn't have to go back to work.'

April tried to disguise her irritation. 'I am perfectly fine and there's nothing to worry about, Mum. I keep telling you I didn't want to go to Cambridge, and I'm very happy doing what I do.'

'OK; it's too late anyway. You're a mother now. You couldn't go to Cambridge even if you wanted to.'

'No, Mum, that's right. I can't go to Cambridge now.' April turned away to hide the frown that had formed involuntarily on her brow.

She had heard this sort of thing many times before, but never ceased to be irritated by it. She would have been highly unlikely to get into Cambridge on the grades she'd achieved anyway, and she had only ever wanted to be a social worker. That was always her ambition, from the time she first started to think about careers.

Jed was waiting by the front door with Demelza in his arms as April pulled into the drive. 'Here's Nanny, Demelza – say hello to Nanny,' he said, waving her little arm.

In a flash, Demelza was snatched from Jed's arms and smothered in kisses, her little face screwing up against the onslaught. 'What has my little angel been doing, then? I expect you've been missing your nanny, haven't you? Yes, you have. Say, "Yes, Nanny." Nanny's going to look after you tomorrow; we're going to play lots and lots of games. Nanny's brought a surprise for you. Would you like to see?' As Diana talked she bounced Demelza up and down in her arms whilst the baby's wide eyes stared at her in wonderment.

Demelza was put down on the floor but, moving along on her bottom, followed Diana to the bag which held the surprise. She peered over the rim before putting her arm inside to take out the colourful package. It was a large book of nursery rhymes, and Demelza, sitting back on her bottom with a thud, started carefully turning the pages. All three adults watched her and laughed as she studied each page as though genuinely intrigued by the text.

After being at home for over a year, April began to look around the house, noticing things she should have done but hadn't found the time for. Things like cleaning the cupboard under the stairs, or sorting out Demelza's many outgrown clothes to take to the charity shop. Time always passes quicker than people expect, but April felt her maternity leave had gone in a flash. She remembered luxuriating in the thought of a whole year at home to enjoy her baby. Alongside the feeling that she hadn't achieved as much as she should, there was a strong sense of dread. She couldn't imagine how it would feel to be separated from Demelza for a whole day.

The rest of the day was spent flitting from one thing to another, knowing it was too late to do all the things she had planned to do at the beginning of her maternity leave, but not wanting to leave them completely undone.

'You go and have a long soak in the bath. I'll put Demelza to bed,' Diana shouted from the lounge.

April didn't want to argue. She could tell Diana was impatient to read the nursery rhymes to her granddaughter once she was tucked up in bed.

April had had a fretful night. At one stage she had woken up in a panic after dreaming that she had left Demelza in the car while she went into the shop, and when she came back, the car seat was empty. The worst thing about it was that she knew she should never have left her in the first place, and it was her own fault that Demelza had been taken. Even once the nightmare had woken her up with a jolt, she couldn't stop panicking; it had felt so real. She'd tried hard to sleep after that, but to no avail. Instead she watched in dismay as the day slowly dawned. What a bad start this was for her first day back at work.

Despite feeling absolutely shattered, April dragged herself out of bed before the alarm went off and whilst Jed still slept soundly. She pulled on her dressing gown and walked on tiptoe into Demelza's room, just to reassure herself that it had only been a dream. Somewhat irrationally, she felt relieved as she gazed at her child lying safely in her cot, stretched out on her back with her light brown curls spread over her pillow, one arm above her head and the other clutching her teddy. She stood for a moment to look at her, heart swelling with pride.

As she walked up the stairs with Jed's coffee in her hand, she heard the radio alarm start up. There was still no sound from Demelza's room so she took the opportunity to have a quick shower. Her clothes were laid out ready for the day: a primrose-coloured dress and white sandals. The yellow was flattering and a lovely contrast with her dark hair. After dressing, she looked at herself in the mirror and was quite happy with what she saw. She had been lucky in that her figure had almost resumed its normal slim shape. She couldn't afford to put on much weight; with her short stature, every extra pound looked like three.

She could hear waking sounds coming from Demelza's room: a whimper, then a yawn. But before she had the chance to do anything, Diana was there, lifting the baby out of her cot and asking her what she wanted Nanny to get her for breakfast. From her room, April watched Diana as she carried Demelza towards the stairs. She was amused by the look of astonishment on Demelza's face at being snatched out of her cot and chatted to before she was fully conscious.

Breakfast over, and the time had come for April to leave for work. Diana brought Demelza to the door, repeating, 'Bye-bye, Mummy, say bye-bye to Mummy' as she waved her little arm up and down.

April needed all her willpower to carry on walking away. As she walked, she was thinking what a bad idea it had been to go back to work, but she somehow managed to keep walking, and turned around to wave and blow a kiss before getting in the car and carefully placing her bag on the passenger seat. Then she drove slowly away, her heart as heavy as lead. *Oh my God, I don't think I'm going to be able to cope*, she thought, fighting back the tears. And then out loud, she said determinedly, 'I'll give it until lunchtime, and if I still feel like this I'm coming home.'

She was soon caught up in traffic. At least there were no appointments to get to, and the first couple of weeks shouldn't be too stressful, until her caseload built up again. She managed to find a space in the car park and started the familiar walk to the office: through the narrow lane and onto the unwelcoming high street with its dilapidated shopfronts which were mostly either boarded up or charity shops. There was an air of deprivation about this town which had once been vibrant with holidaymakers coming from London or the north for the sandy beach and amusements.

The Social Services office was above a clothes shop on the first and second floors of a Victorian terrace. April let herself in by tapping the numbers on the keypad before walking up the dusty staircase, the old wood creaking beneath her feet. Mary the receptionist was still there, behind the glass screen where she had always been, and the same old dinginess hung around the building. Despite its drab appearance though, there was also something strangely quaint about it, with its quirky staircases and little nooks and crannies. It wasn't huge, but one could always find somewhere quiet to go, which was very different to the modern open-plan office she had left behind.

She stood in front of the office door and looked around. It was exactly the same as it had been before her maternity leave; the paintings on the walls beside social workers' desks which had been given to them by children they had worked with, the grubby-looking car seats still in the corner, the scattered papers on the desks. From where she stood, April could see the manager, Maria, in her glass-fronted office in the far corner. She was bent over her desk with the phone in one hand and her head resting on the other. Apart from Janey, the administrator, there were only two other women, neither of whom April recognised. She had been hoping that her good friends Paula and Miles would be there. She had told them when she was due to start back, but they were probably on scheduled visits, at meetings, or doing something else they couldn't avoid.

It wasn't long before Janey noticed her standing at the door and came over to greet her. 'April, welcome back,' she said, giving her a hug.

'Thank you, Janey. It's nice to be back… sort of, anyway.'

'I'll introduce you to the new social workers. Katy's newly qualified and Latifa is a student on placement.'

April tried to conceal her disappointment. For a few seconds she had been delighted at the prospect of having two new social workers in the team, thinking about how that could mean fewer cases for her, but a newly qualified social worker and a student weren't going to alleviate much of her burden at all; in fact, their presence could mean the opposite, bearing in mind the high level of support the team were obliged to provide to such members of staff. Then she shook herself and tried to think positively. This wasn't like her. She had always been encouraging of new social workers and never grudged giving her time. Things were different now, though. She had other priorities.

Janey led her over to the other side of the office to meet Katy and Latifa, who stood up as she approached.

'I'm Katy; it's nice to meet you. How does it feel to be coming back to work? It must be hard leaving your baby.'

April forced a smile. 'Yes, it is hard.'

She always took pride in her appearance, but standing next to Katy made her feel she had made no effort at all. Katy's glossy, shoulder-length light brown hair was highlighted with golden blonde streaks and carefully straightened, and her make-up had been applied perfectly. With sweeping false eyelashes and immaculately decorated fingernails, and a tight-fitting dress hugging a slim but shapely figure, she looked more like a model prepared for a photo shoot than a social worker who would be visiting some insalubrious places.

Latifa seemed genuinely pleased to meet April and shook her hand vigorously. She was short in stature but not in personality, with shiny black skin, tight curls and a broad, infectious smile.

'It's nice to meet you, Latifa. Is this your first placement?'

'No, second.'

April was pleased to hear that.

'I was in adult mental health for my first one. It was OK, I suppose, but I want to work with children. I think what I learned in that team should be useful for me, though.'

'Absolutely. I'm sure you already know that parents with mental health problems commonly require our services. You will have a good idea of what they need and what's available for them out there. I will come to you if I need advice on mental health matters.'

Latifa laughed, thinking that April was joking.

As they continued to chat about previous placements and how things had been since they came to the team, April noticed Maria behind the large glass panel, waving and smiling at her. She turned to make her approach, but had hardly moved when Maria headed towards her, arms outstretched.

'It's great to have you back, April.' Maria stood back and looked her up and down. 'You look fantastic. How have you managed to get your figure back so quickly?'

'Running around after a toddler, and a starvation diet due to lack of time to feed myself. It is getting easier now though, and I've got used to eating cold food so I expect I'll soon start to put on weight as part of my ongoing self-neglect.'

'It's nice being a mother, though. You must be enjoying it, especially after everything you went through.'

April started to glow as she spoke about her daughter. 'Yes, it is nice; she's a bit spoiled, though.'

'You'd better have another one quickly then, I would suggest.'

'Oh, please. I couldn't go through all that again.'

'No, I guess not.' The conversation had taken a serious turn. 'You settle yourself in then, April, get some coffee or something, and then come and see me. We can have a catch-up.'

'OK. I just need to set up my laptop, then I'll be in. Would you like a coffee?'

'Yes please, great. I'll be in my office.'

April found a desk, connected her laptop, then made her way to the small kitchen at the back of the office. She searched through the array of mugs in the cupboard, trying to find two that looked reasonably clean. The social workers had treated themselves to a very nice coffee-pod machine but, most disappointingly, there were no pods to be found. That was a bad omen because nice coffee had been very important in this office. Had everyone been far too busy to think about buying some? Had nice coffee dropped off the priority list?

Carefully, April carried two cups of steaming coffee into Maria's office and pulled up a chair. There seemed to be quite a lot of gossip to catch up on. One of the social workers in the team, Lynda, had been deserted by her husband after more than thirty years of marriage. He'd run off with a twenty-two-year-old.

'She had no idea that he was having an affair.'

'Poor woman,' April murmured.

'Poor or stupid?' Maria replied.

April was a bit shocked at the lack of compassion, but laughed nevertheless.

'I suppose you already know that Paula has found herself a nice lawyer.'

'Yes,' April said. 'I'm glad for her, but I'm going to miss the great dating website stories she used to tell us. I've met Simon a couple of times. He seems nice enough.'

Maria swivelled her chair away from April to face her desk. 'Right, I suppose we need to start thinking about business.'

'I suppose we must.' April turned her focus to the paperwork Maria was moving around. She had clearly prepared well in advance for April's return. She went through each piece of paper in turn, giving a brief overview of the cases she was about to allocate to her.

'Bradley Travers is still in residential. Lynda is looking after him for you for now. He's not doing great, but I'll leave you to read up on that. This is one I think you will like, April,' she added, picking up the next piece of paper.

April bated her breath, knowing that 'like' was another word for 'find challenging or difficult' in social work case allocation.

'Isobel Thorne. She's just come over to our team so it's ideal timing; you'll be her first long-term social worker. She's fourteen. She disclosed sexual abuse; her dad's the abuser. Mum's in denial at the moment; she's standing by the father, says Isobel is lying. You will obviously need to assess this yourself to see if there's any way she might change her mind. Isobel wants to go home.'

'I'll arrange a visit next week. Poor little thing.' April was making notes for herself as they spoke. 'Have you heard anything about Samantha Bushell since I've been away?'

'Oh, you mean the binge drinker, Tayla and Lily Grace's mum. Weren't the girls adopted before you went off on maternity?'

'Yes, they were. They seemed quite settled in their new family, but Samantha disappeared after the court proceedings. I never heard anything from her after that.'

'As far as I'm aware, she hasn't been seen or heard of since then. I'm surprised she hasn't come back to us with another pregnancy.'

'She really wanted to be a good mother to those little girls. It was so sad.'

5

APRIL'S DAD

As soon as she could possibly manage, April was packing up her desk, picking up her bag and rushing down the street to her car in her haste to get home. As she drove, all she could think about was whether Demelza had been missing her; perhaps she had been fretting all day. She couldn't wait to see her little face light up when she saw her mummy was back. It was extremely frustrating that every traffic light she came to was red and seemed to take much longer than usual to change. She edged forward impatiently, and by the time the light turned green, her foot was pressing on the accelerator, ready to zoom away.

At last she was home and, after turning into the drive, jumping out of the car and slamming the door behind her, she noticed her mum with Demelza in her arms, waiting by the open front door. She was slightly peeved that Demelza wasn't jumping up and down with joy at seeing her; just looking bemused. Nevertheless, April snatched her from Diana and covered her with kisses. She was looking into her baby's eyes, hoping, irrationally, for a response, but all Demelza did was point towards the window, saying, 'Look.' April did as she was told, although she had no idea what she was supposed to be looking at. Demelza seemed quite happy with her response.

Demelza was soon put to bed and, as always, asleep within minutes, allowing the three adults to settle into their comfy seats and enjoy the rest of the evening. April and her mum had always been very close and could talk to each other about any subject under the sun, apart from one: April's father. He had left them when April was a baby and there had been an unspoken rule in their house that you never talked about Dad. However, April, during her and Jed's journey through the adoption process before they found out that she was pregnant, had located her father and was now in touch with him. Diana, whom April had considered the most honest, genuine person anyone could hope to meet, had deliberately misled April and Max for more than thirty years about the real reason their dad had left the family.

This was all out in the open now, but still a taboo subject. Diana, still wallowing in shame about her brief affair long ago, remained unable to talk about the past. This had caused a slight rift between them. Diana wanted the past left where it was, whilst April wanted to make up for lost time and build a relationship with her father, which he was also very keen to do. It still annoyed April a lot that even when their chance to adopt a child was in jeopardy, when it had meant so much to them, Diana had remained stubbornly silent.

As they sat watching the television, April started to recall the first time she had met her father after more than thirty-five years. There had been much deliberation around where would be the best place to meet, both of them aware of the awkwardness they were likely to feel. They finally came to an agreement that the best place would be his house, although as she approached his front door on that Sunday evening, a strong pulse throbbed in her chest. With increasing ease they had exchanged photos and engaged in lengthy conversations by phone, but this was very different. This was a real face-to-face encounter in which emotions could be easily exposed.

She'd walked up the short path, which was littered with crumpled maple leaves blown down by the autumn wind. The house was not what she was expecting. Her father had told her it was on the coast, but she hadn't expected it to be quite so isolated and perched on the top of a windy cliff. It looked quite intriguing with its old red-brick walls and peg-tiled roof. The large, solid wood front door was set inside a small brick porch where a pair of green wellingtons and a spiky hedgehog shoe cleaner sat on the step. There was a terracotta pot by the side filled with camomile and thyme, which scented the air pleasantly.

She stood for a moment before ringing the bell, partly to calm her nerves but also to continue enjoying the autumnal smells, the fallen leaves, the fading jasmine which clung to the walls, and the fragrance of the sea. Before she had really thought about it, she rang the bell and there before her stood the stranger who was her father. The fine, wispy hair was the same as in the photo he had sent, and the colour of his eyes the same deep sapphire with flecks of green as hers and Max's, but there was something quite different about him in the flesh. Something she hadn't expected; that she couldn't put her finger on.

He wasn't very tall, though for a man in his fifties, he was quite handsome, but the 'something else' was deeper than appearance. It went below the skin. It was spiritual and binding, like a cord that ran between them. The years they had lost seemed to fade away and the father-and-daughter relationship was as though they had never been parted. She felt sure she would have recognised him even without the photos. There were a few seconds of awkwardness before he stepped forward and took her in his arms. He hugged her so hard her breath was squeezed out of her body, and she knew this was to make up for all the hugs they had missed over the years.

She followed him into the hallway, where the smell of burning applewood drifted towards her. She walked through the oak-panelled door that led into the lounge, and directly in front of her was a huge bay window with spectacular views out to sea. She was drawn to the window and the navy-blue ocean spreading out before her, layers of white foam formed on the rocks as the waves crashed against the cliff below.

'What would you like to drink, April? Tea, coffee, or what about a small glass of bubbly to celebrate this wonderful day?. Oh, I suppose alcohol is off the menu for the time being'.

April slowly turned away from the window and looked at her father's glowing face which radiated joy. 'I would love a glass of bubbly but I'd better not, thank you. A sparkling water would be nice.'

As she took the glass from his outstretched hand, April almost had to shake herself to be sure this was real. All her life, as far back as she could remember, she had longed to know her dad. The stupid thing was that she hadn't even realised how much this had meant to her. She had lived with the longing, it had become part of her being; just like a shadow, it was always there, following her, controlling her. It wasn't until she and Jed had gone through the deeply personal and interrogative process of the adoption assessment that the longing had been exhumed from her subconscious mind. Things had begun to become clear to her; she'd started to understand herself better, including some of her past behaviours such as treating past boyfriends badly because they were too keen. She had been helped to realise that this was a self-preservation tactic; avoidance of another potential rejection. Jed had needed to work really hard to convince her that he was genuinely in love with her and that he would not let her down. He must have enjoyed the challenge because it hadn't been easy.

Her father sat down on the huge armchair with floral cushion covers which was positioned just inside the bay window recess. 'Sit yourself down.' He gestured towards the settee which was close to him. 'I want to hear everything about you. There are millions of questions in my head; I don't know where to begin. I want to know about Max too, and your mother.'

The conversation went on well into the evening; there was so much to catch up on and so much to say. He appeared enraptured by every snippet from the past.

'April, I have to ask this. What does your mum say about us meeting? I presume you have told her?'

'I have mentioned it. It didn't go down well but she has accepted it was inevitable. I really hope there will come a time when I can talk to her about you, but it doesn't seem likely at the moment. I hate this being between us.'

There was a pause of deep contemplation from both of them.

'I was thinking, April. I know you and Jed have been through some dreadful times, trying for a family and all that, but if it hadn't been for that, from what you've said, you probably wouldn't have contacted me, would you?'

'To be honest it was the adoption social worker who was adamant that the family rift was seriously affecting my emotional well-being. She made us put the adoption plans on hold until it was resolved. I'm not sure I would have gone against Mum otherwise. Now that I'm pregnant there's another good reason for doing what I did. My child will want to know about its grandfather.'

April had left the house with so many unanswered questions. Her father had been so hungry to know about her life and about Max that there hadn't been much opportunity to find out about him. That night she struggled to sleep. She couldn't rid herself of the guilt she felt; although it was totally illogical, she couldn't help feeling that she was being disloyal. She realised it was manipulation at the highest level which her mother had managed to do without saying a word.

But that was all in the past and things had moved on since then… to a certain degree. April glanced at her mother, whose head had slumped back, her eyes closed and her breath making soft whistling sounds. She gave her shoulder a gentle shake and the three of them made their way upstairs to bed.

6

FIRST VISIT

The next morning April waved goodbye to Demelza again as she walked down the garden path towards her car on her second day back at work. The parting wasn't quite as traumatic this time as Demelza had coped perfectly fine without her – thanks to her mother, of course.

She made her way up the creaky staircase into reception, waved at Mary as she passed, and walked through the open door into the office. No sign of Paula or Miles again, which was most disappointing. She was planning to go through the cases she had been allocated and read the background history before making arrangements to start her introductory visits. She had already looked carefully at Isobel's case and could see that she needed to meet her as soon as she could. The poor girl was likely to be in limbo at the moment, not really knowing what was going to happen.

Isobel didn't have any history with Social Services so there was not much to read. Her father was a van driver and her mother a classroom assistant. It was clear from reports that had been gathered from school that she was a troubled child. It seemed that Isobel struggled to manage the school environment, and had been excluded a number of times for various things including using foul language to teachers and walking out of lessons. She struggled to maintain friendships and was generally unpopular with the other children who tolerated rather than liked her.

Other social workers drifted in and April was greeted warmly by each one.

'So glad to see you back, April. How is Demelza?'

'She's great, thank you. She's with Mum today but starting nursery tomorrow. I'm dreading that, although it's only for half a day.'

'She'll be fine, but I can understand what you mean.' Janice was a grandmother, so this stage was a long time ago for her.

As April talked, a text message came through. It was from Paula.

Hi, April. Welcome back. Sorry I haven't been able to get to the office to see you. I'm in court at the moment, trying to get Care Orders for five children, so I doubt I will get there this week, but hope to see you Monday. xx

April was a bit disappointed but it couldn't be helped. The two women had remained in contact during her maternity leave but were so busy with their own lives that they hadn't managed to get together for a proper catch-up.

After checking emails and making a few phone calls, April decided to contact Isobel's foster carer to arrange to see her that afternoon. Isobel had been excluded again for telling a teacher to fuck off. April scrolled down the personal details page of Isobel's electronic file to find the foster carer's details. She rang the number and it was promptly answered.

'Hello. It's April Gardiner here, Isobel's social worker. Is that Denise?'

'It is indeed. Hello, April. What can I do for you?'

'I wondered if it would be convenient for me to come around later today to meet Isobel?'

'Yes, of course. She's in her room. What time will you be here? I'll tell her you're coming.'

April had worked out that Denise's house was on her route home. She could arrange to visit around three and then get home a bit early. The workload hadn't kicked in yet and she couldn't see why she shouldn't take advantage of that. After all, once it did kick in, she would struggle to get home on time, let alone early.

She had checked her emails and responded to any which needed a response. Most of them were policy updates or invites to meetings which could be ignored for now. She hadn't had time that morning to make herself a sandwich, so decided to make the most of this settling-in time and go for a walk in the town centre. There wasn't much of interest but there happened to be a little shop where you could buy freshly made sandwiches just around the corner.

Just as she left the office the sun decided to hide behind a cloud, casting a grey shadow over the dilapidated buildings, making them appear particularly bleak. Behind the deprivation and decline, though, there remained an air of faded elegance. She paused to look in the window of one of the many charity shops. There was a woman's grey suit jacket which had seen better days hanging on a headless mannequin. Scattered around this were various unappealing bric-a-brac, well-thumbed books, jigsaw puzzles in shabby-looking boxes; a clear indication of the poverty and deprivation which were rife in this town. Suddenly noticing how much time had passed, she realised she needed to be on her way to meet Isobel.

Isobel had struggled to get through the past few days and was now sitting on her bed waiting for April to arrive. There were too many strangers in her life; too many official people. She wasn't used to meeting strangers and now she was surrounded by them, all wanting to know the most intimate and embarrassing things about her life. She felt too anxious to do anything but sit and stare out of the window. This was a quiet road with hardly any traffic, and when April's car drew up, she jumped off the bed and looked out of the window, curious to know what she looked like. She watched as April got out of her car and leant over to retrieve her bag from the passenger seat.

She pulled the heavy-looking bag onto her shoulder before closing and locking the door. She was dressed in tight pale blue trousers and a colourful short-sleeved top which flapped in the breeze as she walked up the path, her thick dark curls bobbing around. Isobel was relieved to see that she had a kind, friendly face.

She heard April greeting Denise and asking how things had been. There was a mumbled response from Denise which increased Isobel's paranoia. She was sure Denise was complaining about her. This unnerved Isobel somewhat, and her chest tightened. She wasn't sure what was expected of her in this foster home or exactly how she was supposed to behave, and her anxiety was intensified by the whispering coming from downstairs.

There was a knock on her bedroom door followed by a gentle voice asking if it was all right to come in.

'Yeah, come in.'

'Hello, Isobel.' April stood by the open door. 'I'm April, and I think Lynda already told you that I will be your social worker. How are you settling in?'

'I'm not. I want to go home. When can I go home? Lynda said you would let me go home.'

April couldn't help smiling at this. 'I don't think she did say that, Isobel. I think she probably told you that I would find out how things are at home and whether or not it's possible for you to go back.'

'No, that's not true. She said I could go home. She said you would let me go home.'

'Well, I'm sorry if she did say that but I have to speak to your mum. I need to pay her a visit to find out what she intends to do.'

'When?' Isobel demanded.

'I've arranged to see her on Monday.'

April was surprised by how young and childlike Isobel looked. She was fourteen but could have been mistaken for a much younger child. Her brows knitted in a frown as she spoke, like a toddler about to have a strop. A large dimple appeared in one side of her face with every change of expression.

'I know it's all a bit strange and awkward for you at the moment, Isobel, but I'm sure Denise is looking after you very well, isn't she?'

'No!' was Isobel's belligerent reply. 'I have to go to bed at eight. I'm not even allowed my phone.' She spread out her hands in front of her to emphasise her exasperation. 'There's a boy here. I don't like him – he looks at me funny; he's a weirdo. And Denise doesn't like me either.'

April was a bit surprised about the eight o'clock bedtime. That seemed a bit unfair for a fourteen-year-old. 'I will have a chat with Denise about your bedtime and we will see what we can do. What makes you think she doesn't like you?'

'She just doesn't, I can tell. I'm not stupid.'

Before leaving, April had a chat with Denise in the conservatory. Denise told her that eight o'clock wasn't Isobel's bedtime; it was when she liked her to go to her room so that she could read or watch television. She had Sky in her bedroom.

'I think it would be better for her to be included in the family as much as possible. Perhaps you could try to encourage her to sit with you and Harry in the evening. What about Jordan – does he go to his room at eight?'

Jordan was the other foster child, the 'weird boy'.

'He always shuts himself in his room, playing on his computer. I've tried to get him to spend time with us but no; he comes down for dinner, then as soon as he can he's back in his room with the door shut. We often don't see him again until the morning.'

April wasn't happy to hear this but she had other things to think about; it was after five and she was really keen to get home to her own child.

7

ALISON

April was driving to the nursery with Demelza, preparing to leave her there for the first time, now that Diana had gone home. She had brought her to the nursery a couple of times to get her used to it. and watched whilst she played. She seemed happy enough and the nursery staff appeared kind. This time, though, she had to leave without her. Her stomach was tying itself in knots throughout the short journey. At least it would only be until lunchtime for Demelza's first day.

When they arrived, April was greeted by the nursery manager, Celia, who immediately took Demelza out of her arms and began engaging with her. She then placed her down on a large mat where other toddlers were already sitting and various toys were scattered. Demelza picked up a tambourine and shook it violently, narrowly avoiding clouting the child next to her. Oblivious to this close shave, she continued to shake the tambourine vigorously. Celia advised April to say goodbye and leave quickly whilst Demelza was happy. She bent down and kissed her on the cheek before rushing out of the door.

Her mind was soon focused on where she was heading: her planned visit to Isobel's mum. She set the satnav, because although it wasn't far in distance, it was close to the town centre and tricky to find amid the labyrinth of backstreets spreading out like a spider's web from the high street. Within a few minutes she was driving towards the town centre and the satnav was saying, 'You have arrived at your destination', which was confusing since all she could see on either side were shops. She decided to park in the car park and find the house on foot. After walking up and down a few times she noticed a small, obscure alleyway in between an e-cigarette shop and a newsagent. She turned into the alley and almost immediately the door she was looking for appeared in front of her: 2A Taylor's Yard. She rang the bell on the intercom and a female voice responded.

'Yes?'

'It's April Gardiner, the social worker.'

'OK, push the door.'

April did as she was told and walked in. In front of her was an unwelcoming, cold concrete staircase between two unevenly cemented walls with a metal handrail attached to one side. The top of the staircase curved slightly to the left, where there was a small landing with orange linoleum which was torn in parts and turned up at the corner, then an olive-green door. It felt cold and damp, and April shivered as she stood waiting for her knock to be answered. She hoped it would be better inside.

The door opened and before her stood a short, plump woman, probably in her mid to late thirties. Her tight-fitting top hung low over her chest, exposing the bulk of her cleavage. April was intrigued by her hair, which was short and spiky, browny-grey with flashes of startling pink. She had the same large emerald green eyes as her daughter, but that seemed to be the extent of their physical similarities. Isobel had clearly inherited most of her features and her colouring from her father.

This was going to be an awkward visit and April hadn't really had time to plan how she was going to deal with it. As it was, Alison was vocal from the outset, and as was often the case in these situations, things developed rapidly. Before April was properly inside the door,

Alison was confronting her. 'When is my daughter coming back? I want her with me. She needs to be at home with her family.'

April suggested politely that they should go inside and shut the door. 'You don't want the neighbours to hear all your business, do you? Let's go and sit down, then we can talk about what needs to happen,' she said, hoping to calm the situation.

Alison shut the door behind April but persisted with her tirade. 'I know what we need to do; we need to get her back home. She's already got problems: she hasn't been able to cope with school and now she's been taken away from her family. I don't get it. How is that going to help her? I thought social workers were supposed to help kids like my Isobel.' Her face glowed crimson with rage.

April took a few steps towards the chair by the window and sat down. From here she could see over the town. She noticed that, although the window was shut, the noise from the high street was not dulled at all. She guessed that the window, with its thin, rusty metal frame, was as old as the building. The paint on the sill was starting to peel due to the damp coming in. She imagined this room being rather cold in the winter. The chair on which she sat faced an old brick fireplace which could have looked quite appealing but for the old-fashioned two-bar electric fire which had been placed in front of it.

'Do you not have central heating in the flat, Alison?' April asked.

'Yes, but the radiators are old and it costs a fortune. We use the electric fire in the evenings sometimes if it gets cold, rather than keep turning up the radiators.'

'Have you lived here very long?'

'No, we came here just over a year ago. It was the bedroom tax. We had a house with three bedrooms – we'd lived there since Isobel was a baby – but when they brought in the bedroom tax, we couldn't afford it anymore.'

April was pleased that Alison seemed to have calmed down. 'I need to talk to you about the allegation Isobel has made against her father. I know that my colleague Lynda has already spoken to you.

She reported that you are finding it difficult to believe what Isobel has said.'

Alison jerked forward, about to start shouting again, but April interrupted her.

'If you wouldn't mind, Alison, I need to explain how things stand. You will then be welcome to ask any questions you may have.' She waited for Alison to settle back down. 'It is concerning for me that you don't appear to be able to believe your daughter. I understand what a shock it must have been and I can't begin to imagine how it must feel to find out something as horrible as that.'

Alison couldn't contain herself. 'He wouldn't do that to her. If it's true, why did she wait until now to say? Why didn't she tell me before? She's always been trouble. She's told lies in the past. That's what she's doing now. She just wants attention. I want her back, but I won't forgive her. Danny says he will never forgive her for saying those things about him.'

'Why do you think she would say those things about her father if they weren't true?'

'Why?!' Alison shrieked. 'You ask *me* why? How am I supposed to know? Maybe she was jealous of our relationship. I don't know why she would tell lies like this. Do you think I haven't asked myself? I haven't slept since she said it. I'm really confused. I think if I could see her, she would tell me why she's saying it.'

'I can arrange contact for you, but it will have to be supervised, I'm afraid.'

'What do you mean, supervised?' Alison shrieked even louder. 'You mean I have to be watched while I meet with my own daughter?'

'Yes. I'm sorry, Alison, but that is how it has to be. I need you to know that you will not be allowed to talk to Isobel about the allegations. There will be a police enquiry and it could be affected if you say anything to her. She won't be able to see her dad for the time being.'

'That's a joke. See her dad?' Alison gave a high-pitched, cynical laugh. 'He never wants to set eyes on her again.'

There was a brief silence, then, to April's surprise, Alison suddenly leant forward and, hands covering her face, started to sob. Her arms and legs were trembling with grief as tears poured through her open fingers.

April's sympathetic nature got the better of her and she moved towards Alison in an attempt to provide comfort. She stood beside her, stroking her arm. 'I know this is hard for you, Alison. I wish we could resolve it another way, but you must understand that the way things stand, we cannot guarantee that Isobel will be safe at home. You are choosing to believe your husband over your daughter and, whilst that's the case, she's not safe in your care. I know that sounds brutal but you need to know how things stand.'

The aggressive, confrontational stance Alison had presented with initially had dissolved into submission. She was not stupid, and realised quite quickly that she was onto a loser., 'How is she? Is she missing us?'

'Yes, she is Alison, to be honest. I think she is finding it hard to be in a strange house, living with strangers, but it will get easier. If she has to stay there it will get easier for her.'

'When can I see her?'

'I will arrange for you to see her tomorrow. I will supervise the contact, but I must warn you again that you must not mention the allegation. If you do, I will have to stop the contact and there won't be another one until the proceedings are completed.'

'I won't mention it,' Alison said meekly.

By the time April left, Alison was a different woman. She had been all guns blazing, making demands about what she wanted and how things should be, but now she was tearful, and submissive, recognising that anger and confrontation were not going to get her anywhere.

April drove away feeling despondent. She had hoped Alison might have changed her stance in the time since Lynda had visited. It was going to be a long, hard battle with poor little Isobel in the middle of it. One thing was heartening: the fact that Alison wanted

Isobel home. Even though this would not be possible for the time being, it gave April some hope that there could be a way forward in the future. She had been involved with cases like this in which, from the outset, the mother had been adamant that the child would never be welcome back home and that was final. This was heart-breaking for the social worker and devastating and destructive for the child. April, always the optimist, had hope that Alison would change; perhaps after the police investigation was completed. If Danny was charged with sexual abuse of his daughter by the court, perhaps she would be able to accept it, and Isobel could be reunited with her mum. That was a possibility, but there were many cases in which the perpetrator wasn't prosecuted due to what was termed 'lack of evidence'.

April also had to remind herself that there was a possibility that Alison was complicit in the abuse. She may have been party to it or been aware at the time and turned a blind eye, which was equally complicit. April didn't think this was the case but she had to keep an open mind and be prepared to think the unthinkable. It was absolutely crucial that her assessment covered all possibilities, especially if Isobel was ever going to return home.

By the time April had collected Demelza from the nursery and driven home she was physically and emotionally exhausted. Still, she managed to put thoughts of Isobel to the back of her mind for the time being and had a lovely afternoon playing with her little girl.

8

LACK OF SLEEP

On Tuesday morning, April was heading back to the office. She was later than she wanted to be because Demelza had been awake in the night, which was unusual. There didn't seem to be any reason for it. She had been put to bed at her usual time, around 6.30, and April and Jed had relaxed in front of the television before going to bed themselves. April was asleep before her head hit the pillow. She was finding it quite exhausting working as well as being a mother. Jed helped out as much as he could but his long working hours didn't leave him much time and he often had to stay away from home for a few nights at a time. His accountancy firm, where he was a partner, was expanding, and work was coming in from further afield.

It was about two in the morning when the disturbance began. April was woken from her deep, restorative sleep by a loud, piercing yell. She woke with a start and sat bolt upright. All was quiet and she thought it must have been a dream. Lying down again, she sank her head into the comfort of her pillow, but just as the blissful sensation of impending sleep was kicking in, there was another yell, this time more prolonged. She sprang out of bed and rushed into Demelza's room to see what the commotion was about. She found her child standing up against the railings of her cot, looking flushed and bewildered. As April walked further into the room, Demelza's little face puckered, her bottom lip jutted out and tears streamed down her cheeks. She held out her arms to her mother, who lifted her out of the cot.

'Did you have a bad dream, my little angel?' she whispered.

Demelza's cries turned into whimpers and trembling spasms ran through her body. As she walked up and down the room with Demelza in her arms, April could see through the half-open door into the other room where Jed slept peacefully, blissfully unaware of what was going on. She couldn't help feeling irritated by this. *Why is it that he can sleep through anything, and yet with every little whimper Demelza makes, I'm awake?* She decided that it was because he could relax in the confidence that she would see to their daughter if needed. *That's so unfair*, she thought, glaring resentfully at his sleeping figure.

April changed Demelza's nappy, gave her a little drink of water and laid her back in her cot. Snuggling her in with the duvet, she kissed her soft cheek and left her comforted and settled. She climbed back into bed and nestled down into the comfy mattress, sinking her head back into the pillow. But before she had time to drift off again, she was shocked into wakefulness by another loud cry from Demelza's room. Her heart sank. *What on earth can be wrong with her?* she asked herself. She waited for a couple of minutes, really hoping the crying would stop because she felt too tired to move again, but it was no use; Demelza was becoming increasingly fretful and there was no other choice but to get up and see to her once again. She glared resentfully again at Jed, who slumbered on.

'All right, Mummy's coming,' she called.

Demelza's crying soon simmered down and became a whimper after she was gathered in her mother's arms. April walked around with her for a few minutes, talking and singing softly whilst jigging her up and down. Comforted once again, Demelza was settled back into her cot, given her teddy and kissed goodnight.

'I will see you in the morning, my darling,' April said softly, tiptoeing out of the room holding her breath, hoping that would be it.

Unfortunately, it wasn't. Demelza just wouldn't settle. Every time April climbed back into bed, exhausted and desperate for sleep, the cries started again. It was almost 5am when, exhausted with crying, Demelza finally went to sleep, lying widthways across her cot, on top of her duvet and with her pillow at her feet. She had one arm above her head and the other poking through the railings, but April had no intention of moving her. She climbed back into bed ready to grab the time that was left, but could not sleep. Guilt flooded her brain. The early hours of the morning being a ripe time for irrational thoughts, April convinced herself that Demelza was traumatised by being left at the nursery. To make matters even worse, the guilt was coupled with frustration and stress as she needed to be ready to cope with a full day at work. Her head throbbed with the lack of sleep and the mental beating she had given herself for her self-perceived blatant cruelty to her daughter.

At breakfast, feeling wiped out and grumpy, April couldn't resist a snipe at Jed. 'I'm so glad you managed to have such a good night's sleep. Just as well I'm always available to see to our daughter when she needs us.' She took a large bite out of her toast and chewed rapidly as though taking her vengeance on her food.

Jed was just about to have a sip of his coffee, but stopped with his cup in mid-air. Completely baffled, he turned to April. 'April, can you enlighten me, please? Have I done something, or rather, not done something that you think I should have done?' His expression was a mixture of confusion and concern.

'I'm sorry, I'm just a bit fed up. I was up with Demelza half the night. She just wouldn't settle. I don't know what was wrong with her.'

They both glanced over at their little girl, who was sitting in her high chair, happily stuffing a piece of toast into her mouth with buttery fingers. She looked back at them and smiled, happy at being the focus of attention.

'I don't know if I'm going to be able to keep on working. I think she might have been upset by being left at nursery. She's never been like that before. What do you think?'

'She enjoyed it, you said. I thought you said she seemed really happy when you picked her up?'

'She did, but we don't know what she's thinking. She might have thought she'd been left there for good. Oh God, Jed – what if she thought we'd abandoned her? I have to go in today but I think I might give notice. I could stay at home until she's a bit older. I don't think it's right to leave her just now. She's too young.'

'If that's what you want, April. I don't think you should hand in your notice today, though. You should at least try her a few more times; after all, it may have had nothing to do with her being at nursery. Unless you give it a bit longer you will never really know. You only work half the week and you might get bored at home. It's entirely up to you, though. That's just my advice.'

April let out a loud sigh. She knew Jed was right but the thought of leaving Demelza again was cutting her up inside. She hadn't accounted for any of these feelings when she had planned her future with a baby. People are prepared to give you lots of advice about how to bring them up and the best way to care for them, but nobody tells you how strong the ties are and how heart-wrenching it is to be parted from them.

'If you like, I will take her today. I haven't got any meetings this morning so it won't matter if I'm late.'

April's response flew from her mouth before she took a breath. 'You're joking. I'm taking her. You can take her another time, but not today. I want to watch how she is; make sure she's happy with the staff. I need to assess the situation for myself.'

'Of course you do. I will take her another day, then.' Jed stood up from the table, walked over to where Demelza sat in her high chair, kissed her on the cheek and ruffled her hair. 'You have a lovely day at nursery today, my little darling.'

After stuffing papers from the desk in the study into his briefcase, he pulled on his jacket and prepared to leave for work. April went to the door to see him off. Kissing him and giving him a hug, she apologised for being so grumpy.

She was soon ready to go herself, and driving into the nursery forecourt she told herself that if Demelza didn't seem happy to be left she would pick her up, take her straight home and phone the office to say she wasn't coming back.

As usual, Celia was waiting to greet them. She held out her arms to Demelza, who almost jumped towards her in delight. She was carried off by Celia, who chatted away to her as they went. April stood and watched for a few minutes before heading off, then, turning around to see how things were, she noticed another nursery assistant talking to Demelza, who was chuckling and waving her feet. She was put down on the floor and immediately began to play with the array of toys before her. Everything seemed perfectly fine. April decided that it was probably sleep deprivation that had caused the irrational thoughts she was having, and set off without further worry.

The office was unusually quiet, without any tapping of keyboards or phones ringing. Janey was at her desk in the corner and Katy, the glamorous newly qualified social worker, was at another desk with her eyes fixed on her computer, her long, sweeping lashes almost touching the screen. April gave her a quick wave before finding a desk to sit at. Things were beginning to get busy as the cases she had been allocated needed some action. One of these cases was that of the Bailey children: two little boys whose parents were heroin addicts. The older of the two, Florian, who was three-and-a-half, was a difficult child due to the trauma he had experienced whilst living with his parents. The younger child, Leo, who was only eight months old, had been luckier. Soon after he was born his mother had put him in care. The boys were being placed for adoption and April had been given details of approved potential adoptive parents, and she needed to arrange to meet them.

She was halfway through reading the court report which the previous social worker had written, and quite absorbed in the detail of the little boys' past, when she felt a tap on her shoulder.

'April, at last. It's been really cheesing me off, trying to get into the office to see you. I've just been so busy, you wouldn't believe: court, conferences, meetings…' Paula made broad gestures with her hands as she spoke to demonstrate the wide variety of tasks she had been trying to manage.

April stood up and the two women hugged each other.

'Great to see you, Paula. I thought you'd been avoiding me. Only joking. It's lovely to see you, anyway. We've got so much to catch up on.'

'I suppose the pub after work is no longer an option?'

'Afraid not. It's hard enough having to leave Demelza to come to work. I may be able to manage an hour, perhaps one afternoon, if we can all find space in our diaries, or maybe later when Demelza is in bed. Jed wouldn't mind babysitting occasionally, I don't think.'

April sat back down and Paula pulled up a chair beside her. She had been divorced and on her own for many years and, when her daughter Natasha was quite independent, had decided she needed a man in her life. Her tales of internet dating had been hilarious, although not always for Paula.

'I haven't seen Miles yet. He phoned a couple of times whilst I was on maternity leave but didn't come round. What's he doing with himself?'

'I haven't seen much of him, to be honest with you, April. I'm sure he'll want to join us for our evening out, though.'

April was uplifted by the surprise meeting with Paula. It hadn't turned out to be a bad day after all, and after collecting Demelza and feeling comforted by her smiling face, she drove home feeling quite contented with her work-life balance.

9

KERRY

April was driving slowly down Maple Close, looking for Kennedy House. She was confused because this wasn't the type of area she was expecting to be in, and, whilst trying to keep her eyes on the road and one hand on the steering wheel, with her left hand she picked her diary out of her bag and managed to turn the page to the correct date, double-checking the address. It was a wide road with large houses set so far back that some of them couldn't be seen. She noted long, sweeping lawns fronting mainly detached houses of varying ages and styles. Many of the lawns were dotted with large, colourful rhododendrons, blossom-laden trees, and magnolias in full bloom. She couldn't believe this was the right street. The family she was looking for were unlikely to be able to afford to even rent in an area like this. But the address in her diary was Kennedy House, Maple Close, and the satnav had brought her here. There were a few young teenagers in school uniform scattered around, mostly walking home with heavy-looking rucksacks on their backs, staring at their phones as they walked. They looked like serious young people who were heading home to study for exams. There was an air of peace and prosperity; not the sort of area where a social worker would expect to be visiting a family who had been referred to the service due to chronic neglect of their children.

April was just thinking about turning back because, although the satnav was very insistent that she had arrived at her destination, she had still not found Kennedy House. Just a few yards further on was a T-junction, and she decided to turn into it and retrace her journey. As she started to reverse back into the junction, she noticed that the road ahead led into an industrial estate. There was a sign on the corner with a black arrow, and one of the buildings listed on the sign was Kennedy House. This seemed very odd. It appeared that Kennedy House was an industrial building rather than a block of flats. She followed the direction of the sign, and a few seconds later, on her right was a sign saying, 'Kennedy House'. It was clearly a disused office block with large windows and metal frames. It was set between two dilapidated warehouses with green metal roofs and grey exterior walls.

Surely this can't be it, April thought. The concrete forecourt showed clear signs of neglect, mottled and cracked with some weeds poking their heads up ready to spread with a vengeance once the weather warmed up. There didn't appear to be any sign of life and there was nobody in sight to ask, so reluctantly she parked the car and, locking it behind her, walked towards the seemingly deserted building. The whole area appeared deserted too, and had an eeriness which made her feel uneasy. She was just thinking about turning back to her car when a young man in a grey tracksuit and extremely large orange trainers seemed to appear from nowhere. His sudden appearance gave her a start but he was clearly oblivious to her. Not wanting to miss an opportunity, as he walked past, she stopped him by catching hold of the back of his jacket.

'I'm supposed to be visiting a friend somewhere around here but I'm not sure I'm in the right place. She lives in Kennedy House. Do you know if there is another Kennedy House anywhere?'

'No, don't know anywhere else called Kennedy House. Who you looking for?'

'Oh, it doesn't matter; I think I'm in the wrong place. Thank you anyway.'

'You need to go around the back if you want to get into the hostel. The door's round the other side.' He pointed in the direction April needed to go before giving a half-wave and striding off.

April followed his instructions and walked across the long forecourt until she reached the corner of the building. She followed the path down the side and then around the next corner to the back, where she saw a very different picture. Outside the building were clear signs of habitation. Dustbins overflowing with rubbish; a rusty bike with one wheel missing, leaning against the wall; a broken pushchair, wheels facing upwards. A washing line hung between two wooden poles in the small, muddy garden with a few items of children's clothing hanging from it. Incredible as it seemed, there must be people living here, and looking up she could see that some of the windows on this half of the building were curtained. She walked towards the entrance and was able to push open one of the double doors, although it was quite heavy and stiff. It scraped along the tiled floor as she pushed it, increasing the semicircle of white where the surface of the tiles had been scraped off because of the door's poor alignment. As she walked inside, she was hit by a strong, unidentifiable smell. She could hear different sounds coming from various directions, including music and talking from televisions, a child crying, and the voices of adults, although she couldn't tell which rooms the voices were coming from.

On the wall was an intercom, and she pushed the button for Kerry's flat. There was no response and, unsure that it had worked, she tried again, waiting patiently. Again, there was no response, so she decided to go and look for Number 5. The building was huge inside, with long, wide corridors and tiled flooring. She walked around the ground floor, looking at door numbers, before climbing the wide metal staircase to the next floor and eventually finding Number 5. The door was opened and a young woman carrying a child stood before her.

'Hello, Kerry, I'm April Gardiner; I think you were expecting me.'

Kerry looked a bit put out, clearly not very happy about being visited by a social worker, but stood aside to let her in.

April was shocked by what she saw inside. One large room appeared to serve as the bedroom, lounge and kitchen. There were two double mattresses at the far end of the room, and directly in front of them, a ragged two-seater sofa, a small television in one corner with hardly any space between it and the sofa, and, in this space, a small table. There was wall-to-wall carpeting but this was faded, threadbare and scattered with indiscernible stains. One side of the room was completely taken up with clutter, piled almost from floor to ceiling with clothes, saucepans, children's toys, shoes, CDs and who knows what else. Another wall had a sink, and next to it, a small worktop with an electric hob which looked as though its better days had been many years ago. Above this was a cupboard which hung precariously from the wall; the door of which was hanging open. April wondered about fire safety, considering the age and condition of the cooker, coupled with the cluttered environment.

As she started to walk across the room, she felt her feet squelching beneath her. The wet from the carpet was rising up and over the sides of her shoes. 'Have you had a flood?' she asked, looking quizzically at Kerry.

'No,' Kerry said, smiling cynically at April's stupidity. 'That's just where Tamara's potty gets tipped.'

April tried hard to disguise the disgust she felt at having her feet soaked with Tamara's urine.

'She still uses a potty at night and you won't catch me going down those stairs to empty it in the middle of the night. You get druggies, alkies, all sorts hanging around. I keep my door locked.'

April had seen squalor many times before but this was completely off the scale. No family should be forced to live in conditions like this in a civilised country, or anywhere else for that matter. She had been in many hostels during her working life but this was the worst she had seen. Were councils so desperate now for properties that they had to resort to industrial buildings to house their homeless families?

'How have you ended up living in this place, Kerry?'

'Chucked out of my flat. My landlord kicked me out. I got myself in arrears. The Social gave me some money towards it but not nearly enough to pay for everything I needed. I don't know how anyone is supposed to manage on the money they give you. I had to buy food for the kids. Tyler needed school uniform, which I did get from the school second-hand shop, but it was still thirty quid. That took all my money. I couldn't even buy him shoes; he had to start after Easter with his old trainers.' She was gesturing to the corner of the room behind her where the mattresses were, and April saw the little boy sat on the edge of his bed, staring at a mobile phone.

'Hi there, Tyler,' she called out.

Tyler didn't look up from the phone but mumbled a response which sounded like some form of greeting.

Kerry could have only been in her early twenties at the most, but the streaks of sunlight which shone through the window revealed crow's feet spreading from her eyes, fine lines starting to form around her mouth, and a deep furrow that marked her forehead where her brown hair was pulled back from her face; the visible marks of a lifetime of deprivation and hardship.

Being a social worker and having a natural empathy for people suffering disadvantage, April's immediate instinct was to do whatever she could to help her. As they talked, the little girl Kerry had been carrying was put down. She had a dummy in her mouth which was almost the size of her face. There was a strange look of sadness about her, and her large blue eyes, with which she scrutinised April, were glazed with a film of unshed tears. There were no signs of the natural joy, curiosity and mischievousness of a normal two-year-old, but then there was no room to play, no suitable outside area for fresh air and exercise, and her mother was struggling to cope. Where would the joy come from in a situation like this? April felt incredibly sad, as well as angry that an already vulnerable family should have to struggle like this.

She turned her attention back to Kerry. 'How long have you been living here?'

'Nearly a year. Tyler had to start his new school halfway through the term. He couldn't stay at the other one because it's too far. We would have had to get the bus and I can't afford that. He didn't want to leave his friends because he's known them since he was in nursery, but there was no way I could get him there. I asked them to give me somewhere closer but this was all they had. I don't know what's going to happen. I can't get another rented place because they think I'm a bad person who won't pay the rent. That's not true, though. I always paid my rent. It was only because I couldn't. I got into debt and then couldn't catch up.' She wiped away a tear with the back of her hand.

All of a sudden there was a big crash from upstairs, just as a motorbike started up outside.

'Oh, here we go. They're at it again. It's the people upstairs. They shout and swear at each other, then he starts riding his motorbike around the building, revving it up as loud as he can. It's usually through the night he does it, just when everyone's asleep. I've been on to the council but they're not bothered. You watch; in a minute she'll be effin' and blindin' out the window. They've got kids up there, you know. How come they don't get social workers round? They need social workers more than I do. Those poor kids, having to live with that all the time.'

Some shouting did follow, but the motorbike roared off into the distance – thankfully, as it was deafening on the forecourt. The windows clearly didn't block any of the noise from outside.

'I can see that life is very difficult for you at the moment, Kerry.' April felt quite embarrassed at the scale of the understatement but nevertheless felt the need to express this observation. 'You are aware that the health visitor has made a referral to Social Services because she was worried about Tamara's development. She feels that you need support.'

An expression of anger crossed Kerry's face. 'How am I supposed to look after my kids properly in this shit-hole? I'd like to see you do better. I expect you've got a house with a garden, and you don't have to worry about whether the money will last until the end of the month so that you can feed your kids.'

April moved the conversation on quickly. 'Have you got any family to help you at all?'

'My mum lives over in Brookside but she can't help much. She's on her own. She's got COPD as well so she can't walk much. She gets depression a lot, *and* she's trying to get some extra benefits because she can't work. They keep saying she can work, but she can't get out of bed sometimes so I don't know how they figure that out.'

'Is she still working age, then?' From Kerry's description April imagined a woman in her seventies.

'I think she's forty-five; could be forty-six, not sure. It's her birthday in June.'

'What about the children's fathers?'

'Tamara's father still comes to see her but I don't get any money. He's a bit of a smackhead but to be fair, he does love Tamara.'

As Kerry talked, April noticed Tamara pulling something from under the clutter by the wall. It was a small doll, which she grabbed by the hair before trying to push her dummy into its mouth with some force. Although strange and unusual, at least it was a form of play, which was encouraging, but since the start of the visit April had not heard any form of verbalisation from either Tamara or Tyler. The only sounds were Tamara's loud sucking on her dummy, and repetitive music from the phone Tyler was playing on. There didn't appear to be any other toys but who knew what else was under that rubble? April was intrigued that Tamara knew exactly where to find the doll.

'I think the first priority is to get Tamara into nursery, Kerry, what do you think? I will make a request for it to be funded. Tamara needs stimulation.'

'OK, if you pay for it. That's fine by me.'

‘I’m going to arrange a Child in Need meeting for both children, and I will invite the school, the nursery, the health visitor and someone from Housing. We need to get a plan together and see what we can do to make things better for you and your children.’

Kerry looked quite pleased at the thought of getting some help. April wondered what type of mother Kerry would be in different circumstances. Nobody could argue that living in these conditions would impact on parenting ability, and most people would struggle.

10

CONTACT WITH MUM

'Can you bring those clothes down, Isobel? I don't want to have to tell you again.' Denise was calling up the stairs again.

'OK, I'm just sorting them out; give me chance. Moany old cow,' Isobel said under her breath as she sorted through the huge pile of clothes on her bedroom floor.

Isobel was fed up with Denise. The only times she seemed to talk to her were to complain about something she hadn't done that she should have done. She hated mealtimes because she was forced to sit with Denise, Harry and Jordan. She didn't like any of them. Harry tried to be friendly but he gave her the creeps. Jordan seemed to hate everyone; didn't say anything, just grunted when someone spoke to him and disappeared as soon as he had finished his dinner. Isobel always did the same. Her room was lonely but it was the only place she felt comfortable. This wasn't her home and she didn't feel wanted in it.

She'd been feeling really nervous when she'd got up this morning because she was about to start at a pupil referral unit. Her school had excluded her and didn't want her back after she took another girl's phone and stamped on it. The girl had called her a slag. This was the end of the road for the school. They felt they had done everything they could to support her but she couldn't be managed in mainstream school any more. The head decided that a period in a PRU would be the best way to meet her educational needs for the time being.

A taxi picked her up at 8.15 and another girl was already sitting in the back.

'I'm Isobel,' she said, turning to look at the girl beside her.

'Gina,' the girl answered.

They spent the rest of the journey in silence. After around half an hour, the taxi turned off the road onto a long, winding dirt track. As they followed the bend around, a green single-storey building came into view. It looked more like a long shed than a school.

'This isn't the school, is it?' Isobel exclaimed, looking out of the window in disbelief as the taxi pulled up outside.

Inside were a couple of rooms, each with a large round table which seated about eight people, a small kitchen, and a toilet. Isobel was met by Greta, the unit manager, whose broad Glaswegian accent was hard to interpret. She showed her around and explained the set-up. Greta was a tall, heavily built lady with an abundance of red curls. She seemed quite kindly, which helped allay Isobel's nerves.

'There're only two wee girls in yer group, Isobel. We ainly work till twelve on a Monday sae ye'll be home early.'

Isobel nodded.

'We kin give ye more work tae do at home if ye like, bit ye'll get homework anyway. We want ye tae be able tae keep up wi' the level o' work yer capable of. It won't be long before yer doin' yer GCSEs 'n' we want ye to do as well as ye kin. I'm sure ye do too.'

She stared at Isobel, waiting for an answer. Isobel just stared back defiantly. She had understood enough to know what Greta was saying, but Isobel couldn't give a damn about GCSEs. She didn't want to be here; she didn't want to be in foster care. She just wanted things to be normal.

One of the boys, James, seemed to take a liking to Isobel. He jumped into the chair next to hers and played up persistently throughout the morning. He swore at the teacher, refused to do anything he was told, and made rude comments about others in the class, whilst throwing glances at Isobel to see if she was impressed. She was not, but she found him intriguing, the way he kept looking at her. He was quite nice-looking, taller than her and slim, with blond hair. He reminded her of someone she had seen on the television but she couldn't think who it was.

Greta was not impressed with him at all and, although she managed to maintain an air of patience, became increasingly exasperated. 'Right, girls 'n' wee jimmies, fur the lest half an hour we're off tae do art,' she said whilst handing out large sheets of white paper and placing jars of colouring pencils on the table.

'I ain't doin' any art. I 'ate drawin',' James protested, stretching his legs out and slouching in his chair.

'Yer very good at drawing, James. I'm not goin' tae tell ye whit ye have tae draw. I just want ye tae imagine a bonny scene, full o' colour. Something that, whin we look at it, will brighten our day. I will leave it tae ye to decide whit ye want tae do.'

The children began drawing enthusiastically. Isobel was happy because there was nothing she loved more. She struggled at first to think of a beautiful scene, but then she recalled a happy time in her life when her nan took her to Blackpool. Her nan had adored her. Isobel was eight when she died. Her memory of being on a little train which ran along the seafront was vivid. It was a lovely day and the beach was packed. The train hooted and its bells rang as the sun shone down. Her nan held her close as they trundled along, both laughing. She relived this scene as the different coloured pencils slid fluently across the page.

All of a sudden, everything stopped as Greta snatched James's paper. 'What is this?' she demanded, shaking it in front of his face in rage.

James's cheeks coloured slightly but there was an arrogant smirk on his face.

'I asked ye tae tell me whit this is?'

The images on the page were clear: a large pair of breasts with defined nipples, and an erect penis positioned between them. Below this was the start of a drawing which was obviously going to be a vagina. Gina screeched. Isobel froze.

'OK, we wull stoap there, folks. A'm off tae tear this picture up 'n' put it in the bucket where it belongs. A'm very disappointed, James; ah ken yer capable o' much better than this.'

James was leaning back in his seat, looking back at her defiantly. Another boy was trying hard but failing to stifle a giggle.

At the end of the morning the taxi was waiting for Isobel and Gina to return them to their foster placements. Isobel had found out that Gina was also in foster care.

Isobel was distracted on the journey back. She was going to be seeing her mum for the first time since coming into care. She was in quite a turmoil about it, not knowing how she was going to be. They were meeting at the Family Centre and April was going to be there with them.

When she got home, Denise was waiting for her. She didn't ask what kind of day Isobel had had; just pointed her in the direction of the kitchen and told her to get herself something to eat before April came. Isobel pulled a face at her retreating back.

April arrived at 1.15 as she had promised. She chatted to Isobel as she drove, but all Isobel could think about was what it was going to be like when she came face to face with her mum after all these weeks and all that had happened. Her stomach was churning, making her feel queasy.

Her mum was waiting in the family room when they arrived, looking as anxious as Isobel. The two of them stood, one on each side of the room, staring awkwardly at each other.

Finally, Alison broke the silence. 'Hello, Isobel, how are things?'

'All right,' Isobel replied. She was looking down at the carpeted floor awkwardly, avoiding her mother's gaze.

April could see that her intervention was needed. 'OK, I can see that this is very difficult for both of you. I want you to pretend I'm not here. I will go and sit over there,' she said, pointing to the far side of the room. 'I know you're happy to see each other, so try to forget everything else; just enjoy being together. Isobel, you can tell your mum about the PRU you started today. Give each other a hug and then go and sit over there on the sofa. I will just disappear.' She waved her hand in front of her face as though she was holding a magic wand.

April wouldn't normally dream of intervening so explicitly, but on this occasion she felt it was necessary, and it worked. Alison walked over to her daughter, put her arms around her and hugged her tightly. Isobel wiped tears from her cheeks. In next to no time they were sitting together on the small two-seater settee, chattering away. Alison wanted to hear everything about Isobel's placement – what the carers were like, what she was given to eat, and were they nice to her? Isobel answered, 'All right' to most of the questions, which was a relief to April, who knew she wasn't really happy at Denise's. She was impressed that Isobel had the maturity and sensitivity to protect her mum from the worry of knowing how unhappy she really was. Alison had bought a few presents for Isobel – some underwear and socks – and watched with delight as Isobel unwrapped them.

The parting was heart breaking. To pretend that she was happy to go back to her placement was more than Isobel could manage, and the tears flowed. 'I don't want to go back, Mum. I want to come home.'

Alison looked helplessly at April, who waited patiently by the door.

On the journey home, Isobel persisted. 'My mum won't let my dad hurt me now she knows about it. Anyway, he will go to prison, won't he? Why do *I* have to leave home when it's him that did wrong? I hate it in foster care. I hate Denise.'

April knew full well that there was no choice at the moment; that Isobel had to remain in care. There was the possibility that changing her placement could help, but it didn't seem worth moving her at this stage as she didn't know what was going to happen. Further disruption at this time would not be in her best interests. 'I know you don't like it at Denise's, Isobel, but I still think it's because it's new and strange to you. It will get easier. I'm hoping you will be able to go home eventually, but if not, I will find another foster carer for you. Try to be brave for now. This is just for a short time.'

April felt quite desperate, wanting to make Isobel feel better, but not having much she could offer. To be honest, she wasn't very keen on Denise either, although she would never let Isobel know that. Some foster carers did a wonderful job for the children they cared for. Although it was their profession and they got paid, they did it for love. They chose to do the job so that they could help and support vulnerable children, and they did a great job of it. A minority, though, did it because they thought it was easy money. They provided for the child's basic needs but offered no more. Children, especially children who were away from their birth families, needed so much more.

There was hope for Isobel. Her mum loved her. She just needed to recognise that the choice was either her husband or her daughter. She could not have both. The contact session had been positive and the bond between Alison and Isobel was strong. April really hoped that Alison would come to her senses and see what she needed to do for the sake of her daughter. It was hard to witness Isobel's distress without having the power to change it for her. The police had started the process of investigation and all April could do for the time being was wait and see what happened.

11

DANNY

Alison let herself in, and by the time she reached the top of the stairs Danny was waiting, leaning against the open door with his arms folded.

He spoke quietly. 'I asked you not to go.'

Alison was shaken up. She had hoped to be home before him. He had obviously left work early. He moved aside to let her in, his icy stare following her as she walked nervously past him. As soon as she was in, he slammed the door behind her and leant against it, his stare piercing her like a sharp blade. He then slowly started to move towards her, forcing her to move back against the wall.

'You think I did it, don't you? You think I abused my own daughter. You do, don't you? Admit it, Alison, you do.'

He was moving closer, his tall, strong body within an inch of hers as she shrank back as close to the wall as she could manage.

'No, Danny. I don't, honestly.' Her bottom lip quivered.

'Why did you go behind my back? Why did you do it, Alison?'

The anguished look on his face triggered guilt in Alison as well as fear. She couldn't think what to say. She had been on the wrong side of his moods before and it wasn't pleasant. He had never been physically violent towards her but there was a menacing silence and an unpredictability. In some ways this was worse because she never knew what to expect.

He suddenly, surprisingly, pulled her towards him and kissed her. 'You know I love you, Alison. You do love me too, don't you?'

She looked up into his pleading eyes. 'Of course I do, Danny. You know I do.'

'Then promise me you won't go behind my back again. If you love me you'll stop seeing that bitch of a daughter. If you really loved me you wouldn't want anything to do with her after what she said about me.'

Alison's emotions were in shreds. She couldn't move or speak.

Danny gently took her arm and led her to the sofa. 'Let's get a takeaway and some beers. The silly cow will come to her senses in the end and admit she was lying. I won't forgive her, though. I'll never forgive her.'

Alison did as she was told, wiped away the tears that were forming and sat down dutifully, waiting for Danny to return with the takeaway. A few beers might help her to sleep for the first time in weeks.

It was nearly 2am when she woke up. She was crying. Her pillow was saturated; she had been crying in her sleep. Without thought or reasoning, the sobs continued. Her heart was breaking and she felt she would never stop. Her sobs became louder. Danny stirred slightly and turned in his sleep. She sat up and, head resting on her bent knees, continued to sob until there were no more tears in her eyes. She was exhausted but managed to drag herself out of bed and into the lounge. She missed her daughter desperately, and was eaten up with guilt. The pain of being torn in so many directions at once felt almost physical.

For some reason she found herself drawn to the wall cabinet and the drawer where family photos were kept. The photos were loose and mostly of Isobel. Isobel with Alison, or with Danny, and some with the three of them together. Alison lingered on the one which showed Isobel, aged about five, on a pedal boat with Danny. Danny's arm was around her shoulders, keeping her safe, and her little, dimpled face beamed up at him. Alison remembered this picture being taken on one of their caravan holidays.

She was blissfully lost in the past when all of a sudden Danny appeared in the doorway.

'What are you doing Alison?' he said softly.

The hand that held the photograph trembled as he swiftly snatched it from her. In a flash, he tore it in half.

'You won't be looking at that again, will you?' He then pulled out all the rest of the photos before slowly tearing them up, one by one, all the while his eyes fixed firmly on Alison, deriving gratification from her pain.

'Please don't, Danny.' She tried to grab his hand but he shook her away, his eyes continuing to stare at her, cold as ice.

Alison continued to plead but his face was transfixed as the tearing and ripping intensified. She sank down onto the settee. There was nothing more she could do but watch as the physical memories of Isobel's childhood were torn to shreds.

On Friday evening, April was bending down putting washing in the machine when the front door opened and in walked Jed. His striped shirt was undone at the collar and his tie was hanging loose around his neck. His thick brown hair was dishevelled and he had bags under his eyes. He dropped his small suitcase behind the door before hanging his jacket on the peg above. April came out to greet him with a hug and a kiss. He had been away for two nights. He worked long hours when he was away so that he could get the job done and come home as soon as possible.

'I've got baked cod with samphire and new potatoes in the oven and a bottle of Chablis to go with it. Demelza is fast asleep. I tried to keep her up for you but she was really tired. I think nursery tires her out. Mum's coming tomorrow so she can have a few days at home. I think she needs that.'

'I'll just go and have a look at her, then.' Jed went quietly up the stairs, although it wouldn't have mattered how loudly he did it;

Demelza rarely woke once she was asleep. He then showered and changed into casual, comfortable attire before joining April in the kitchen and helping to prepare the meal.

'How on earth am I going to get around the issue with Mum and Dad?' she mused. 'Dad desperately wants to see Max but he won't have anything to do with him whilst Mum isn't happy. I feel as though I'm betraying them in some way.'

'Right, April, with your social work skills and my accountancy training, surely we can find a way to resolve this between us.'

'Well, I can tell you, I've had some awkward people to deal with during my career, but these two… well, what can I say? I just can't for the life of me fathom out why Mum can't forgive him. In fact, I can't even work out what she should be forgiving him for. Wasn't she the one who had an affair? Yes, admittedly he walked out of our lives after that, but surely they are both to blame in their own ways. He is willing and wants more than anything to make amends. I know that he wants to see Max, but I have a sneaky feeling that he would also love to see Mum.'

'Has he actually said that?'

'No, not exactly… but his face changes when I talk about her. He tries to look normal but he kind of flushes and his whole demeanour changes. It's quite subtle but it's definitely there.'

'I suppose she's still bitter about him walking out of her life and leaving her with two very young children.'

'Yes, but he did try to make amends, didn't he? So he tells me, anyway. He told her he had forgiven her for having an affair and wanted to put it all behind them. She said no and then ignored any correspondence from him. He said he had no choice but to leave her alone.'

Jed was already aware of all this but was happy to let April air her frustration yet again.

As always happened when this subject was raised, April had stirred herself up. She stood up and paced around the room as she spoke. 'They're like kids, aren't they? I hope we wouldn't act like that, leaving Demelza to sort out our problems.'

'I hope you don't have an affair. We won't need Demelza to sort us out then.'

'That's true. I won't have an affair, then. Mind you, you need to be on your toes. Miles is still just as gorgeous; maybe even more so.'

She smiled as she watched Jed's response.

'Huh.'

She sat down beside him and put her arms around his neck. 'I still prefer you though'.

Diana arrived the next morning, and as usual April was there to collect her from the station. She was laden with a suitcase and bags which April took from her and loaded onto the back seat.

'I hope you haven't been buying too much for Demelza again, Mum.'

'Only a couple of things I saw in that lovely children's clothes shop in the high street. They have such beautiful things in there for little ones.'

'Yes, I know they do, but they're really expensive, and she grows out of things so quickly.'

'I know, April. But you wait till you see what I've bought. She's going to look absolutely adorable in them.'

April tutted as she drove off, but felt secretly delighted and couldn't wait to see what her mum had bought.

12

FLORIAN AND LEO

April's diary was beginning to get busy. She was finding it a struggle to fit all her appointments into the two-and-a-half days she was working. She was determined that she wouldn't do any more than she was paid for now that she had Demelza to think about. There was a lot going on with her cases, though. The two little boys, Florian and Leo, who were waiting to be adopted were one of her priorities. A number of potential adopters had expressed an interest in them and April had narrowed the list down to two couples. She was due to visit both.

She was just typing the last line of her report for Tyler and Tamara before getting ready for the visits when she was tapped on the shoulder. She turned with a start, and within seconds she was pulled up from her chair and being hugged tightly in Miles's strong arms.

'I've been trying to get into the office to see you but I've been caught up in court for the last two weeks. I bet you're really glad to be back,' he said with a cynical smile.

It was less than a year since April had last seen him but he appeared to have aged a bit in that time. His jawline was more defined and his lovely thick blond hair had started to recede a bit at the front.

The boyish glow had gone from his cheeks. In a strange way, the new maturity suited him.

'In some ways I am, but I don't like leaving Demelza. I missed working, though. How are you? I thought you were going to come and see me while I was off.'

'I'm sorry I didn't make it. I have lots going on myself at the moment. I would tell you about it but I don't suppose you can come to the pub after work anymore now you've tied yourself down with responsibilities. Paula's all settled down with her man from the internet. I haven't got any drinking buddies anymore.'

'Surely Paula can manage to come sometimes, can't she? Simon must be at work as well, I should think.'

'You would have thought so, wouldn't you, but I haven't managed to persuade her yet.'

'As it happens, Paula and I had the same conversation recently. She seems to think it's you who doesn't want to come. OK then, I will see if Jed minds babysitting one evening. I'm sure he won't. Things have changed now, with Demelza. I can't go out straight after work like we used to, but I could come later in the evening occasionally, when she's asleep and Jed's there. Shall we do that?'

'Great. I will leave it to you to persuade Paula, though. I think she's so absorbed with *Simon*,' he said this sarcastically, 'that she doesn't want to do anything else.'

'I'm sure she'll come. We always had such a good laugh. Social workers need to get together to share their sick sense of humour. No one else understands what we're laughing at.'

'By the way, I saw that woman you used to work with – what was her name? You know, the one with the two little girls, the binge drinker… Samantha Bushell?'

'Oh, really?' April said, surprised.

'Her daughters were adopted. I visited them a couple of times at their new home before the order went through and they seemed to be doing really well. Tayla was the older child, wasn't she? Their parents, Phil and Hannah, were trying to teach her that she wasn't responsible for Lily Grace. She kept mothering her, apparently, telling Hannah that Lily Grace was tired or needed her lunch. They did say it was getting better, though, and they are people who can manage that kind of thing. I'm sure they will be absolutely fine.'

April was really pleased to hear that Lily Grace and Tayla had settled and were doing well, and that their Adoption Order had been granted. She really wanted to know about Samantha, though. In many ways, she was just as needy. Her development had been affected by the abusive family environment she was raised in and she struggled to function in the adult world. Neither did she have any positive supportive networks to go to for help.

'How is Sam, do you know? Where did you see her?'

'She was sitting in a shelter on the seafront. She was with a gawky-looking male who looked like your typical drug addict. I'd say they were probably homeless. He had a flea-bitten mongrel on a lead. She… well, she didn't look very clean, let's put it like that.'

April was really sad to hear this. She had always hoped Samantha would be able to get herself together and make something of her life after the girls were taken from her. She was aware of her precarious housing situation, though.

April decided to pay a visit to the foster carers of the Bailey children to see how they were getting on before setting out to meet the two sets of potential adopters. Florian was holding his foster carer Melanie's hand when she answered the door. He looked like a little cherub, with his tussles of blond curls and his chubby cheeks.

'Hello, April. Do come in. Leo is asleep at the moment but you can go up and take a peek if you like.'

'I will do, thanks. Hello, Florian.' April knelt down beside the little boy, who immediately looked down at the floor. He was dressed in a yellow plastic apron, and his hands, arms and face were covered in purple and bright pink paint. 'What have you been doing today?' she asked, trying to coax him to look at her.

He continued to look at the floor.

'You look as though you've been painting some lovely pictures.'

'We've been having a bit of a tantrum, haven't we, Florian? It's all forgotten now, though.'

April immediately picked up on Melanie's cues that it had been dealt with and wouldn't be helpful for Florian to hear it being discussed. She would wait for the chance to talk to her alone to find out what had happened.

Florian soon relaxed as April showed an interest in the large pieces of white paper streaked with brightly coloured paint. 'This is lovely, Florian,' she said, picking up one of the brightest pictures. 'Is it a rainbow?'

Florian nodded.

She picked up another one. 'This is lovely too – is it another rainbow?'

'Rainbow,' he answered. He had a limited vocabulary for a child of almost three. Since being in foster care it had improved and he now used the occasional distinguishable word. Melanie was doing a great job with him.

Florian was set up again at the table with the paints and quickly became absorbed in his art. In the meantime, Melanie led April into the kitchen.

'What happened earlier then, Melanie?' April could tell she was keen to talk about it.

'It was another of those tantrums. It's the first time he's done that for ages. I was hoping they were in the past, but I'm afraid they're not. This one was every bit as bad as they were when he first came to me. It started because he wanted a biscuit. I had just emptied some into a tin and he was asking for one. I said he could have one after breakfast, but I had hardly finished speaking when he swept all the paint pots, the water, the brushes, everything, off the table. There was paint everywhere. He threw himself onto the floor and just screamed. He wasn't crying, just screaming. I just sat down and waited, but the next thing, he stood up and was kicking and stamping on the paints. There was such a mess. Oh my God, April, you wouldn't believe it.'

'What did you do?'

'Do you know what? I know I'm too soft but I can't help thinking about what the poor little thing has been through. What must be going through his brain. I did make him sit on the stairs for a minute but he was so upset. His little face was crumpled up and I've never seen tears like it. It melts your heart.'

April couldn't help smiling. 'You probably are too soft, Melanie, but I'm glad you are. I'm sure a lot of foster carers would be saying they've had enough and can't cope anymore.'

'You can be assured that there is nothing on this earth that would make me say that. I just hope the people who adopt him love him enough to help them cope with all this. You *will* make sure they know how to look after him properly, won't you, April? Make sure they know what they'll have to deal with.'

'Don't worry, Melanie. The adopters will have every bit of information about the children that there is to know. Of course, we don't know the extent of the trauma Florian has suffered, but we can be sure that at the very least he was severely neglected. You spotted within a few days that he didn't seek comfort from you. Do you remember when he collided with the brick wall on his scooter and scraped his fingers? It was only when you saw the blood dripping from them that you realised how much he'd hurt himself, wasn't it? He just carried on as though nothing had happened.'

'Yes. I do remember. I realised he didn't expect anyone to comfort him when he was hurt. There were other times, though, when he had minor scrapes and he would scream the place down for ages. Anyone outside would've thought he was being tortured. It was impossible to comfort him. I always make a big fuss of him now, even if he only has a little bump. He still doesn't respond very well but he is starting to learn that if he hurts himself there will be someone who cares.'

'Adopters are very carefully screened to make sure they have a good understanding of what they might have to deal with. They will have attended training sessions to prepare them. Before I make my mind up as to who is going to have them, I will want to be sure that they can manage anything that might be thrown at them. Adopters must be able to understand that it isn't the same as having your own child and there will be part of their adopted child's life that they will never know about.'

Having reassured Melanie, April set out to meet the potential adopters. The first couple, David and Sarah, were very nice and fell into the 'average' category for adopters: middle class, early middle age, childless. David was a music teacher and Sarah a nurse. Sarah planned to give up work to be a full-time mum for the boys.

They made April welcome, gave her tea and offered cake, which she declined. Their anxiety and desperation to be the chosen ones was clearly evident in their manner. April tried to make them feel at ease but it wasn't easy. When people were highly anxious, she found it rubbed off on her and she struggled to appear at ease herself. David and Sarah had been given information about the boys and were already aware of the difficulties which could arise in the future. They had read books and attended courses for potential adopters, done all their homework, and there was not much April could say was not right about them. She felt this would be a good home for Florian and Leo.

After stopping off to buy a sandwich, which she ate in the car, she made her way to the home of the second couple, Matthew and Lawrence Ryan.

The house was small but cosy, and the couple, Matthew and Lawrence, were very welcoming. April was invited in and offered a comfortable chair to sit on. Looking round, she noticed photos on the walls of the couple with children. Matthew in a swimming pool with a little boy on his shoulders, both laughing; Matthew and Lawrence on the beach, digging sandcastles with the same boy and an older girl. By the beam on his face, it was clear that Matthew was enjoying the activity as much or more than the children.

Matthew was warm, flamboyant and gregarious, whilst Lawrence was the quiet one. While Matthew took control of the meeting in his open and friendly way, offering tea or coffee and placing a plate of chocolate biscuits in front of April, Lawrence watched with a proud smile, enjoying the chance to observe his partner's social flair. Although he didn't say much, April felt he was probably the strong, dominant one. She noticed Matthew intermittently catch his eye as though looking for approval. They had been together for ten years and the bond between them was clearly strong. Lawrence was an artist and had a little shop just off the town centre, and Matthew was a chef. They had desperately wanted a child for years but had had to wait until they could afford for Matthew to give up work.

'Who are the children in the photos?' April asked.

'They're my sister's two children, Maisie and Ben.' Matthew walked over to another photo of an older lady sitting in a deckchair, eating an ice cream and smiling at the camera. 'This is my mum. She adores being a granny and can't wait to have more grandchildren. You should have seen her when we got our approval. She sobbed enough tears to fill the garden pond.' Matthew chuckled as he told this to April.

April had to make the very difficult decision as to which of the two couples would be the best parents for Leo and Florian. Whilst both couples appeared to have the ability to provide adequate care for the children, with a gay couple there was always the added consideration of how this could affect the children as they grew up, and their sense of identity. However, Matthew and Lawrence had a very good insight into how being raised by two men might affect the boys, and had thought carefully about how they would manage it. April knew before she left their house that they would be her choice. Whereas the other couple would be able to offer a perfectly good, stable and settled family life, Lawrence and Matthew offered the same but April sensed something special in their household which promised lots of fun as well as a loving environment. She came away feeling absolutely confident that this was the right decision. She would now need to spend a bit of time with the boys to prepare them for the move, as well as helping them to get used to the idea of having two dads.

13

DAMIAN

At lunchtime, Isobel, James and Gina left the school premises and walked across the field to the open parkland that backed onto the school building. They had started to make a habit of this, although it wasn't strictly allowed. They were usually the only people there, and the three of them just sat on swings or leant against the brick wall of the disused cafe and talked – or groaned, rather – usually about being bored out of their brains at the PRU, and the stupid teachers who were idiots and didn't know anything.

'I'm not staying at that shithole until I'm sixteen,' James told them. 'I could work if I wanted. My stepdad does bikes and I help him sometimes. I can make loads of money doing that; I don't need to get GCSEs or any of that shit.'

'What do you mean, "does bikes"? What does he do with bikes?' Isobel asked.

'Fixes 'em; what do you think he does with 'em, stick 'em up his arse?'

'I don't know, do I?'

'Do you mean motorbikes or ordinary bikes?' Gina asked.

'All bikes; any kind of bike. It wouldn't just be one sort of bike, would it?'

Gina pointed out that it was time to go back.

'I don't feel like going back. I'm staying out. I might walk into town. Why don't you come?' James asked them both.

'I'm not doing that,' said Gina. 'I'm in enough trouble at home at the moment. If I skive off, I'll get grounded again. She grounds me if I breathe too much.'

Isobel was tempted. She didn't really feel like going back to the PRU either. 'What will you do in town?'

'I dunno, look in some gaming shops, I suppose.'

'I'm going back,' Isobel decided. She didn't want to get into trouble with Denise. She knew that Denise didn't like her much and she didn't want to make it worse. She would never admit it to anyone – or even to herself, for that matter – but deep down, she desperately wanted Denise to like her.

She had been sitting down, and as she stood up and started brushing the grass from the back of her skirt, she noticed a tall, thin man striding towards them.

'What you kids doin' hangin' around 'ere? What you up to?'

Isobel noticed a large tear in the sleeve of his leather jacket which started at the shoulder and ran down to the cuff. Following the line of the split back up to his face, she noticed a parallel scar where the skin was healing, but still looked red and sore. It looked as though he had been slashed with a knife. She shuddered at the thought.

'We're supposed to be going back to school but I'm not going,' James said. 'I'm fed up with it; it's stupid and you don't learn anything. The teachers are crap. They're not even proper teachers anyway.'

The man introduced himself as Damian. He seemed quite interested in the PRU. 'I went to something like that but it wasn't called a PRU. It was for kids who got into trouble. I was one of those kids.' He smiled as he said this, and continued to boast proudly about some of his escapades.

'I'm going back to school now,' Gina said. 'I don't want to get into trouble.'

'I'm coming too.' Isobel joined her and they started to head back.

'Do you want to come to a party on Saturday night?' Damian called after them.

Both girls stopped and turned around. Damian had caught their interest.

'What party's that, and where will it be?' Isobel asked.

'It's not far. About three miles from here. I can pick you up and bring you back. There're some other kids comin'. You might know 'em; they're about the same age as you '.

'I would come but I know I won't be allowed. She wants me in bed by eight, out of her way,' Isobel said.

James then piped up with, 'I'm comin', will you pick me up? My mum doesn't make me come in; I just come back when I please.'

As they started to walk away, James had an idea. 'If you have to be in your room, Isobel, how will your foster carer know if you sneak out? She won't, will she?'

Isobel thought about this. It was true that Denise didn't check on her. Once she went to her room, unless she went down for a drink (which she did sometimes), she didn't really see anyone until the morning. 'I could; I don't think she would know.'

'Right, that's sorted then. I'll meet you on the corner of Harbour Street at 8.30. It'll be a great party. You'll have a ball,' Damian said, before setting off back in the direction he had come from.

All three children went back to school. They were feeling buoyed up by the thought of going to a party, and James decided it would be best to go back after all, not to get into trouble. He didn't mind being in school so much now because he had Saturday to look forward to. He had never been to a proper party before.

April was unable to sleep. It was really frustrating because Demelza had gone off straight away and as usual Jed was dead to the world. She was thinking about Samantha Bushell, scolding herself for letting her walk away from the court that day and not checking up on her afterwards to see if she was OK. Although Sam was not her responsibility and once the children had been removed from her care any duty she had to Sam was finished, she could have checked to see if there was anything she could have done to help, just as an act of kindness. She found herself full of guilt and remorse, imagining Sam sleeping through the winter on cold pavements with no one to turn to. She made a decision to find the time to walk around the area where Miles had spotted her. Friday was a day off and she was due to meet with her father for lunch. She decided to walk along the seafront afterwards to see if Sam was around.

She arrived at the restaurant early. The waitress helped her manoeuvre Demelza's pushchair into a corner so that it wasn't in anyone's way. It was only 12.30 but already the place was busy. It was a small restaurant on the seafront which allegedly sold local fresh fish. The view from the window where she sat was just sea and sky, as though the restaurant was afloat. April put Demelza in a high chair and made herself comfortable whilst she waited for her father to arrive.

The decor was pale blue and cream with rustic wooden tables and paintings in pastels of ships on the water. There were fishing nets and lobster pots hanging from the ceiling, replicating the inside of a fishing boat. The restaurant had a lovely calm feel, and despite Demelza rhythmically banging her chair with a large spoon, April felt her mind and body relax as she looked out over the vast expanse of blue sea and sky.

It wasn't long before her father arrived and she stood up to greet him with a hug. He then grabbed Demelza from her high chair and swung her up in the air. 'How is my little darling today? Have you got a kiss for your grandad?'

Demelza's lower lip shot out before she emitted a piercing scream. She was startled by the sudden change in her situation.

'Dad, let me take her,' April said, protectively taking her baby out of his arms. 'You've scared her. Don't forget, she hardly knows you.'

A dark shadow moved fleetingly across his face.

'I'm sorry. I didn't mean to…'

'Don't worry. It's my fault. I have to learn to live with the guilt of not being around for you. I can't change the past, however much I would like to.'

April didn't answer. She couldn't deny that there was a part of her that felt resentful. She still couldn't really understand why he had not tried to contact her and Max when they became adults. He had explained that her mum had made it very clear that she didn't want him in their lives when they were growing up, although this was only his story. April didn't know whom or what to believe. None of it really made sense.

Demelza was comforted and put back in her chair. Although settled, she continued to throw mistrustful glances in her grandfather's direction, as though worried he might suddenly snatch her out of her chair again.

April had lovely fresh herring with hand-cut chips and tomato and chilli marmalade. She didn't want pudding because she was still trying to lose the last few extra pounds she needed to shed to return to her pre-pregnancy weight. She was pleased that she and her father had been completely relaxed with each other. Even Demelza appeared to have got over the initial upset and allowed him to take her out of her high chair and put her in the pushchair. There was a disagreement about who was going to pay the bill but her father won the argument, stating that he had a lot of years to catch up on.

As they were getting ready to leave, he turned to April and asked how her mother was. 'I know she doesn't want to see me but I live in hope that one day she will. I probably shouldn't say this to you, April, but you will never know how much I grieve over what we lost, your mum and me. All those years when we should have been together. I never met anyone else and neither did she'.

'I can't understand it myself, Dad. I just can't imagine how anyone can bear a grudge for so long. Mum isn't that kind of person. She is a forgiving person in every other aspect of her life, except with regard to you.'

'And how are Max and his family?'

'They're absolutely fine. We don't see a lot of them but they are hoping to come down in the summer. I speak to him on the phone and he does ask about you but he still won't see you because he thinks Mum won't like it. I'm sure he would like to otherwise.'

They said their goodbyes and April set off with Demelza to make her way home. She was just about to turn into the high street when she remembered Samantha Bushell. She turned the pushchair around and headed back towards the seafront. There was a chilly wind blowing in from the sea, and a few spots of rain fell as the clouds darkened. She carried on walking along the promenade, looking for signs of rough sleepers. She looked inside the shelters as she passed them but they were mostly empty, apart from one or two, where pensioners sat reading the newspaper or looking out to sea. She ended up walking the length of the promenade, but to no avail. It was getting cold and the sky was darkening further, so she decided to get Demelza home.

14

ON THE STREETS

By the time Samantha reached the town centre some of the shops were starting to open. She could see the lights from McDonald's ahead of her, looking warm and welcoming, drawing her towards them. She was going to get a cup of coffee and a Big Mac with the bit of money she had in her pocket. By the time she reached the building her toes and fingers were stiff with the cold. It was turning into one of those bitterly cold, sunny January days when those with nice homes and warm fires loved to get wrapped up in their cosy scarves, mittens and bobble hats and romp through the woods with their children and frisky pet dogs.

She sat in the window, watching the world go by. The traffic was building up; people rushing in different directions, heading to their various workplaces. There was a department store opposite and she watched the shutters being raised by women with poles, a young man putting a sign outside which advertised special meal deals in their cafe. The town was waking up. Samantha wanted to stay in McDonald's where it was warm and she sat there for as long as she dared, until it became cringingly embarrassing every time a young woman dressed in a McDonald's uniform came again to her table to ask if she was OK.

She couldn't say how she got through the day but somehow the hours went by and it was dark once again. She still had no idea what she was going to do, but although she hadn't wanted to face the fact, it was becoming clear that her only option was to make a bed on the pavement. What else could she do? She dreaded the thought, sure that she would either be murdered or freeze to death.

By eight o'clock she was exhausted and sat down in a shop recess where a bit of light shone from inside. Further up the high street she could see a shop assistant putting some cardboard into a bin. As soon as the girl had gone back inside, she rushed over and took it, hoping it would provide a bit of a barrier between her and the cold concrete beneath her. She placed it on the ground and sat herself down, but the cold still seeped through. Having been awake since four o'clock in the morning, and with all the emotional trauma she had experienced of late, she felt completely exhausted and her body longed for sleep. The shop was close to the road where traffic ran constantly, engines revving impatiently whilst waiting at nearby traffic lights, blowing dusty fumes directly towards her. At the same time, she couldn't stop shivering. A powdery white frost was forming on the pavement. By now her fingers were so numb she could hardly move them.

She was thinking that she needed to move or she would die of cold there in the shop doorway, but her body was stiff and unresponsive, and she didn't know where else she could go. Although the noise was dreadful, she didn't want to be anywhere quiet. The busy noisiness of the high street was strangely comforting. She wrapped her arms around her knees to try to warm her body. She had a blanket with her, and although it was thin it helped a bit. She drew her knees up to her chin and made a platform with her hands to rest her head on. The combination of lack of sleep and fighting off the cold made her weak with exhaustion, but she couldn't find a comfortable position and the constant noise was becoming intolerable. The hard concrete and being so scrunched up made her ache, and she longed to stretch out her legs. If she did, though, the blanket would no longer cover them.

She was on the edge of despair and close to tears when, above the din, she thought she heard a voice. She lifted her head up, and standing before her was a tall man in a long brown coat with a beard and long, tangled dreadlocks hanging over his shoulders.

'You can't be planning to spend the night here, can you, young lady?'

Samantha couldn't quite work out what was happening. She thought at first that she might be dreaming.

'I'm from the shelter. You are welcome to come with me if you like. I really don't think you should be sleeping outside on a night like this.'

'I… I'm not sure. I don't know. My landlord kicked me out. I've got nowhere to stay.'

'Well then, you must come with me. It's not quite the Ritz but there is a mattress you can sleep on and some hot food to eat. I expect you're hungry, aren't you?'

This sounded like bliss to Samantha, who, stretching out her stiff limbs and shaking away the numbness from her legs and arms, stood up obligingly and followed the man through some narrow little backstreets and down a long, winding alley which ran parallel to the station. She started to wonder when they would get to the shelter. It dawned on her that this man could be intending to harm her. He could be anyone. But she was too tired and hungry to care. Anything was better than spending the night on that pavement in the freezing cold.

Eventually they came to a long single-storey building with a sagging roof. The man opened the door and stood aside, smiling kindly at her whilst she walked inside. She could see line after line of mattresses, inches apart, which covered the floor space of the huge room. Just in front of the door was a counter with a notepad where she was asked to sign her name. Some of the mattresses were taken by sleeping bodies who looked dead to the world, but there were also people, mostly males, sitting on rickety kitchen chairs at the far end of the room, chatting. One man who she thought might be about her age was sitting apart from the group, rocking back and forward and mumbling to himself.

She was shown to a mattress and given a sleeping bag to put on it before being taken to the kitchen for some food. The place was squalid and lacking in basic homeliness but it was safe and warm. The warmth of the room, the thought of a mattress and a cosy sleeping bag, and some hot food were everything she could have wished for at that moment in time. She was given a plastic bowl full of chicken stew and dumplings. It tasted heavenly, and after eating it she collapsed on her mattress and slept better than she had in years.

When she woke in the morning, people seemed to be leaving the shelter with their bags on their backs. Sam wondered why they were leaving. She then spotted a woman walking towards her.

'Get yerself some breakfast, luv, have a shower and clean yer teeth, then come and see me over there. My name's Sydney by the way'. She pointed to a room in the far corner before handing Samantha a little pack with a tiny tube of toothpaste, a toothbrush and a mini bar of soap.

After getting dressed, Sam did as she had been asked and went to look for Sydney.

'Somebody brought these in yesterday; you can look through them if you like to see if there's anything there you would like.' On the floor was a huge pile of clothes – jumpers, coats, shoes, gloves, scarves. 'We get a lot of things given to us by kind people, so help yourself; you'll need things to keep you warm out there.'

Sam looked curiously at her. She'd thought she would be staying here. Sydney, recognising her confusion, explained that this was just a night shelter. She would have to leave during the day, but she could come back in the evening. Sam sorted through the pile of clothes and tried on various coats before settling on a brown corduroy three-quarter-length jacket with a fur collar. She found some colourful stripy gloves, a scarf and a bobble hat; none of which matched, but they felt warm, which was all that mattered. After taking note of

Samantha's situation and the circumstances which had led to her being there, Sydney offered to take her to the homeless charity which helped people obtain housing. Her name was added to their long list.

Sam spent a few nights in the shelter, wandering around during the day and selling *The Big Issue*. She soon began to realise that this wasn't the utopia it had appeared on the first night when she was so cold and so tired. She spent much of her time fighting off sexual advances from other residents.

There was one man called George who seemed OK. He looked a bit grubby with his unwashed hair and broken teeth, but despite those things he wasn't too bad to look at and sticking with him meant the other men left her alone. They started to spend their days together and Sam felt so much better not being on her own. George was quite savvy and familiar with the etiquette of street life. He had spent long periods on the streets from the age of sixteen, in between being a resident in a young offenders' institution and later in prison.

15

KATY

On Monday morning April was in the office, discussing Tyler and Tamara Phillips with Katy. A few decisions had come out of the Child in Need meeting and one of them was for the family to have extra support from the social work team. This was a good opportunity for a newly qualified social worker to gain experience whilst also meeting the requirements of their portfolio. A neglect case with these complexities would give Katy a perfect balance. It would also help April, who could offload some of the work she would otherwise have had to do herself. She had arranged for Katy to meet the family that afternoon. She couldn't help feeling amused at the thought of Katy, in her beautiful cream-coloured open-toe stilettos, stepping onto the urine-soaked carpet in Kerry's flat. Perhaps she should have warned her, but it was too late now.

Following the visit with Katy, April intended to go straight to Lawrence and Matthew's home to tell them the good news: that they had been chosen to be parents to Florian and Leo. She couldn't wait to see their faces.

On the journey to Kennedy House, April discussed the case of Kerry Phillips and her children. 'You will probably be shocked at the conditions this family are living in, Katy. In all my career, I haven't seen anything quite as bad. It's a disused office block, not even built to be a home. Hostels are never good, but they are often converted Victorian or Georgian houses where there is at least a semblance of homeliness. The challenge for us here is balancing poor parenting and neglect issues against inadequate living conditions. We need to try to help Kerry improve her situation, but we also need to be sure that she's doing her best for the kids, despite the conditions.'

As the car pulled up on the forecourt in front of Kennedy House, Katy looked at April in disbelief. 'You're not telling me this is where they live?'

'This is where they live. And they're not the only family here.' Instead of turning to get out of the car, April turned to Katy. 'I think I should warn you, Katy. You may need to tread carefully when we get inside the bedsit. I should have said earlier but I'm afraid I have been so busy I quite forgot.'

Katy's arm, which had stretched out to open the door, now stopped in mid-air.

April continued. 'There's an overflowing potty problem in the flat, so you might want to avoid walking across the carpet.'

Katy appeared surprisingly unperturbed.

'What do you think might be your first priority then, Katy, for this family?'

'Housing, I would guess. I could write to the Housing Department on their behalf.'

'Yes, and there are some charities who might be worth getting in touch with. I will leave that to you to find out what there is out there. Keep me informed, though, won't you?'

'I know I probably shouldn't say it, but to be truthful I'm quite excited about this, you know, April. It's going to be great for my portfolio.' Katy was clearly thrilled by the impending challenge.

'Despite the urine-soaked carpet?'

They both laughed.

After climbing out of the car, April double-checked it was locked securely before showing Katy the way to the back of the building and the entrance. April pushed open the heavy glass doors and then led the way up the open staircase towards Kerry's room. She watched with amusement as Katy's mouth fell open with astonishment as the door was opened and she looked inside. She wondered how prepared Katy was for encountering this kind of environment. Surely she must have seen squalor before in her placements, but April was still baffled that a social worker would go to so much trouble with their appearance, knowing the kind of situations they might find themselves in.

Tamara was lying on the mattress at the back of the room. She had the teat of a bottle between her teeth, but she sucked fruitlessly because the brown-tinted liquid was not coming through. April noticed that neither Tamara nor Tyler had changed their position in acknowledgement of the social workers' arrival. Tyler seemed to be in exactly the same position he had been the last time she visited: sitting on the edge of the second mattress, holding the phone and with earphones in his ears. There was an unpleasant odour, and distinguishable within that was something recently fried, as well as the strong acidity of stale urine. April noticed there were dirty dishes piled in the sink and a used frying pan on the portable cooker. Dark shadows circled Kerry's eyes. Her hair was loose, unbrushed and falling into her eyes. She wore a black silky top with shoestring shoulder straps which kept falling down. The hair and the straps were clearly trying her patience.

'Katy is a newly qualified social worker. She's going to do her best to help you. She will support you in trying to find more suitable accommodation. In the meantime, we need to think about how you can make the best of what you have and improve things for the children. It seems to me that you are giving up a bit, Kerry. I acknowledge that it must be hard living in these conditions but there are things you can do. I've arranged for Tamara to start nursery. It's quite a walk from here but it is doable. She can start by going two mornings a week and gradually build up to four. Tyler can go to Breakfast Club at his school and After-School Club two or three times a week.'

'That's fine with me. I don't know what difference it will make, though. I just need somewhere proper to live.'

'I understand that,' April said, 'but at least they will get some stimulation. There will be opportunities for them to play. When they're at home you could always take them out somewhere. You could take them for a walk or to the park, get some fresh air.'

While they were talking, Tyler put his earphones down and walked over to his mum. Like Kerry, he had dark circles under his eyes. April wondered if this was due to lack of sleep or poor nutrition, or both. 'I need a drink.' He was pulling on Kerry's top to get her attention as she was talking to April.

She said, 'In a minute' a few times, but he persisted.

'I'm thirsty, Mummy. I need a drink.'

Eventually, Kerry turned towards the sink, which was behind her. She searched through the stack of dirty dishes and found a plastic beaker. Without washing it, she filled it with water from the tap and handed it to Tyler, who took a big gulp before returning to his place on the side of the mattress, putting his earphones back in and resuming his game. Kerry half-turned towards April. 'Can I get you a cup of tea?'

April looked at the dirty crockery in the sink and, trying not to show the disdain she felt, answered politely, 'No – thank you for the offer, though. We had a drink before we left the office, didn't we, Katy?'

Katy nodded a bit too vigorously. 'Yes, we did, thank you.'

April decided that Katy would need to get to know Tyler. Building a relationship with a child was a vital part of the practical training, and was also necessary in this case to gauge how they could be helped, and to get a clearer picture of what was going on for these children.

Katy had quickly come to the conclusion that this was a lazy, inadequate mother who would be so even with adequate living conditions. She agreed some weekly appointments with Kerry; some during the day and other times when she would take Tyler out to get to know him.

Back at the office, April was handed a note with a telephone number for the police officer who was dealing with Isobel's case. *At last*, she thought. *Maybe I'll find out, finally, how the investigation is going.* As soon as she could she called the number, and the phone rang for quite some time before being answered by a woman.

'Hello, it's April Gardiner here. Is it possible to speak to DC Gilligan?'

'I'm afraid she's not in the office. Shall I leave a message for her to call you?'

April tried to disguise her frustration. They kept missing each other. 'I really need to know how the investigation is going. If she could call me as soon as possible I would be grateful. She has my mobile number, I think, but I will give it to you again, just in case.'

She recited the number and then, with a sigh, turned her attention to the next thing on her list. She still felt frustrated. She could never understand why it always took so long to investigate these matters. As far as she was aware, Isobel's father had not even been interviewed yet.

16

THE PARTY

When Isobel finished at the PRU on Friday afternoon, she was picked up by Norah, a social work assistant, who took her to the Family Centre to meet her mum. Norah had been at their last contact so Isobel was used to her by now. She was chatty and friendly, and Isobel felt comfortable in her company. She always seemed genuinely interested in her, which helped to lift her mood a little bit.

Norah and Isobel were a bit early so they sat on comfy chairs in the family room, chatting together. Isobel found herself opening up to Norah more than she had with anyone else. She was quite young, probably not much older than Isobel, and they were able to talk about the music they both listened to, television programmes they watched, and who they fancied. Isobel really enjoyed this.

After about half an hour, she started to look out for her mum. 'What's the time?'

'It's 4.15,' Norah said after checking her phone.

'She was supposed to be here at four.'

Norah did her best to reassure Isobel, but by 4.30 Alison still had not arrived. 'I will give her a ring to see where she is.'

Alison's phone rang for a while before the answerphone kicked in. Norah left a message asking her to get in touch.

By 4.45pm Isobel was becoming fretful; it was clear her mum was not coming. Norah watched helplessly as Isobel rushed to the window each time a car stopped outside or voices were heard, but they were not Alison, and reluctantly Norah suggested that they go home. She assured Isobel she would find out what had happened, reassuring her that there was probably a reasonable explanation.

Although Isobel felt exhausted that night, she found it hard to settle. She was trying to think of all the possible reasons for her mum letting her down. She wanted to believe there was a reasonable explanation but somehow, deep down, she knew what it was. Her mum didn't love her; she loved her dad more. The emotional intensity of this realisation caused her physical pain. Her insides were rolling and churning. She began to wonder why she had been born; why she would want to carry on living, even. There was nothing likeable about her, she thought. She had never been popular at school; although the other children tolerated her, she knew they really thought she was a bit strange, which she was. Her father had used her as an object, there for his own sordid and deviant satisfaction, and her mother believed she was a liar. As the night drew on and the dawn approached, her anger at her mum turned to despair. She felt desolate, alone and unloved. She buried her head in her pillow to muffle the sound of her sobs until exhaustion overwhelmed her and she finally slept.

She was woken early the next morning by a sharp, loud knock on her bedroom door. Her eyes flew open with a start. She had been in a deep sleep after her turbulent night.

'Isobel? Isobel, can you hear me? I want your sheets. Can you get up now, please?'

Isobel forced her eyes open and looked at the clock on the side table, which said 7.30. 'Yes, coming,' she groaned.

'We're going out today, Isobel. We're going to see my sister in Dartford, so get up now, please.'

'Dartford?'

'Yes, Dartford,' Denise replied with annoyance.

‘I don’t want to go to Dartford,’ Isobel mumbled.

There was no response to that.

She dragged herself out of bed. The anger inside her felt just as intense. She hated her mother now with a vengeance. She shrugged into her dressing gown and started to pull the sheets off her bed. Denise had a thing about sheets. She was always changing them – or making Isobel change them, anyway. If she wasn’t nagging about sheets, it was something else: leaving dishes in the sink, taking coffee upstairs, the television being too loud. Isobel put the sheets on the landing before getting in the shower. Whilst she was showering, she could hear Denise moaning that she hadn’t put the sheets in the laundry bin. She mumbled to herself, ‘Why don’t you fuck off, you stupid old bitch?’

She sat at the breakfast table without speaking to anyone, a scowl on her face. Her eyes never left the inside of the bowl from which she was eating her Coco Pops.

‘Have some fruit,’ Harry suggested, pushing the overflowing fruit bowl towards her.

‘No thanks,’ she replied without looking up.

‘We need to set off as soon as we can. It takes about two hours to get there,’ Denise said as she fussed around the kitchen.

‘I’m not coming,’ Isobel said.

‘You are coming,’ Denise answered.

‘I’m not.’

‘You are. You have to come, otherwise you will be here on your own.’

‘I’ll stay on my own then. Anyway, I won’t be on my own, Jordan’s here’.

Denise threw the teacloth she had been folding on to the chair in front of her and stomped towards the table where Isobel and Harry still sat.

‘Jordan is old enough to stay on his own, you’re not!’

Harry joined in with a more gentle and persuasive manner. ‘You have to come with us, Isobel, I'm afraid. It won't be that bad. Steffi has a daughter a bit older than you. You might get on with her.'

'I'm not coming,' Isobel persisted.

Harry and Denise looked at each other despairingly.

'Well, you have no choice: you are coming whether you like it or not. You have to come. I have to go and you can't stay here, so you have to come.' Denise was becoming increasingly rattled.

'I'm *not* coming.' Isobel stood up and stormed out of the room, slamming the door so hard the house shook.

Upstairs, she sat on her bed and let the tears flow. She hated the idea of meeting Denise's sister and her family. She was shy and nervous around strangers at the best of times, and Denise and Harry were still strangers as far as she was concerned. Besides, she was going to a party later and she wouldn't be back in time if she had to go to Dartford. There was no way she was going and she couldn't see how they could make her.

She continued to sit on her bed with her arms wrapped around her knees, staring out of the window and waiting to see what would happen next. She could hear muffled voices from the hallway downstairs, and strained her ears to hear what was being said. The next thing she heard was Denise saying goodbye to Harry, telling him she would be back late in the evening. Harry had clearly offered to stay with Isobel. She could tell by the tone of Denise's voice that she was not happy.

Isobel spent the rest of the morning in her room as she always did. She occasionally went downstairs to get a drink or a biscuit from the kitchen, but only when she thought the others were somewhere else. She was starting to feel a bit better about helping herself to food but still felt awkward. Harry was much easier to get along with than Denise and Isobel felt more relaxed when it was just him and her in the house. She had been suspicious of his kindness towards her to begin with, but had come to realise that there were no sordid intentions behind it.

Just after one o'clock she was feeling peckish and decided to go downstairs to get herself a sandwich. Harry was in the kitchen, making himself something to eat. He tried to make light conversation but Isobel wasn't really in the mood to talk.

'I'm going for a walk with the dog. Why don't you join me after you've had your lunch?'

'No, I'm OK, thanks.'

'I didn't ask if you were OK, did I? I asked if you would like to come for a walk.' There was warmth and friendliness in his smile.

Suzie, the little cocker spaniel, was sitting restlessly beside Harry, long nose pointing upwards and eyes pleading. Her paws began scraping the wooden floorboards in her eagerness to get on her way.

'A bit of fresh air will do you good and I would really like some company for a change. I get fed up walking just with the dog. You can hold the lead if you like.'

Despite Isobel's expression remaining bored and solemn, she was secretly lifted by Harry's words. 'OK, I'll come then.'

'That's great.' Harry turned to Suzie. 'We've got company today, Suzie. You can show her what a good swimmer you are. You should see her when she gets in those waves; she looks like a bottlenose dolphin.'

Despite herself, Isobel smiled. She had started to almost like the idea of a walk along the beach with the dog. She was fond of Suzie, and sometimes, when she had been in the house on her own, which had happened occasionally for a short period of time, she had taken her into her room, put her on the bed and talked to her about how she was feeling.

Suzie panted and wagged her tail vigorously as they drove the short distance to the seafront. Isobel, by this time was feeling almost completely relaxed in Harry's company. He was a short, tubby man with a bald patch at the front of his head. His face was open and friendly and always had a smile. It was a pity that he wasn't the one looking after her at home instead of Denise, she thought. Harry worked long hours and she hardly saw him during the week.

When they came home, Isobel's mood had lightened after the fresh sea air, the fun with the dog, and Harry's infectious sense of humour. She started to turn her mind to the party. Damian was picking her up at 8pm. She was feeling a bit anxious about it, not knowing who would be there. She wasn't sure what to wear either as she had never been to a party before. She went through her wardrobe and found a pair of tight jeans and a salmon-pink top which clung to her body like a second skin.

By 7.30 she had told Harry she was going to have a shower and go to bed, saying she felt really tired. He wasn't the least bit perturbed by this, bearing in mind that she spent most of her time in her room.

'OK, Isobel. Have a good sleep, won't you? We can take Suzie out again tomorrow if you like; I think she enjoyed your company.'

At 7.50 Isobel had changed, sneaked out of the front door, and was heading off towards Harbour Street where she was due to meet James and Damian was picking them up. She stood on the corner where Damian had told her to wait. It was quite a busy road but there was a lay-by where Damian said he would pull in. Isobel looked both ways, hoping to see James.

Within a few minutes a sleek black saloon pulled up beside her and she could see Damian at the wheel. He leant over and opened the passenger door for her to get in. She looked inside through the open window and was a bit unsettled when she saw there was no one else in there. 'Where's James?'

'He's already there. He wanted to make his own way.'

She continued to stand on the pavement. 'How did he know where to go?'

'I texted him. Stop standing there asking silly questions. You're going to be fine; just get in and let's get on our way.'

Isobel hesitated but could sense that Damian was getting a bit impatient with her, so with some reluctance she climbed in. The second she shut the door, Damian sped off.

'Who else will be there? Are there other kids coming?'

'Yes, they'll be there, stop worrying.'

Isobel began to feel more relaxed and, for the first time, settled into the comfort of the soft leather seat. She noticed the car was quite plush, and in the middle of the steering wheel she saw the letters 'BMW'. She was very impressed that Damian was the owner of a BMW; quite a new one as well, by the look of it. She didn't know much about cars but she did know that you had to be rich to own a BMW.

'This is a nice car. Is it yours?'

'Yep, glad you like it.'

He seemed different than when they had met in the park. He was dressed in jeans as before, but smart jeans, not baggy and frayed. The tight olive-green T-shirt looked attractive against his smooth, dark skin. His features were symmetrical with an aquiline nose, and his hair a mass of dark curls. His skin looked bright, and the scar on his cheek less noticeable than before.

They seemed to be driving for quite some time before turning into a long street with identical terraced houses on both sides. There were cars parked all the way down the road as far as one could see, but Damian, not a bit perturbed, drove straight down the middle without slowing. Quite a way down, he suddenly jerked to a stop, touched the gearstick and, in no more than a few seconds had reversed and parked against the pavement.

'This is it,' he said, turning his smiling face towards her. 'Come in and meet the gang.'

'Gang?!'

'Just a joke, it's not a real gang; crowd, I mean.'

Damian opened the small metal gate, then, with his keys still in his hand, unlocked the front door, which was reached by a couple of steps. From the hallway where Isobel stood just inside, she could see into the lounge and part of the kitchen at the end of the hallway. The flooring throughout was laminate, but with no signs of homely touches, such as rugs or mats, there was a cold, empty feel about it. A couple of old armchairs in the lounge appeared to have been dumped rather than arranged. Isobel followed Damian through to the kitchen. A cupboard door was ajar and there was nothing inside. The feeling of emptiness resonated throughout. A small saucepan stood on the cooker, and on the worktop next to it was a kettle. The only other visible items were odd pieces of cutlery on the draining board and two mugs on the side.

'Where are all the others?' she asked, feeling more than slightly perturbed.

'Don't worry, they'll be here soon.' Damian took her hand and led her into the lounge. 'Come and sit down in here. Don't look so worried. I'm going to look after you. You're my girl now.'

Isobel felt confused. Whilst she was a bit alarmed, at the same time she was flattered. She had never had a boyfriend before, and now Damian – who wasn't bad-looking, who had a BMW – seemed to be saying *he* was her boyfriend.

Within half an hour a woman and two men arrived. Isobel saw them from where she sat in the lounge, opening the gate and walking up the path. She wasn't sure what to think because they didn't look like the type of people she'd been expecting to be at a party with. They were too old. She'd been expecting teenagers. The woman must have been in her forties at least. One of the men looked a similar age, and the other – somewhat younger, but still a lot older than Isobel – probably in his twenties.

One of them had a key and Isobel heard the lock being turned and low voices. The older man and woman went straight upstairs without introducing themselves, but the younger man came into the lounge.

'Well, hello, young missy,' he said, circling her like a tiger eyeing up its prey. 'Damian's a lucky bugger. Where did he find you?' He looked her up and down slowly, his eyes lingering creepily around her breasts where her tight T-shirt was stretched to capacity.

Isobel felt jittery. She was regretting wearing such a tight top now, and found herself hunching her shoulders against his leering stare. 'When does the party start?' she asked, a slight quiver in her voice.

The man, who had told her his name was Joseph, gave a cynical laugh. 'Don't you worry, little missy, we know how to party, don't we, Daim?' He seemed to smirk as he caught Damian's eye.

17

MISSING

On Monday morning, April was in the office typing up the adoption report for Florian and Leo. She needed to complete the paperwork before the end of the week so that it could be submitted to the panel for approval. It was going to be tight as she only had two-and-a-half days to do it, and hundreds of other things to do as well. She had just about finished the first section when she was tapped on the shoulder. It was Paula.

'Oh! Paula. I was hoping to see you. I've been meaning to text you. We were planning to meet for a catch-up with Miles.'

When they'd discussed it previously Paula had been enthusiastic, but now she appeared surprisingly reticent.

'Don't worry if you're a bit busy. Just let us know when you can make it. It's a bit frantic on the work front at the moment, isn't it? I'm finding I have to work some evenings despite promising myself I wasn't going to do that this time.'

'Yes, it's busy. I'm trying to get as much done as I can during the day. Simon isn't happy about me bringing work home. He says he doesn't work at home and he earns more than me, so why should I? He has got a point, I suppose. Only thing is, I can't always manage to get everything finished. Well, you know what it's like.'

‘I can see what he means but if you’ve got deadlines for reports there’s not a lot of choice in the matter, is there?’

‘I will try to arrange it so that we can have a night out with Miles, April. I would really like that. I’ll let you know soon.’

They sat down at opposite desks and began typing away, trying to make up for the time they had wasted chatting. April was a bit surprised by Paula’s response. She had always been the instigator of the pub sessions, sometimes dragging April along after work when she wasn’t really in the mood. But now she was in a relationship, her sessions with her friends were not so important to her, which was understandable, especially as it was a relatively new relationship.

April suddenly realised she hadn’t checked her emails. There were, as usual, quite a few standard ones: notifications of legislation updates, team meeting dates. She scrolled down, hoping to get through them without any further distraction, but stopped abruptly when she saw one from Out of Hours. It was regarding Isobel Thorne. April gasped as she read it.

> *This is an Out of Hours alert notifying you that Isobel Thorne went missing from her placement on Saturday 17th May. Her foster carer noticed she had gone at 9.15pm and OOHs was notified at 9.30pm. There has been no contact since and her mobile phone is switched off.*

April was aware that Isobel’s mum hadn’t turned up for contact on Friday. She was completely distracted by this, and as well as being worried, she wondered how she was going to carry out the necessary time-consuming procedures required when a child goes missing from foster care, and also finish the report she was working on in time for the deadline.

She read the full report from OOHs before phoning Denise, who told her how Harry had gone to Isobel’s room, knocked on her door to say goodnight, and when there was no reply, went in to find her gone. They had no idea where she could have gone. The police had checked her family home and Alison hadn’t heard anything.

She had no close friends with whom she might be staying. It was a complete mystery.

Before April had time to get her head around the catastrophe, her phone started to ring. Just like many times before in these kinds of situations, she was tempted to leave it. However, it rang and rang and she finally answered it.

It was Alison. 'Have you found Isobel yet?'

April had to take a deep breath. How was she supposed to have found Isobel? She had only just heard that she was missing, and the police hadn't found her even though they'd had the whole weekend. 'No, I'm sorry, Alison; as far as I am aware, she hasn't been found yet.'

'What are you doing, then? Are you going to look for her? Is anyone looking for her?'

'Everyone is doing their best, Alison, I can assure you of that. I am about to arrange a strategy meeting with the police to get a plan together. I will let you know what happens.'

April hesitated before asking about Friday. She could tell Alison was very worried about her daughter, but at the same time, it was important to know what had happened. 'I was wondering why you didn't turn up on Friday for contact, Alison?'

There was silence.

'Are you there? What was the reason for not turning up? Did something happen?'

'No. I wanted to come.' There was another pause. 'I had a migraine…j. I was really ill.'

'Too ill to phone?' April queried.

There was another short silence.

'I'm worried. Do you think something's happened to her? Do you think it was because I didn't turn up?' Alison's tone was becoming more like a screech as her anxiety rose.

'I'll come and see you shortly to discuss this further, Alison.' April felt it was too important for a phone discussion, although as she said it, she wondered how on earth she was going to fit it in.

After hanging up, she had to hold her head between her hands for a minute to stop it spinning as her stress levels began to reach crisis point. 'Right. The first thing to do in situations like this is have a cup of coffee,' she said out loud.

Paula looked up from her keyboard and said, 'Yes please, if there's one going.'

April stood in the kitchen, thinking over what she had to do whilst waiting for the kettle to boil. It was clear that the report she had been trying to finish would have to be left for the time being. She needed to arrange the meeting with the police, the foster carer and someone from the PRU, and then she would visit Alison on her way home. Having put things in some order, she was able to think straight and get on with the task in hand.

Denise was the first to turn up for the meeting, which gave April the opportunity to quiz her about what had happened and what had led up to Isobel's disappearance. Unfortunately, this led nowhere. As far as Denise was concerned, Isobel had been her usual self and there had been no indication that she was going to run away; on the contrary, she had enjoyed her afternoon with Harry and the dog.

The police had nothing much to offer. They had made all their enquiries but there were not many leads. The only piece of helpful information was from James, whom they had interviewed. He'd told them about the party, but unfortunately he had no idea where it had been held, and all he knew about the young man who'd invited them was that he'd said his name was Damian. Alarmingly, James had told them that he had been expecting to go to the party but had been texted by Damian to change the place he was to wait to be picked up, and then Damian hadn't turned up. James had tried to text Isobel but had no reply.

Alison was beside herself with worry when April arrived at her flat. She paced up and down, frequently asking why no one was doing anything. The guilt she felt for not turning up to the contact session was overwhelming her and she was struggling to focus. Unfortunately, April couldn't provide much comfort.

That evening, after putting Demelza to bed, April sat down on the sofa with her laptop on her knee and finished the report for the adoption panel. It was after ten by the time she finished, absolutely exhausted. Jed was away until Wednesday. She ran a lovely hot bath which she sank slowly into, enjoying the luxury of the rich, foaming lather bubbling around her. The scents of camomile and rosemary from the very expensive bath soak Jed had bought her for Christmas did the job of calming the rapids in her brain. Afterwards she made herself a cup of hot chocolate before setting off for bed with the novel she was halfway through. She had hardly found the page she was up to before her eyes closed and she drifted into sleep.

At 3am she sat bolt upright, her eyes wide and her brain swirling in panic. Isobel had now been missing for two consecutive nights and nothing had been heard from her. April started to question whether she had done everything she could for Isobel. Maybe there was something else she should have done to keep her safe. Isobel had told her she didn't like it at Denise's. Perhaps she should have let her move somewhere else. Whilst she was very worried about Isobel, she was also very worried about herself. What if something terrible had happened to her and April was blamed? She was her social worker after all. It was her job to keep Isobel safe. There was bound to be an enquiry, and the work she'd done, every decision she'd made, and every action she had taken since Isobel had come into care would be pawed over and scrutinised.

April tossed and turned. She envisaged her name being splashed across the tabloids. She thought of other cases nationally in which, despite the social workers doing everything they could possibly have done, they were blamed for tragedies that they couldn't possibly have prevented. Although she tried hard to think positively and confidently that she had done everything she could, she couldn't help recalling other cases. There was one high-profile case where a little boy died at the hands of his mother's boyfriend, and although the social worker had done everything within her power to protect him, she was sacked, as were her manager and managers further up the line. Other professionals should have taken more of the blame but had got off scot-free.

She was now thinking that she shouldn't be expecting the police to resolve the matter, although she couldn't think what else she could do. She was desperate for morning so that she could get up and do whatever else she could to find Isobel.

18

BOW & ARROW

Miles had been persistent in his aim to get together with April and Paula, and the three had managed at last to set aside a late afternoon. They'd agreed to meet at 3pm at their old haunt, the Bow & Arrow; a fifteenth-century pub with a beautiful garden. They had spent many a Friday evening there before the big changes – April going on maternity leave and Paula meeting Simon – winding down from their frenetic, action-packed week at work with a drink and a chat.

Miles and April arrived in the car park at the same time, but by the time they had been served at the bar and found a table Paula breezed in.

'Why are we sitting indoors? It's glorious out there.' She had already turned towards the open door at the back of the bar where a beam of bright sunshine split the darkness in the room.

The other two picked up their drinks and without comment followed her out of the door and down the three concrete steps, bending to avoid bumping into the abundant array of flowers dangling from baskets on either side. The scent from the colourful mix, mingled with freshly cut grass, was glorious.

Paula stood still for a moment, taking deep breaths and slowly exhaling. 'Wonderful. Let's sit over there where we can look at the stream,' she said, pointing ahead.

'I can't believe this is the first time we've managed to get together since you came back, April. Do you think things have got busier or are we more dedicated social workers than we used to be?' Miles asked as he slumped back into the thick cushion that lined the wooden chair.

'I don't know about more dedicated. I don't seem to get as much done, though, I can tell you that much. I never seem to finish anything before the next emergency crops up,' April replied.

'You've got different priorities now, though, April,' Paula pointed out. 'I remember when I started work, Natasha was still small and all I could think about was how quickly I could get back to her.'

It felt a bit strange at first, since the three of them hadn't got together for well over a year, but they were soon back to their old selves, laughing and talking as though they had never been apart. April was studying Paula as they talked. She wondered how things were with her and Simon, but wasn't sure whether she should ask. She noticed how radiant her friend looked. Her hair looked great; the new short style really suited her, with its wispy fringe and the edges shaped around her ears. She had lost a bit of weight too, which April thought must be a positive sign. She had been a bit worried about Paula because she hadn't seemed quite her old self, but seeing her now, appreciating the joys of nature and the warmth and smells of summer, made her think that things couldn't be too bad. No relationship was plain sailing, after all.

It had always been agreed between them that discussing work was not acceptable in social settings and they were usually quite good at sticking to that rule, but sometimes it was inevitable. April wanted to know if Miles had seen anything more of Samantha Bushell. 'I meet my dad sometimes for lunch at a little fish cafe on the seafront. You saw her down there a while ago, didn't you? I've looked out for her but haven't seen any sign. There are often homeless people around there but I've never seen Sam amongst them.'

'I haven't seen her either, to be honest. I haven't really looked out for her, though. I have some children in foster care down that way so I will make a point of looking out next time I visit.'

April was just about to say more when Miles turned the conversation around.

'How are things between your parents now then, April? Is it still awkward?'

'Oh, don't ask. I get frustrated with them. I just can't understand why they don't act like adults. Mum had an affair thirty years ago or whatever it was, and for years Dad couldn't forgive her, but then she couldn't forgive herself so blamed him. It's just all too much for me.'

'Do you want to know what I think?' Paula asked.

'Go on then.'

April and Miles waited quietly to hear Paula's thoughts.

'I think they're still in love with each other. That's why they're behaving irrationally. Love brings out the worst in people, don't you think?'

She looked expectantly at them as though waiting for their applause for her astute observation. Nothing was forthcoming; just looks of blank curiosity.

'If they didn't still have feelings for each other they would act like everyone else: turn up at family gatherings and make polite conversation with each other. Yes, I believe I am on to it. They're still in love.'

April looked at her as though she had lost her senses. 'You must be joking – they detest each other. Well, Mum hates Dad, anyway.'

'Hmm… I don't think so somehow.' Paula tapped her forefinger against her cheek with a discerning smile.

The dappled sunlight was glinting through the trees, bouncing off Miles's tanned skin and making his blond hair shimmer. His expression was clear: he thought Paula was right, and perhaps he too had thought this all along.

April looked from Paula to Miles and then back again. 'That's preposterous. Why would they refuse to see each other or be in the same place if they love each other? They'd do everything they could to get back together, wouldn't they? Nobody's making them stay apart, only themselves.'

'You're not taking into account what proud people they are, April, are you?' Miles almost sang.

She just laughed sardonically. 'I won't take any notice of that; it's ludicrous. Let's talk about something else.'

April noticed how much Paula was enjoying herself. She appeared to have become the woman April used to know before she met Simon. Curiosity got the better of her. 'Talking about love, how are you enjoying your new life with Simon, Paula?'

'It's wonderful,' Paula said fervently. 'We've had a few ups and downs. I think he thought he was going to control me to begin with, but he realises now that that's not how it's going to be. Do you know what? I think he respects me now more than he did.' Her eyes shone with happiness. 'We've booked a holiday.' She looked at them both, waiting for the inevitable question.

'Lovely; where to?' April asked.

'Namibia. A week in a safari lodge and a week at the beach.'

'Wow. Sounds great,' Miles said.

'What about you, Miles? Have you got any plans for a holiday?' April asked.

'I want to get a train somewhere. I'm thinking about the environment – you know, like we all should be.' He nodded accusingly at Paula.

April wondered if he really was going on his own as he seemed to be saying. 'I need to get going, I'm afraid,' she said as she gulped down the last of her Diet Coke. 'It's been great. Why don't we try to set aside this time every month? Let's face it, we all need a bit of sanity amidst the madness of work, home, and trying to fit everything in. Just to sit here under the trees for a couple of hours once a month and unwind – it's not asking too much, is it?'

'Well, I'm game. What about you, Paula?'

Paula kind of agreed, but without conviction.

As April drove home, Paula's observation about her parents kept churning over in her mind. It had seemed incredibly stupid at the time, but the more she thought about it, the more she wondered if there could be some truth in it. It would explain why their behaviour seemed so weird. Miles had perceptively worked out that it could be excessive pride which had caused the long-standing rift, which was all very well but there wasn't much chance of anyone being able to change things.

April thought back to the times when she had tried to get information from her mother about her dad when she and Jed were going through the adoption process and she had been asked to provide background history, including on both parents. On the verge of being approved and about to be considered for a child to be placed with them, the adoption had been put on hold due to the circumstances regarding her father. The adoption social worker had perceived that the situation was still affecting April and could potentially affect her parenting in the future. Even though it prevented her and Jed getting the child they so longed for, and the grandchild Diana longed for, her mum remained obstinately determined not to talk about her father.

In the end April had been forced to go behind her mother's back and make her own enquiries, which had ultimately led to the reunion with her dad. The unspoken rule of her childhood continued to prevail: *Dad is not to be mentioned in any capacity. He is banned from all conversation; wiped out of history.*

19

NEGLECT

Kerry was in the laundry room on the ground floor, loading the huge washing machine. Tamara stood behind her, chewing on the teat of a bottle which she held in one hand, whilst holding on to her mum's long skirt with the other.

'Hiya, Kerry. Washing again? Costs a fortune, doesn't it? I put three quid in yesterday and I've got another lot to do today. I do some in the sink sometimes but then it takes forever to dry.'

'Yeah. I've just put a couple of quid in and there's another load to do upstairs. It will have to wait till I get my money on Monday.'

The two women chatted for a bit longer but Tamara was getting quite fretful. Her nappy was full and so heavy it hung below her knees. The stench was becoming nauseating.

'I need to go and get tidied up before Miss Snotty Snob-Face turns up. "Oh, Kerry, you haven't washed the dishes today,"' Kerry mimicked. '"Oh, Kerry, you haven't hoovered up – look, there's a crumb on the floor."' She held her palm against her forehead in mock disbelief. '*Why don't you come and live in this shithole?* That's what I feel like saying to her, anyway. *See if you can keep it any cleaner.*'

'Who's coming, then?' Briony asked, idly twisting thin strands of long blonde hair between her fingers.

'Oh, it's that stupid social worker. Well, she isn't even a proper social worker, she's a new one, but she thinks she knows everything. I don't think she's even got kids. She's taking Tyler to McDonald's after school. At least that'll save *me* a few quid.'

By now the two young women were walking together out of the laundry room and making their way upstairs, Tamara still clinging to her mother's skirt.

'Come around to mine later when the kids are asleep. Frank's bringing some smoke.'

'Oh, I don't know. I might, but Tamara wakes up sometimes and I won't hear her. Do you remember when I did that before? She was wandering around the room looking for me when I got back. I couldn't stop her crying. I felt guilty for ages – no, I can't do that again.'

'You just need to check on her every half-hour or so. She'll be all right. It's only along the corridor.'

'I'll see.' Kerry unlocked her front door and waved as she ushered Tamara into the room.

There was never much to keep her occupied during the day. She sometimes went to her mum's but all her mum ever did was moan about her own problems. She never seemed interested in Kerry or her kids. After changing Tamara's nappy, she got her dressed and decided to walk into town. At least it'd get them out for a bit.

She carried Tamara down the stairs and walked around the building to the large wooden shed, which was crammed with all kinds of rubble. Some old plastic garden chairs had been piled on top of the pushchair and, after pulling it free, she put Tamara in the seat and strapped her in, ready get on her way. She wasn't really intending to buy anything; she didn't have much money to buy anything with. It was just something to do to pass the time. She bought a few bits of food that she needed, some milk and some sweets for Tamara. She didn't bother looking in many shops because she couldn't afford what they were selling anyway.

As she was walking back home, she passed a charity shop. A mannequin dressed in a tight-fitting black dress with silver thread running through it caught her eye. She stopped to look closer at it. She loved it. She pictured herself in it, with its low-cut neckline and short length. Tamara was asleep so she guided the pushchair into a corner of the shop whilst she arranged to try on the dress. The price was more than she could afford but she would ask for a discount.

Just as she had imagined, it really suited her. She stood in front of the mirror, let her thick hair loose over her shoulders and pulled in her stomach as much as she could. The material seemed to quiver like silvery moonlight on a frosty night. The price on the dress was twenty-five pounds and there was no way on this earth she could afford that. Once out of the changing room, she held up the dress to the woman sitting behind the counter and shouted across. 'Excuse me… excuse me.' She managed to attract her attention. 'I'll give you ten quid for this.'

The woman asked her to bring it to the counter so that she could see the price. 'I'm sorry, my dear, I can't sell it to you for ten pounds. I can give you a discount of five pounds but that's all.'

Kerry was really disappointed and annoyed at the same time. 'I can't afford twenty pounds for a dress. I'm not *rich*. I could give you fifteen pounds.' She was a bit worried about how she would afford that, but she really wanted that dress.

'I'm sorry, lovey, but I can't. I would be in lots of trouble if I gave you it for fifteen pounds. As you can see, it's designer, and there will be plenty of women happy to pay twenty-five pounds for it.'

Kerry left the shop feeling quite despondent. Sometimes she felt as though her life was not worth living. She loved her kids but there was no pleasure in constantly struggling to make ends meet. The money she got barely covered necessities, let alone any extras for pleasure. She had tried to get jobs, but with no qualifications and only minimal literacy skills, she struggled to complete an application form, and if she did manage to get as far as an interview, she was so nervous that, if she managed to turn up, she could hardly speak. She had been badly bullied at school due to her shabby clothes and dirty appearance. Her mother had been virtually an alcoholic, although she was teetotal since becoming ill. She didn't know who her father was.

Tyler was returned to her at five, just as Katy had promised. He had a plastic toy from the Happy Meal which he seemed to be enthralled with.

'By the way, Tyler has a reading book in his bag with a reading diary. It might be a good idea to read it with him before he goes to bed.'

Before leaving, Katy pointed out that there was a bit of a mess on the worktop and that it was unhygienic to prepare food there. She set a few tasks for Kerry to do, including washing the carpet again where the potty had been tipped, and changing the sheets on the children's mattresses. As Katy left, Kerry thrust two fingers up behind the door she had just closed.

By 8.30, Tamara and Tyler were fast asleep on their mattresses. Kerry normally got herself comfortable with a few cushions on the floor and watched the small flat-screen television at the other end of the room, but she didn't want to do that tonight. She was feeling really fed up with everything. The social worker had said she was going to help her get somewhere better to live, but she hadn't done it. She hadn't even mentioned it again. As far as Kerry was concerned, Katy was just a nosy cow who wanted to know too much and poke around to find fault with her.

Kerry was desperate for some adult company. She spent most of her days and evenings on her own. She used to have friends calling in all the time where she lived before. She had lived in that area most of her life and had known people there for years. She didn't know anyone around here except Briony. In her opinion, some of the other residents in the hostel were a bit rough, and she tried to keep out of their way.

Kerry was unable to relax, and became more agitated and restless as the evening went on. She couldn't stop thinking about Briony's invitation. After sitting around for an hour or so, she saw that the children were still sleeping soundly and the call of Briony's room and someone to talk to became overwhelmingly tempting. She decided to pop in for a bit. It was just along the corridor and she wouldn't stay for long. Tyler rarely woke up; Tamara did sometimes but not too often. She pulled open a small drawer next to the sink which was crammed with papers, old letters, pamphlets, packets of plasters and various medicines, in search of a hairbrush. She tipped her head to one side and pulled her hair over her shoulder, brushing vigorously until it shone. She then tossed it back, before picking up her keys and walking out of the flat, locking the door behind her.

Briony was surprised to see her. 'I thought you weren't coming.' She stood aside and Kerry could see that there were two young men in the room. 'This is Frank and his friend Ed.'

They both looked up at her as she walked in, feeling very self-conscious. Neither of them spoke. They had some weed and were rolling it into cigarette papers. Kerry had smoked weed in the past but hadn't really had the opportunity or the money to do it on a regular basis. But she was desperately in need of something to lift her mood.

The room was the same shape and had the same layout as Kerry's, with the bedroom space at the back and the kitchen at the front. It seemed quite neat and tidy compared to her own, and she wondered how Briony managed it. Briony's baby, Angel, was three months old and always asleep.

Kerry sat down on the floor with her back leaning against the small sofa, and it wasn't long before she was handed the spliff. The four's friendly banter became gradually more absurd as the evening wore on and the cannabis seeped into their brains. Although strangers, they were soon relaxed with each other, and nothing seemed out of bounds. It wasn't long before Frank and Briony were on the bed and Ed and Kerry were rolling around the floor, laughing as they pulled each other's clothes off.

It must have been about three in the morning when Kerry came to. It took some time to figure out where she was, but gradually she remembered what had happened and panic set in. She hadn't checked on her children at all. She imagined Tamara crying for her and not knowing where her mummy was. What if she had woken Tyler up? They would be scared. She dragged herself up off the floor and, only half dressed with her top under her arm, staggered out of Briony's room.

Relieved that her room was silent, she unlocked the door expecting and hoping to see everything as she had left it. It wasn't. Tamara was lying face down on the floor, whimpering, and Tyler was beside her, trying to comfort his little sister. The sight of her children in that state almost broke Kerry's heart. She ran to them and hugged them both at the same time.

'Where've you been, Mummy?' Tyler looked up at her with his tear-stained face.

Tamara, who had been lying on the floor with her head resting on her folded arms, lifted her head and murmured, 'Mummy.'

'I'm sorry, my darlings. I'm really sorry. Mummy is back now and she's not going away again. Mummy will never do that again. I'm so sorry.'

Tears of guilt poured down her cheeks. The children clung to her and she squeezed them tightly, trying desperately to banish the terror they must have endured.

20

PAULA AND MILES

April's weeks were getting busier and busier. Having settled Demelza at the nursery on Monday morning, she hurried out of the building, jumped into her car (which she had left virtually outside the gate, despite the yellow zigzags), slammed the door shut and drove in haste to see Lawrence and Matthew. There were a lot of things to fit into the day but this week Florian and Leo were to transfer from their foster carer, Melanie, to the care of Lawrence and Matthew. She had been through the programme with their new dads a number of times and they had a written schedule, but she just wanted to do a last-minute check to make sure they were still happy with everything.

Transferring the boys' attachment from their foster carer, whom they had been with for nearly a year and who was effectively a mum to them, was quite a complex process and needed to be handled with caution and care. It began with Lawrence and Matthew visiting them at their foster home and spending time with them there. They would build up the length of time they spent there and gradually take over their care – giving them their meals, playing with them and, by the end of the week, bathing them and putting them to bed. The next week would entail the boys being taken to Matthew and Lawrence's home, and culminate in overnight stays before they moved in permanently. April had already spent time with the boys, showing them photos of Lawrence and Matthew and explaining that they were going to be their daddies. They'd been shown pictures of the house, their bedroom, the garden, and even the area around where they lived, including the local park. April had been through this process many times with children and it never failed to astonish her how young children were able to adapt to having a different carer in such a short time. They did, of course, miss their previous carers, but arrangements were made for them to visit and write to them to ensure they didn't feel abandoned.

When April pulled up outside Matthew and Lawrence's house, she could see them both peering out of the window at her, anxiety written all over their faces. She smiled and waved as she got out of the car. Before she reached the front door it was opened and both men followed her into the lounge, gabbling frenetically.

'We've been wondering if we should take the boys something. Lawrence said we shouldn't but I wasn't sure. What do you think we should do, April?'

'Such as?' April couldn't help being amused by their high state of anxiety. Of course this was a major event in their lives, but for her it was all in a day's work. She enjoyed nothing more than seeing children who couldn't live with their own family due to abuse, neglect or other reasons being placed with loving people who wanted to adopt them, but she was just there to facilitate and ensure the process ran smoothly.

Lawrence walked swiftly out of the room and returned carrying two carefully wrapped presents adorned with bows and ribbons. 'They're only teddies but we thought it would be nice to give them to the boys when we meet them.'

'It's a lovely thought, Matthew,' April said, leaning forward to take papers out of her bag. 'I think it's probably best not to at this stage, though. They might expect something every time you come, and that would be disappointing for them, wouldn't it? I think it's best to just be present without making too much of an impact, especially in the early stages of the transfer. What about giving them the teddies after they move in – a gift for their new home?'

She sat back in her chair and waited for their response, but, quickly realising she was only going to get a stare from both men, she continued. 'I know it's easy for me to say but you need to try to relax and enjoy the experience. If you have any worries after today's visit you're welcome to phone me, but I will be surprised if you do. I would really like to know how it goes, though, if you do get the chance to phone me.'

April was smiling inside at the two men's fretful faces. They looked just like two nervous little boys about to start a new school. All they needed were the short trousers and satchels. She handed them the paperwork they needed and left, reiterating that everything would be fine and, once the first meeting was out of the way, there would be nothing else to worry about.

April headed straight back to the office. She had a number of urgent matters to deal with including catching up with Katy to discuss how her visits to Kerry and her children had been going, and phoning the police once again to find out the progress (if any) on Isobel's investigation and, most importantly, if there had been any news about Isobel herself.

The office was busy; social workers at their desks, heads down, typing away, trying frantically to catch up with paperwork. She could see Miles across the room, his blond hair falling forward and his eyes glued to his screen. He hadn't seen her so she decided to sneak in, find a desk and get down to work. She might feel like a chat once she had made a dent in her outstanding tasks.

She was just settling down, had adjusted her chair and was turning on her computer when she heard her name being spoken. Katy was rushing towards her.

'Morning, April. I'm glad to catch up with you. Is it a good time to talk? I could wait until later but I do have to go out on a visit by one.'

'No, that's fine, Katy. Let's go into the interview room; it's a bit noisy here. I was hoping to see you today anyway for a catch-up.'

They threaded their way through the office, past the hard-working social workers who mostly didn't look up from their desks, out of the door, across the corridor and into the small interview room, which fortunately was empty for a change. April had her obligatory notepad and pen.

As they sat down, Katy began to talk about her visits to Kerry and the time she'd spent with Tyler. 'I am really worried about those two children, April. I understand it's hard for Kerry being in that awful place, but I do think she could do better than she's doing. I don't get the impression she ever talks to the children, let alone plays with them. I think she just goes through the motions of basic care, and I mean *really* basic.'

She paused, expecting to see shock on April's face, but April just waited, without expression, and, disappointed, she carried on.

'Tamara wanders around with a grubby-looking bottle dangling from her mouth all the time. She's way below where she should be in her development. And I know I shouldn't really say this, but Tyler is a bit weird. When we were in McDonald's he ate his burger within seconds. He crammed it into his mouth as though he was scared someone was going to snatch it off him. I kept saying to him, "Slow down, Tyler, you'll get tummy ache." He didn't, though. He doesn't look at you when you talk to him, and he hardly speaks back. I would have thought a boy that age should be really chatty. I've got a nephew that age and he never stops talking. I asked him how he likes school and he just shrugged his shoulders. I would say he's hypervigilant as well because he just didn't seem to be able to settle. He wanted to eat his food as quick as he could and then go.'

'You've made some good observations there, Katy. You probably need to do some research now to see what could possibly be the cause of his behaviour.' April paused for a minute to get her thoughts together. It dawned on her that she had been preoccupied with everything else that was going on. It had been good to pass the work involved with this case over to Katy but it wasn't going to be as straightforward as she had hoped. It seemed there was more to worry about than just the home conditions. 'I think I'll join you on your next visit. We may need to think about a Child Protection Plan for them. Sounds like they need a higher level of input and scrutiny from what you're saying.'

After their conversation ended, April went straight back to her desk, carrying her unused notepad and pen. Somebody had placed a piece of paper on her desk with a message saying, 'Please phone Denise' followed by a phone number. This was something that couldn't be left until later. There were many thoughts racing through April's head; thoughts that she had during her wakeful nights, worrying about Isobel and imagining all sorts. Her heart was thumping as the phone continued to ring and she waited for someone to answer. The phone rang and rang but, hugely frustrated, she had to give up, as there was no answer and no option to leave a message. She hadn't realised before, but when she opened up Isobel's record on her system she noticed that it was her fifteenth birthday. She wasn't really religious but she did utter a silent prayer: *Dear God, please let her be OK.*

'Right, this is as much stress as I need for one morning. I'm making myself a cup of coffee and nothing is going to stop me.' She spoke out loud, and Celia, who was sitting in the desk opposite, looked up and smiled.'

'You rebel, April. Make me one while you're there, will you?'

On her way to the kitchen, April passed Miles's desk. He spotted her approaching and swivelled his chair round to face her.

'It's only 11.45 on Monday morning and I'm just about sapped.'

'Sapped?'

'Well, you know what I mean – I've had enough. I need a year off.'

'You've just had a year off.'

'Well, we won't go into that one. How many times have you been at home looking after a little one?'

'OK, April. Point taken.'

They walked towards the kitchen, where they made coffee before sitting down at the little table in the middle of the room.

'Miles, do you think Paula is avoiding us? I did say to her about going for a drink again one evening and she seemed to agree. Well, she didn't say no anyway, but since then I've hardly seen her. What do you think of Simon?'

'Can't say I've had much chance to get to know him, really. She seems to be happy enough with him.'

'She's not the same, though, is she? She isn't the Paula we used to know. I can't put my finger on it but she's definitely changed.'

'That's what being in love does for you, April. Not that I would know.'

April really wanted to follow that one up, but somehow it didn't seem right. She always felt that if Miles wanted her to know about his private life he would say, and she didn't want to seem intrusive. Tempting though it was, she had to quell her curiosity once again.

When she returned to her desk there was another note waiting for her, again asking her to call Denise. This time the phone was answered, and April held her breath.

'Hello, April, I wanted to let you know that Isobel is back.'

'Thank God for that.' She sank back into her chair with a long sigh of relief. 'Is she OK? Where was she?'

Denise explained how she had been returned by the police in the early hours of the morning, looking bedraggled and filthy. 'I told her she wasn't getting into bed without having a shower or a bath first. I made her egg on toast with a sausage. Honestly, April, I don't think she'd eaten for weeks. You should have seen her guzzling it down. She went to bed and slept all right after that, but when she woke up in the morning she didn't have a clue what day it was. She certainly didn't realise it was her birthday.'

'I'll need to come and see her later then, Denise. Thank you for letting me know.'

Before leaving the office, April phoned Matthew and Lawrence. Matthew answered and said the day had been 'absolutely wonderful'.

'We're so excited, April. We love them already. The minute I sat down, Florian came and sat on my knee. He just seemed to belong there. He isn't a shy boy, is he?'

Being a social worker, April saw this differently to Matthew. It was more of a worry to her that Florian was happy to sit on a stranger's knee the minute he walked in the door. She didn't want to dampen Matthew's spirits by telling him this, though, and spoil their enjoyment of the day. They would have had the training on attachment and normally would probably recognise that this wasn't what you would be hoping to see.

'They both sat between us and we read *The Very Hungry Caterpillar* to them. Can't wait until tomorrow; we're going to stay for lunch.'

'I'm so glad it all went so well, Matthew. I will give you a ring tomorrow.'

21

ALARM BELLS

By the time Isobel woke up, it was almost midday. She lay in bed, staring at the ceiling for some time, thinking about the things that had happened to her while she was away. It all seemed strange to her and she wasn't quite sure what to make of it. Her feelings about Damian were confused. He was her boyfriend and had told her he loved her and was going to look after her. He'd bought her things – a new phone and some designer jeans, as well as jewellery and perfume. He'd introduced her to his friends, who'd all made a fuss of her. There was also another young girl, Lucy, whom she had got to know a little bit. She was in foster care too and often stayed at the house.

There were times when they had other friends around, and one night Damian gave her some white powder to take. He said there was nothing to worry about, it wasn't dangerous and would make her feel great. She felt a bit worried but could tell Damian was keen for her to take it, so she did as he said. Both she and Lucy took the powder and very soon she felt her spirits lifting. She found herself carried off into another reality; a kind of euphoria. They had some alcohol as well; she wasn't sure what it was but she didn't care because it was the best fun she had ever had. They were dancing, singing loudly and laughing.

She didn't remember much else until she woke up in the early hours of the morning with a naked man sleeping beside her and no sign of Damian. She still felt a little bit nauseous from the drugs and alcohol but was alert enough to recognise that something was amiss. Then the haziness in her eyes started to lift and she was able to really see the man lying beside her. She lay there for a few minutes, trying to make sense of it. He looked very old, she thought; bald and grey with wrinkles. He was breathing steadily with his mouth open, revealing broken stubs of tobacco-stained teeth. She suddenly felt terrified.

There were vague memories of something horrible, although she wasn't quite sure what it was. She edged her way slowly out of the bed, watching his face anxiously to ensure he was not disturbed. Walking slowly and on tiptoe, she gathered up her clothes and slowly crept out of the room. Gathering speed, she fled downstairs and into the street. Dressed only in a skimpy nightie and the sandals she had slipped on her feet, she ran as fast as she could without looking back, worried that someone might come after her. She hadn't been out of the house since she'd arrived there over a week ago. After reaching the end of the road and turning a corner, she leant, panting, against the side wall of a garage, trying to catch her breath. She quickly got into her clothes, then phoned 999, and within a short time, two policemen arrived in a car, ready to take her back to Denise's.

Now she lay in bed, worrying about how she was going to face Denise and Harry. She had no idea what kind of response to expect from them. She had to go downstairs soon because her mouth and throat were sore; she desperately needed a drink. What if they insisted on questioning her about what she had been doing? She just couldn't think what she would say to them. She didn't want anyone to know about the things she had done; some of which she had consented to, for which she felt riddled with shame.

She eventually climbed out of bed, walked over to the window and opened the curtains. The sun streamed in, filling the room with a light so bright she had to cover her eyes. She opened the window and felt the warmth of the sun on her skin. It was a beautiful day; a stark contrast to her bleak mood. For a minute she thought about walking out of the house again. She was desperate to think of anything to get her out of having to face Denise. She knew if she went to her mum's she would only bring her back, because that was what she had been ordered to do by April.

Just then there was a knock on her door, and a soft voice. 'Isobel? Isobel, are you awake?' It was Denise. 'I've brought you a cup of tea.' The door opened slowly and Denise popped her head around. 'Is it all right to come in?' She had brought a tray with tea and a chocolate-covered wafer, which she put on the bedside table after moving some of Isobel's bits and pieces out of the way. 'When you've eaten that you can come downstairs if you like. There's no one else home so you won't have to talk to anyone if you don't want to.'

Isobel looked blankly at her, all the time thinking, *Why is she being nice to me?*

'It's all right, you don't have to explain anything to me about where you've been. April is coming around later and you can talk to her.'

'I don't want to talk to anyone.'

'OK, well, she's coming around anyway, so see how it goes.'

April arrived in the late afternoon. Isobel was sitting in one of the wicker chairs in the kitchen-diner, watching the television, whilst Denise was busy preparing food for the evening. April walked in and took the seat opposite.

'Hello, Isobel.'

Isobel didn't divert her gaze from the screen but mumbled, 'Hi.'

'We need to have a chat, don't we? Shall we go into the conservatory?' April moved her eyes to indicate Denise's presence, and Isobel took the cue.

'OK.' She moved her feet from under her and stretched her legs before standing up and leading the way to the conservatory, waiting for April to go in before shutting the door behind her.

'So, how are you, Isobel? You know that everyone has been extremely worried about you.'

'Yes, so I keep being told,' she said, almost with a yawn.

April explained that she had to fill in some forms and that there was a list of questions she needed to ask. She wasn't a fan of the procedural nature of the missing child process but it had to be done. Isobel was clearly not giving anything away, though. She said she had been with her boyfriend, Damian. She wouldn't say where he lived or if there was anyone else in the house they had stayed in. Luckily, April was very experienced at disguising frustration. She wanted to take Isobel by her shoulders and shake her, but was somehow able to maintain a facade of absolute calmness.

'Isobel, I do need to ask you if you had sexual intercourse with anyone while you were away. You won't be in trouble if you have. I just need to know so that I can help you.'

April was sitting forward on her chair, holding out her hands to Isobel in a plea for the truth. She waited patiently, whilst Isobel just shrugged her shoulders and continued to stare at the floor.

'Would you agree to come with me to the sexual health clinic just to make sure everything is OK, then? You could have a chat to the nurse on your own if you wanted to.'

There was no response and still no eye contact.

April took a deep breath before settling back into the chair. There was no use persisting. 'So, tell me then, Isobel, what's Damian like? Is he at school or does he work?'

Isobel looked at April as though she was stupid. 'No, he's too old for school; he's twenty-three. He doesn't work either.'

'Don't you think he's a bit old for you?'

Isobel shrugged again.

'I will make an appointment for you to see the nurse. Would you like me to take you or do you want to go with Denise? Your mum could come if you want her to.'

Isobel was very quick to answer. 'I don't want Denise there and I don't want my mum there. She doesn't give a shit about me anyway. She didn't even want to see me.' She sat quietly for a moment but her decision was clear. 'I will go, but I want you to come with me.'

April had mixed feelings. She was relieved that Isobel was agreeing to attend the clinic, but at the same time this left no doubt that she had engaged in sexual activity. Whilst this wasn't really surprising, April had been hoping against the odds.

'It's your birthday today, Isobel, isn't it?'

'Is it? I didn't know. What's the date, then? I thought it was only the 23rd.'

'No, it's the 25th. Denise has made a special meal for you and she's got a birthday cake. You weren't here to choose it but she thought you might like coffee and walnut. I would think she's got presents for you too. By the way, your mum has been really worried about you. She was on the phone every day, asking if you had been found yet. She does care about you, Isobel. Sometimes things are much more complicated than they seem.'

'I know that. I'm not stupid,' Isobel snapped. 'But she takes my dad's side. She doesn't believe what I said about him. I know that's true. I've been thinking about it.'

April tried to smooth things over but what could she say? Isobel was right; at the moment her mum was believing her dad. She also noted with sadness that there was no present or card from her family. Isobel was bound to have thought about that fact herself and internalised it. April did her best to lighten the conversation before leaving Isobel in the kitchen with Denise, who opened the fridge and invited Isobel to choose what she wanted for her lunch.

April left there ready to head straight to the nursery to collect Demelza. The car felt hot and stuffy, so after slamming the door shut, she opened the two front windows to let in the warm, fresh air and the scent of spring flowers from the surrounding gardens. She took some deep breaths before letting her body relax into the seat, setting the gear into drive and slowly moving away.

Demelza had been hand-painting and her nails, arms and legs were streaked with scarlet. April wondered if it would ever come off. Although she was engrossed in her activity, she looked up at her mother and beamed, holding her arms up towards her. April immediately picked her up and squeezed her, without worrying about the paint on her white top.

When they arrived home, April walked up the short path, heavy work bag in one hand and Demelza on the opposite hip, managing to talk to her at the same time. 'Have you had a lovely day today, Demelza? You were doing some beautiful paintings, weren't you?' She opened the front door and put Demelza down on the floor before picking up the post which was scattered on the mat. Sorting through, she spotted one which was handwritten. She thought she recognised the writing but couldn't recall where from. She ripped it open and it was a letter with a card inside. It read:

Dear April,

I remembered that it's your mum's birthday on Saturday and I have enclosed a card. Would you mind passing it on to her? I realise she may not accept it but I thought it would be worth a try. At least she will see that I wish to make amends in the hope that one day we might be friends again.

Love,
Dad

PS: I am looking forward to meeting again. Perhaps you could bring Demelza to my place for lunch one day?

April gasped. She couldn't decide if she was annoyed that he had put this on her or pleased that he was trying to mend the rift. At the same time, she was in a dilemma. Her mum was aware that she had been seeing her dad but wasn't particularly pleased about it. It was dealt with in the same way they had dealt with him leaving the family all those years ago: it was not spoken about. If April were granted one wish it would be for her mum and dad to be friends. It was quite surprising that it mattered so much since she was now an adult herself with her own family. She could remember how, as a child, she'd often fantasised that her father would return. In her imagination he was a tall, good-looking man, with tousled hair and a big smile. She pictured him helping her and Max ride their bikes, burying them in the sand at the beach, chasing them through the woods; all the things she had seen happy families do on the television. It was surprising to her that her longing for that complete family which everyone else appeared to have had never quite diminished.

The best thing she could hope for now was that her parents could become friends. Demelza had had a lovely family christening but April's father had been excluded because of the problems his presence might cause. Her mum always came first so there was no other choice. She decided to put the letter on the side and see what Jed thought when he came home. Diana was coming to stay on Friday and Max and his wife were coming on Saturday for the birthday party.

22

FREDDIE

April had arranged to visit the Simmons family on Tuesday morning but she wasn't due to call until ten. She decided to work at home until then, rather than go into the office where she could easily get caught up in unplanned situations. By 9.30 she had finished all her case notes, written a report for the Child Protection Conference for Tyler and Tamara Phillips, and got herself ready for the visit.

She drove slowly down Cleverly Road, looking for Number 79. There were rows and rows of small terraced houses fronted by tiny gardens with low brick walls which all looked identical. After driving quite a way down this long road, she finally came across Number 79. The house was very different to the one the family had lived in previously when there was so much worry about Freddie, but one thing that was exactly the same was the state of the garden. The little square of garden had woody lilacs which were so entangled with weeds that most of the flowers had failed to materialise. There were wild saplings which were spindly but tall enough to spill over the wall and block some of the pavement in front of the house. The growth was so high in front of the window that it must have been blocking the light.

April pulled up against the pavement directly outside the house, and walked up the short path, stepping over the nettles and brambles that spread out in front of her. The bell to the side was hanging crookedly from a piece of wire, so she decided to knock. Whilst she waited for an answer she looked more closely at the variety of weeds and the wildness of the garden. Interestingly, a hanging basket of brightly coloured plastic flowers hung from a hook to the side of the door, and below on the step, a brightly coloured pot with the same plastic flowers. She had to smile at the absurdity of this.

The door was opened and in front of her stood Becky Simmons, holding two-year-old Wesley in her arms. She had put on a lot of weight since April last saw her but she looked happy and healthy and her skin glowed. 'April!' Becky seemed really pleased to see her. 'Come in. This is Wesley; you haven't met him yet, have you? You've got a baby now too, haven't you? I always ask how you are when social workers come.'

April was invited into the tiny lounge. She could see through to the kitchen from where she was sitting; a pile of dishes waited by the side of the sink to be washed. She could see cluttered worktops and a heap of dirty clothes on the floor waiting to be put in the machine. Freddie was home because he had a day off school following the May bank holiday. He was sitting on the floor surrounded by Lego, and looked up curiously at April as she sat herself down.

'Hello, Freddie. Do you remember me? I'm April. I used to come and see you when your mum needed help.'

The little boy looked up at her, with a furrow in his brow, trying to remember where he had seen her before. 'I'm making a *PAW Patrol* helicopter. Do you like *PAW Patrol*?'

'I don't think I know it. Is it on the television?'

'It's in a book as well, *and* a comic,' he answered, exasperated by her stupidity. He then turned back and focused on his task, his thoughts written all over his face. *This woman is not worth talking to; she's far too stupid.*

'Can I get you a drink? Leon's on nights this week. He should be back soon.'

'No thank you. I had a coffee earlier. How is everything, Becky? Have you settled into the new area?'

'I like it here. I didn't really want to move but Colin just wouldn't leave me alone. The police used to arrest him but he still kept doing it. One night, about two or three in the morning, he was banging on our window, yelling that he wanted his baby, and threatening to kill Leon. We were petrified. The council found us this house. It's Housing Association so we're not on a shorthold tenancy any more. We can stay as long as we like. The rent is a lot but we manage it.'

Just as Becky finished speaking, the door opened and Leon walked in. He smiled at April before taking her hand to shake it vigorously. 'It's great to see you again, April. We missed you.'

This was such a treat. To be told by a family she was working with that they had missed her was an extremely rare occurrence. Becky and Leon had never forgotten how April had fought for them to keep Freddie during the court case. Although Becky had been the perpetrator of Freddie's frequent injuries the bond was strong between them. This had been a classic case of how one man could control a woman to the extent that it changed her whole personality and she didn't even realise it was happening. It had been a difficult decision for April and not without risk, but her intuition had played a role and she'd felt strongly that the right thing was for Freddie to go home to Becky and his biological father. The court eventually agreed with her, and from what she had seen and heard from other social workers who had visited, it appeared to have been a good decision.

Leon had already picked Wesley up and was bouncing him up and down, and with him still in his arms he bent down next to Freddie and expressed admiration at what he had made, despite there being nothing recognisable amongst the thousands of pieces. The house may have been cluttered and left a lot to be desired with regard to cleanliness but there was a lovely feeling of warmth and love in the home which rendered the clutter of little significance. April thought about how timid and meek Becky had been when Colin Lyons was in her life. How she'd covered herself in thick, dark make-up and stared at the floor when she spoke. How the house had been so immaculate you would have had to use a microscope to detect any dust. Now there were toys and books everywhere, where previously there had been none, and both children were clearly happy and secure in their reconstituted family. Freddie was doing well at school and Wesley was meeting his milestones.

This was a great relief to April. The decision she had made during the care proceedings to allow Freddie to return to his mother after he had suffered injuries by her hand had been a precarious one. It would have been much easier to go along with the guardian at the time and agree to Freddie being placed for adoption, but she had chosen to fight against that. Sometimes it was necessary for social workers to go by their gut feelings, although they had been based on what she had seen, how much Freddie's mother loved him, and her intensely controlling relationship with Colin Lyons which had caused her to behave in a way that was completely out of character. April realised that history could repeat itself and she could never be absolutely certain about the future, but she really didn't believe it would, and so far she had been proved right.

She left the house feeling really pleased with herself. The case was due to be closed shortly as there were no further concerns. She was only visiting now because the court had, at her request, made a Supervision Order which lasted for two years.

Diana arrived on Friday evening and again April picked her up from the station. She and Jed had come to a mutual agreement that Diana should be told about the birthday card and could then decide for herself if she wanted to open it. Their guess was that she would say, 'Absolutely not' and it wouldn't be mentioned again.

After the family had finished their evening meal, Demelza was bathed and put into her unicorn pyjamas. She looked adorable with her flushed cheeks from the warm bath and her damp curls clinging to the sides of her face. Diana sat in an armchair and watched her granddaughter play. She was quite tired after her journey. Demelza had been pulling herself up against the furniture for a while now, but as her grandmother watched, she pulled herself up on the small coffee table, stretched out her arms towards the chair Diana sat on, and took two-and-a-half steps before flopping with a thump onto her bottom.

Diana was beside herself with excitement. 'She walked, April, she walked! She just took her first steps right in front of me.'

April, who had been in the kitchen, came running in. She looked down at Demelza, who was beaming up at them with pride. She was still very young but she already knew she was a star and there was no doubt in her mind that she was a very important person and had just done something exceptionally clever. April, though, was more than a bit miffed that her mum had been the one to witness this important milestone. Illogically, it increased her persistent underlying guilt about going back to work.

Max and Joanna arrived on Saturday morning, with some wine, flowers for Diana, and presents for Demelza.

'You shouldn't be buying her toys; she's got loads. She's going to think it's Christmas every day.'

'I've only got one niece and I had to wait years, so sorry, you'll have to get used to it, April.'

April smiled at him. She was quite pleased really. It wasn't easy for Max to do anything which April disapproved of. Although they were twins, he always acted like the older brother. He was quite a bit taller than her and was the firstborn, although only by less than two hours. Joanna, as usual, looked elegant in her Iris & Ink striped satin dress, her long chestnut hair hanging neatly over her shoulders. Their two children, Alistair and Elinor, were away at boarding school, much to April's annoyance. She felt she had missed out on watching them grow up because she hardly saw them. It had been different when they were little; she was very much a part of their lives, and although Max lived in London, they always spent a lot of time together.

The conservatory doors were open and the family sat outside on the small patio. Jed had brought the garden chairs out for the first time that year, and they sat enjoying the sunshine and being together. The patio was quite small, but April had made the most of the space. She had hanging baskets full of pink and white pansies on either side of the patio doors, and late spring flowers were coming up in the borders. The patio was sheltered from the cool sea breeze by a brick wall on one side and a high fence on the other, which made the day feel warmer than it was.

In the afternoon, April and Jed started to get the party food ready, laying out a buffet of cold meats, cheeses, dips, various breads, and in the middle a beetroot and dark chocolate cake which April had made the day before. In the centre of the cake was an elaborate candle in the shape of a tall, slender woman with blonde hair piled on top of her head and wearing silver shoes and a long ballgown the colour of the sky. Beside the candle, and stuck in the cake, was a large silver '60'. Jed opened a bottle of sparkling wine and they all clinked their glasses together.

April wanted to tell Max about the card and what she and Jed planned to do, and her opportunity came a bit later when he took himself off into the kitchen to pour a glass of wine. She followed him in. 'Max, I just thought I should warn you; Dad sent me a birthday card to give to Mum. We were talking about it last night, Jed and I. We decided she should be told.'

Max stopped what he was doing. 'I don't think that's a good idea. Why would you want to do that? She'll be annoyed. It will spoil her birthday. Leave it, April; don't mention it. Just put it in the bin and pretend it didn't happen.'

April wasn't a bit surprised by his response. Max was always in favour of the easiest way out; not rocking the boat. 'What if she finds out somehow and gets annoyed because she wasn't told? She's not a child, Max, she should be given the chance to decide for herself what she wants to do.'

'Yes, but you're the one who brought him back into our lives. We were all right before you got in touch with him.' There was a slight quiver in Max's voice as he tried hard to disguise his annoyance.

April was stung by this. 'You know why I did it. Anyway, that's in the past now, and I believe it would be wrong not to tell her.'

'OK.' He raised his hands. 'If that's what you want to do. I hope you don't regret it.' He continued filling his glass from the bottle and then turned toward the garden to make his way out.

'Max,' April said calmly, 'you must have some thoughts about him. I can't believe you wouldn't like to meet him. He's desperate to make amends. We know it wasn't all his fault. Mum had an affair and couldn't forgive herself. It was all such a big mistake on both sides.'

As she said this, she spotted Diana coming through the conservatory doors. 'What's going on here? Do you want me to do anything?'

They both turned and looked at her without answering. Their conversation had been quite emotional and they struggled for a moment to focus on the present.

'Honestly, you two. Even at your age, you've still got your little secrets. I thought that had changed. Anyway, are we going to do the cake?'

They smiled at their mum, then followed her out onto the patio as though nothing had been going on. Demelza sat on Diana's knee while they sang 'Happy Birthday to You' and she tried to help with blowing out the candles by puffing air through pursed lips.

Diana started to open her cards. There was one from Demelza which had a piece of yellow cotton wool stuck to it, and inside April had written, 'Love you, Nanny. Happy birthday from Demelza.' Underneath was a line of blue where Demelza had pulled the crayon across with April's support.

'Mum, I have another card for you.'

Everyone fell silent, including Demelza.

'It's from Dad.'

Her mother's face paled instantaneously from pink to white.

'You don't have to open it if you don't want to. I'll just throw it in the bin. I just thought you should be told about it, that's all.' April looked defiantly at her brother.

They all sat waiting in nervous anticipation. Diana suddenly stood up, her chair scraping backwards and almost toppling over, then stomped through the conservatory doors and disappeared.

Max turned to April. 'I told you not to tell her. It's spoilt her birthday now. You know how much she hates him. I wish you had listened to me.'

April didn't answer. She was upset, but at the same time she still felt she had done the right thing.

A few minutes later, Diana reappeared. 'I will look at it,' she said stonily.

'Oh… right… good. I will just go and get it.' April went inside and took the card out of the drawer in the kitchen where she had put it, not expecting it to be needed. She handed it to her mum and they all waited and watched.

The card was quite neutral. It wasn't funny, romantic or gushing, just 'Have a lovely birthday. Best wishes from Anthony.'

'Right, shall we move on then?' Diana said, putting the card on top of the pile. April noticed a pink flush spreading across her cheeks and wondered what this meant. Anger, embarrassment… or even joy?

The afternoon continued without any further mention of the card. Diana was her usual self, giving her views based on her limited knowledge of politics, and making a fuss of Demelza. Politics was always a difficult subject due to Joanna and April having totally different opinions on it. Joanna had led an extremely privileged life: upper-middle-class parents, private-school education and ultimately a place at a top university. By the time she married Max both she and he had successful careers and the lucrative salaries that went with them. She had never wanted for anything. She was basically a kind person and generous to needy causes such as malaria control and famine relief, but she had no understanding of or empathy for British citizens who required state assistance due to their impoverished and unfortunate circumstances. She just couldn't understand why they didn't work harder at school, get a decent job and take care of their own needs. When they were younger, she and April had fallen out regularly over these differences, but now they were just careful to avoid discussing them. Diana wasn't quite so diplomatic and would often spout her views, usually about the dreadful government and what they were doing to public services.

They all helped to clear up the dishes and the leftover food before Max and Joanna set off on their journey home. After putting Demelza to bed, April and Diana sat down together in the lounge, leaving one of the windows wide open so that they could listen to the blackbirds chirping in the treetops outside.

April folded her legs underneath her, sighing as she sank back against the cushions. 'I am absolutely shattered.'

'Shall I get us a cup of tea?' Jed said. He hadn't sat down yet and was standing just inside the door.

'That would be marvellous.' April rested her head on the back of the chair and briefly closed her eyes.

'That was very thoughtful of him, wasn't it?'

'It's only a cup of tea, Mum. He does do that for me sometimes, you know.'

Diana laughed. 'No, I mean your dad.'

'Oh!' April was so taken aback that she couldn't reply.

Jed came in with the tea, and April waited for Diana to continue. She really wanted to discuss it further, but unfortunately nothing more was said.

23

BEHIND CLOSED DOORS

The conference for the Phillips children went as April had expected, with all the relevant professionals present, including Tyler's teacher and the health visitor, expressing concerns about the children. Unfortunately, no Housing professional attended even though invitations had been sent. There was therefore no one present who was able to suggest how the family's housing situation could be resolved. Kerry was objectionable throughout the meeting, although April couldn't blame her. She was an angry woman who felt she was being blamed for something that was out of her control. She felt that if she were given a reasonable place to live, back in the area where she had friends and family, she would not be where she was now with her children being placed on Child Protection Plans. Regardless of this, it was unanimously agreed that CP Plans should be in place, and that without them there was a risk that the children would suffer significant harm.

Katy updated the conference on the housing situation. She had been in frequent contact with the Housing Department, only to be told the same thing each time: that the family was not a priority case. April wondered who would be considered a priority if this family living in appalling conditions weren't. She could see that Kerry was becoming more and more angry, which was hardly surprising. She had thought the professionals were there to help her and her family, but it seemed as though all she had heard was criticism and blame.

When the conference ended, April asked Kerry to stay behind for a chat with her and Katy. The three of them went into a side room which was set aside to be used for interviews. Before April was properly inside or anyone was seated, Kerry was yelling. 'How the fuck am I supposed to bring my kids up in that shithole? How the fuck would *you* bring your kids up there, or anyone else? I can't cope much longer. You'll have to take the kids into care. It's not fair on them. It's not fair on me. I thought someone would help me. I thought *you* were going to help me.' She jabbed her finger accusingly at Katy. 'I thought that's what you lot were for.' She was becoming red in the face and her eyes blazed.

April jumped to Katy's defence. 'We are doing everything we can, Kerry'. 'Unfortunately we have no control over housing. In the meantime it's important for you to focus on what you can do to try to make it better for the kids. Nursery is helping Tamara but she needs more interaction from you at home, and so does Tyler. You need to take them out more. We're having lovely weather at the moment. Take them to the park; it doesn't cost anything.'

Kerry didn't answer at first. She wasn't happy about this approach: putting the focus on her. She felt they should be helping her get a house, not telling her to take her kids to the park. Finally, she spoke. 'Oh yeah, that's going to solve everything, isn't it? "Take them to the park, Kerry" – everything will be fine then, I suppose. Until we have to go back to that shithole. Have you seen how far it is to the nearest park?'

'Of course everything isn't going to be fine. It's called not giving up, doing your best. I know it seems as though it will never end, but it will. You will get somewhere to live sooner or later, but in the meantime you need to do the best you can for your kids,' April repeated.

After the conference, April set off to see Florian and Leo, who had just moved in permanently with Matthew and Lawrence. It dawned on her that she would be passing close to Taylor's Yard, and she decided to call in to see how Alison was feeling about Isobel and what her thoughts were now about having more contact with her, since she seemed to be experiencing some guilt. April also needed to tell Alison about the planned visit to the sexual health clinic. She parked the car in the nearby car park and walked up the busy high street before turning left into Taylor's Yard. She knocked loudly, and the door was soon answered by Alison.

'Hello, Alison, I hope you don't mind me calling unannounced. I was just passing and realised I hadn't had time to see you since Isobel returned.'

Alison didn't look too pleased but reluctantly she let her in. The cold of the concrete on the walls and below her feet made April shiver as she walked up the narrow staircase. Seeing the door was ajar, she stepped inside, directly into the lounge. To her surprise, a man with dark hair and long legs was sprawled out on the armchair next to the window. Without making any effort to stand up or even sit upright, he stretched out his bare arm towards her, revealing angry-looking red lines criss-crossing from the inside of his elbow to his wrist. April immediately recognised these as marks of self-harm. She assumed this must be Danny, whom she had never managed to meet. He had always been at work when she visited and never attended any meetings. It was going to be more difficult to talk about Isobel and contact with him present.

'What can we do for you today then, April? I've had the police around this morning so I don't really want to be answering any questions from you,' Danny pronounced. He was smug, disrespectful and arrogant.

'Don't worry, I'm not here for that. I just wanted to know how things are and to talk about plans for Isobel's future.' April sat down on the small, hard armchair opposite Danny. 'Since you're here, Danny, I will take the opportunity to find out from both of you what you would like to happen now and in the future with regard to Isobel.'

She turned first to Alison. 'You haven't had contact with Isobel for some time now, Alison. Would you like me to arrange a session for you? I'm sure Isobel would like to see you.'

Before Alison had the chance to open her mouth, Danny stood up, towering over April. 'Alison doesn't want to see her and neither do I. The police came round and they're not pressing charges. I told you the whole thing was a pack of lies, didn't I?'

This was an incredible bolt from the blue for April. 'Is that what they told you?'

'Yes, they said she was making it all up. They couldn't find any evidence.' The arrogance in his tone was clear. *I did do it but no one, including you, can prove it* ,was unspoken but written all over his face.

Unusually for her, April felt an overwhelming desire to stand up and swipe the smug expression from his face. She hoped that he was lying, that he was making it up for Alison's benefit, but she had a horrible feeling about it, although she was sure the police would not have said that Isobel had made it all up. That must be what he was telling Alison. She had seen this so many times in the past. Young people placed their trust in the system that was supposedly there to protect them, only to be told that nothing would be done. All she could think of now was how quickly she could get back to her car and contact the police to check what she had just heard.

'So what are you hoping will happen now, then, with regard to Isobel?' April looked first at Alison, who immediately looked down at the floor, before focusing her gaze on Danny.

'Well, she ain't coming back 'ere. Not until she apologises, anyway. I don't know why she made up all those horrible lies about me,' he said, looking convincingly mystified. 'We used to have a really good relationship. She was a proper Daddy's girl, wasn't she, Alison?'

Alison nodded vigorously. 'Yes, she always wanted to be with Danny rather than me when she was little.'

April wondered why Alison wasn't curious about the change in her daughter's behaviour. She wanted to say, *Why do you think that might have changed, Alison?*, but decided that might be best kept for another time. It wasn't going to help things currently. 'So, I just need to make sure I am clear about what you are saying. You are both saying that you don't want to see Isobel unless she apologises?'

Danny was adamant in his answer, whereas Alison's sounded uncertain and hesitant.

'Would you consider writing to her, Alison?'

Alison looked directly at Danny, who glared back at her. 'No. I can't do that unless she apologises, she said meekly'.

April left the Thornes' home with a very heavy heart. It was such a sad situation. She had hoped Alison would put her daughter first. It was going to be really hard to tell Isobel what her parents had said. After getting into her car, she took her phone from the front zipped pocket of her bag and found the number for the police child protection unit. Frustratingly, as usual, the answerphone asked her to leave a message and someone would return her call. She cursed under her breath as she put the phone back in her bag. She was annoyed that, if Danny *was* telling the truth (and she guessed he probably was), the police had not informed her.

24

NO JUSTICE FOR CHILDREN

April stood on the doorstep of Lawrence and Matthew's home, waiting for someone to answer the door. There didn't appear to be anyone at home. She thought it was a bit strange if they had gone out because she had arranged the visit and wasn't late or early.

She was just thinking about phoning them when she heard a commotion: a male voice mingled with the laughter and squealing of a child above the sound of rubber and metal against concrete. April stood on tiptoe to see over the privet hedge into the street where the noise was coming from, and could see Lawrence's back as he ran beside Florian, who was pedalling fast on his little bike, wobbling from side to side as the stabilisers touched down on either side against the pavement.

'Keep going, keep going, you're doing great. Lift your feet up. Great!' Lawrence was shouting encouragingly.

Lawrence was holding on to the bike as he ran, trying to stop Florian from veering into the hedge or the road. They were closely followed by Matthew who was carrying Leo on his shoulders. They looked rosy-cheeked and windswept.

'Sorry, April. We didn't realise what the time was. We've been down to the park; did a bit of pond fishing and then went on the cycle trail. Florian is very good at riding his bike. It won't be long before we have to get him a big boy's bike, will it, Florian?'

Florian nodded. 'I went really fast,' he said, making a whooshing motion with his arms to demonstrate his speed.

April followed Matthew into the lounge and they sat down whilst Lawrence made the boys a drink. Then Lawrence popped his head around the door. 'Anyone for coffee?'

'Yes please, that would be lovely,' April answered.

Florian came in with his plastic sipi-cup and Leo was put in his high chair before being given his. April was really pleased to see how settled they both seemed. It was as though they had always lived there.

'Things seem to be going very well.'

'You should have been here yesterday; you might not be saying that,' Lawrence said as he joined them in the lounge.

'Oh. Was there a bit of an upset?'

'More than a bit.' April was relieved to see that he was smiling. 'I'll let you know more in an email, April. It's nothing to worry about. We managed it and it's nothing we couldn't handle.'

'FC has been mentioned a few times recently by F,' added Matthew. '"Where is she? When are we going home?" – that sort of thing – but it passes really quickly. They've both been sleeping really well.'

'It's early days yet and it may not seem like it to you, but it's good that F is missing her. It shows that he formed an attachment, which is actually a positive thing for the future.'

Whilst they were talking, Florian pulled a little plastic tea set from a box in the corner of the room. He laid out the plates and cups on the carpet, poured imaginary liquid from the teapot, placed a cup on a saucer and carried it, wobbling, to April, who took it, thanked him and pretended to drink it.

'He's got a wonderful imagination, hasn't he Matthew?' Matthew nodded, smiling proudly.

'Yes, I would say in lots of ways he's right where he should be'.

April smiled. 'Yes, I think you're right.' She didn't really think that – Florian was right as he should be – but it didn't do any harm to let his new dads think otherwise. In reality they were fully aware of all the help he was going to need,

By the time April left the Ryan household it was nearly five o'clock. She had to get to the nursery to pick up Demelza before 5.30. The trouble was that she needed to phone the police again before five, otherwise she'd have to wait until Monday to check out what Danny Thorne had told her. She hurried back to her car, climbed into the driver's seat, took out her phone and rang the number again. It was answered this time.

'I would like to speak to Fleur Gilligan, please.'

'I'm sorry, she isn't in the office at the moment. Would you like me to ask her to call you?'

April couldn't help herself; she groaned loudly with frustration. 'No. I have been trying to get hold of her for some time now. Is there anyone else I can speak to in the child protection unit, please?'

'Can I ask who's calling?'

'My name's April Gardiner. I'm the social worker for Isobel Thorne.'

'If you'd like to hold on, I will see if there's anyone I can put you through to.'

'Thank you.'

April waited, listening for what seemed like ages to the silence on the other end. Then, finally, 'Hello, DC Anderson here. How can I help you?'

April explained again who she was. 'I have been told there has been a decision regarding the case of Danny Thorne. Can you tell me if this is true, please? If what Danny has told me is true, I need to tell his daughter as soon as possible, but I want to make sure I have the correct information.'

'OK, I will just have a look. Won't keep you a moment.'

April could hear the tapping of a keyboard and occasional muttering from DC Anderson as he searched through the data.

'Oh yes, here it is, Daniel Thorne.' He was reading out loud. '"Case closed. No further action."'

April struggled to keep her voice calm. She'd had a dreadful feeling that this would be the answer but had hoped she'd be wrong. 'How can that be? Isobel described everything in great detail. It all fits in. How can she not be believed?'

'I'm just looking at the notes now.' He hummed as he scanned the notes, as though he was looking for a package holiday, rather than a decision that was going to impact on a young girl's whole future. 'There wasn't enough evidence. The notes also say that Isobel would not be considered a viable witness by the DPP.'

'*What?!*' April gasped. 'How can that be?'

'I'm just reading through…' Another pause. 'Yes, here we are – it looks like she's a bit unstable. Her mum says she's always been a difficult child. It says here that she admitted to having a sexual relationship with someone. She's considered promiscuous. Her mum says she's always told lies. I see she was excluded from school. Goes to a pupil referral unit. Couldn't be managed in mainstream.'

April was dumbfounded. 'Of course she's a difficult child. What do you expect? She's an abused child.'

'I know that as well as you do, but we both know how the court will see it. The defence will argue that she can't be trusted and that will be the end of it. I know how you feel, and believe me, I've been in this job for nearly three years now and I never fail to be astonished by how many abuse cases never get to trial. I'm sorry but that's how it is. We need radical changes in our legal processes when it comes to abused children as witnesses.'

April was seething. She had heard the same story so many times, how men could abuse children and not be charged. So many were never charged. All she could think about was how she would tell Isobel, who had been waiting for her dad to be prosecuted so that she could go back home and be with her mum. It was more than likely that she would never go home now. At least the weekend was coming up, so April would have time to think about how best to tell her. She needed to somehow convince her that the decision not to press charges against her father did not mean that nobody believed her. It just meant that they couldn't prove it in court. As she drove off, she started to think about Isobel's future. She would need to apply for a Care Order to make sure that she stayed in care.

April collected Demelza from nursery and seeing her little girl's smile as she walked in the door was like sunshine breaking through a cloud. She picked her up and swung her around before covering her in kisses. Demelza fought against being strapped into her car seat, but April won in the end and they headed home with April's thoughts turning to how they would spend her days off.

25

DEMELZA

On Monday morning, April was awake early as usual. Eyes wide open, staring at the ceiling, wondering what to prioritise out of the many urgent matters she had waiting to be dealt with. It wasn't long before she heard murmuring from Demelza's room. Jed, was still asleep and would probably stay that way until the alarm went off. He lay on his back, the duvet pushed down, revealing a covering of dark hair on his bare chest; his strong jaw wobbling slightly in unison with his steady breathing. She pushed the duvet aside, and as she did Demelza's voice became louder. She was shouting out now in protest at the lack of response to her calls.

Demelza was standing up in her cot, holding on to the bars, and April noticed that her cheeks were blazing. She felt her forehead, which seemed hotter than usual, but she was clearly all right in herself. April decided she must be teething again.

After dropping Demelza at nursery she was able to go back to her thoughts about what to prioritise. The most urgent matter for the day was to visit Isobel to inform her of the police decision. She was really not looking forward to that but needed to let her know as soon as she could in case Isobel heard about it from another source. Unfortunately, that would have to wait until Isobel came home from school.

Now that Tamara and Tyler were on Child Protection Plans, visits to the family would have to be increased. Katy was still going to continue to see them but April would need to be more involved too. Unfortunately this meant visiting late in the day when Tyler returned from school. April resented any visits that made her late collecting Demelza from nursery. There was plenty of paperwork to be getting on with, though, and she was relieved to have found some time to sit down and tackle it.

April had only just started on her paperwork when, to her annoyance, her phone rang. She was a bit taken aback to hear the voice of Celia from the nursery. 'Hello, Celia, what can I do for you?' she asked apprehensively.

Although she asked the question, she had already guessed what was coming.

'I'm sorry to call you, April, but Demelza just isn't well. She seems to have a temperature. We made up a little bed for her but she's not settling and needs to be at home, really.'

'Oh my God!' April gasped. 'I'm on my way. I should be there in about twenty minutes.' She packed up her papers, threw her phone and pencil case in her bag and turned off the computer. She could see Maria in her office with her head down, working, but decided not to bother her. She would email from home to explain.

When she got to the nursery she went straight to Demelza, who was lying on a little makeshift bed, looking very hot and bothered. Her hair was damp around her neck and forehead, and her cheeks were blazing. April wrapped her up in a thin blanket and carried her to the car. She was racked with guilt. She beat herself up all the way home for not realising, not taking enough notice of her child, ignoring the signs, prioritising her work over her child. Apart from all this, she was really worried about Demelza. She seemed listless and whiny, which she had never been before; even when she was teething or had a cold she seemed to shrug it off and breeze through. April decided to take her to the clinic rather than go home, and get her seen by a doctor.

After a brief wait she was called in to see the emergency doctor, who took Demelza's temperature and looked in her mouth before checking her body. The doctor lifted her top before turning her over to look at her back, and there, as clear as day, was a large patch of redness which was dotted with angry-looking spots. April saw it at the same time as the doctor and her heart seemed to stop. 'Meningitis!' she exclaimed.

'No, there's no need to panic; it's not meningitis, Mrs Gardiner. It's chickenpox.'

April let out a long sigh of relief. 'Oh, thank God for that.'

'I will give you a prescription for cream, and you might want to give her some oatmeal baths which should help reduce the itchiness. You will need to keep her at home for a week.'

April felt so relieved that her little girl didn't have a life-threatening disease that she hadn't given a thought to how she would manage. It wasn't until she had collected the prescription and some oatmeal and taken Demelza home that she started to think about it. She was certain that her mum would come and stay but didn't want to take advantage of her by expecting her to drop all her own plans. She thought it could be possible for Jed to work at home, and decided she would try that option first. They had discussed this possibility, along with other potential scenarios that could arise, during her pregnancy and it had seemed that any issues of this nature could be easily resolved between them, with April's mum as a backup.

Demelza was lying on her back on the settee, her orange teddy tucked under her chin. She was dressed in a cotton T-shirt and had a thin blanket covering her legs. She was still, and by the way her eyelids were drooping, it was clear that she was about to fall asleep, so April decided it was a good time to make some phone calls. She called Jed first.

'How did she get chickenpox?' There was panic in his voice. 'She had the vaccination. Can't they go blind? Children can go blind if they get chickenpox. She must have caught it at nursery. Parents aren't getting their children vaccinated now, are they, because of the stupid autism scare? Now our child's got it.'

April was surprised by his response, but also amused. He was a new father, after all; what would he know about children's illnesses? 'No, Jed, you're confusing it with measles. They don't vaccinate against chickenpox and it's not serious. It's just not very nice. The doctor said it will only be a few days before she's feeling better, but the spots take some time to go. It's just that she can't go to nursery. I was wondering whether you might be able to work from home for a few days? I've got some really important matters to deal with at work. They can't be left until next week.'

'I don't think so. Can't someone else do those things for you? If your daughter's not well, someone else will have to do them for you, won't they?'

'Oh, I see. Your job is much more important than mine, then, is it? Why can't *you* stay at home and let someone else do *your* work?' Tears of frustration sprang to April's eyes. It was a combination of the worry about Demelza, the guilt around sending her to nursery when she wasn't well, and the difficult issues that were waiting to be dealt with at work.

'I'm supposed to be out on an audit tomorrow. It won't go down very well if I have to cancel it. Have you asked your mum if she'll come up? I'm sure she would jump at the chance.'

'Don't worry, just leave it to me. It's obviously my problem.' She put the phone down abruptly.

As she had thought, Diana was delighted to be asked. Even whilst they spoke on the phone, she started getting her things together, ready to set off. She said she would be there before teatime. It was a great relief for April, although she still felt miffed that Jed clearly valued his own work above hers, and she intended to discuss this further with him as soon as she had the opportunity.

Even though her mum was at home with Demelza, the next day when she was leaving for work, April felt terribly guilty as she got in her car. Demelza was a bit brighter now but she still wasn't well, and all April wanted to do was sit and cuddle her to make her feel better.

It was so hard to leave her that she had left it as late as possible before leaving the house. In fact, it wasn't far off lunchtime when she arrived at the office.

After replying to urgent emails and talking to Maria, who had stopped by to ask about Demelza, April started to prepare to set off to see Isobel. As she drove her head was spinning with the stress of trying to catch up with everything. She had hardly managed to give a thought to how she was going to break the news to poor Isobel.

Denise was looking out of the window when April pulled up beside the pavement, and by the time she had walked up the garden path, she was waiting with the front door open.

'Can I have a word before you see her, April?'

'Of course. Is there a problem?'

Denise gestured towards the kitchen and stepped aside whilst April walked inside.

'I presume Isobel is in her room?'

'Yes, that's where she always is. I still try to encourage her to come down and join us but she won't. I'm worried about her, April. I know I'm no expert but she seems depressed to me. I think she needs to be seen by someone.'

'It's not really surprising, I suppose, Denise. Unfortunately, once she hears what I've got to tell her today, she's going to feel even worse.'

April explained the police decision not to pursue prosecution, and Denise clasped her hand to her mouth in disbelief.

'This is just awful. Poor little thing. I wish I could help her, but I'm afraid it's beyond me.'

April could see that Denise was completely genuine in her concern, which was heartening. She had thought her cold and uncaring, but that clearly wasn't the case now. Perhaps seeing the way things had gone for Isobel had melted her heart.

April made her way upstairs to Isobel's room and knocked on the door.

'Yeah, what do you want?' Isobel called out.

'It's April. Can I come in, Isobel?'

'If you want.'

Isobel was propped up on some pillows on her bed. It looked as though she had been listening to music, as the white cord from her earphones still hung around her neck. Her hair was a tangled mass of thick, unbrushed dark locks which tumbled over her shoulders. Although she was now fifteen, her tiny, solemn features gave her a childish countenance.

'How was school?'

'Crap.'

'It can't be that bad.'

'It's crap. You don't learn anything. I did all that stuff in primary. They think we're all thick. I want to go back to my old school. At least I learnt something there.'

'OK, Isobel. We'll talk about that another time. In the meantime, I have some news for you, and I'm afraid that it will probably make you feel very angry.'

Isobel's head shot up and her back straightened. 'What?'

'It's about your dad.'

'Yes, what about him?' Her eyes widened and focused intently on April. She seemed to be holding her breath.

'I hate to have to tell you this because I know it's going to be hard for you to hear, but I have spoken to the police and they are not going to prosecute your dad for the offences against you.'

There was silence whilst Isobel took this in. After a pause, she put her hands up to cover her face and her eyes. She left them there for some time before slowly moving them away; then, with a stoical expression, she looked towards the door and said, 'OK. I will go home now, then.'

'Isobel, you can't go home. Just because he isn't going to be charged doesn't mean it didn't happen, does it? I know this makes you unhappy but it is my job to protect you. I can't let you go home. It wouldn't be the best thing for you. You wouldn't be safe.'

'What about Mum? She will want me to come home. I don't think she would let him touch me again. She might make him move out. She does want me to come home, doesn't she?'

April's stomach churned. 'Isobel, at the moment your mum is saying that she believes your dad. I do believe she is just trying to keep the peace and that this may change in time.'

She watched as Isobel's expression hardened like stone; void of all feeling, shut down, too much for her to take in. April was deeply concerned by this internalisation. This was one of those rare situations when she was at a loss for something to say. Nothing she could say would take away the pain.

'I know it's hard, Isobel. I wish it had turned out differently for you. As it is, we have to make the best of it. I am going to be here to help you get through this, and Denise and Harry want to support you as much as they can. It might be that in the future your mum will change her mind. I do know she loves you and cares about you. Sometimes, though, mums can find things difficult and get it wrong. It might be that she is frightened of being on her own. She might think she can't manage without your dad. Things can change, though, and she might think differently in time.'

'I'm not staying here. I hate it here. If I can't go home I want to move somewhere else.'

'That's a shame, Isobel; I thought you were beginning to settle here. I thought your relationship with Denise was better now.'

'No,' Isobel said angrily. 'What made you think that? Denise hates me. She talks to me as though I'm a piece of shit. She just doesn't do it when you're here.'

April was worried about this. It was a difficult one because it could be Isobel's perception of things, but it might also be true. How was she to know? 'If you are still unhappy here, Isobel, I will look for another foster carer for you. I would like to find you a placement where you can settle and really feel at home.'

She prepared to leave, but stopped in her tracks when Isobel suddenly spoke. 'Has Mum asked to see me?'

April felt a surge of compassion. How could she tell her now, after the worst news one could imagine, that, no, her mum hadn't asked to see her? She walked back into the room and sat on the bed beside her. 'Everything is still up in the air, Isobel,' she waffled. 'Try to remember, this has been extremely difficult for your mum too. She's trying hard to deal with the terrible shock of it all, but she's not dealing with it very well at the moment.'

'She hates my guts,' Isobel asserted before turning her face determinedly towards the wall.

April left the foster home with a heavy heart. If things continued as they were, life was going to be very difficult for Isobel. At least she hadn't gone missing again, and Damian hadn't been mentioned.

By the time April arrived home after giving Isobel the news about her father, Demelza was bathed and in her pyjamas, ready to go to bed. She was sitting on Diana's knee, looking at nursery rhymes. She looked much better than she had that morning.

26

STREET LIFE

For the next few months Samantha spent her time begging during the day, and on some occasions going back to the shelter. Things had been better because she wasn't on her own anymore and the weather was warming up, although the temperature dropped considerably at night. What she found most difficult to cope with were the disdainful looks from some passers-by. Most people looked the other way as they passed in case they had to acknowledge the human degradation of homelessness and begging, but others were blatant in their contempt. This made Sam shrivel up inside.

There were kind people too, though, and she always managed to get some money for food. Sometimes she and George had enough between them to buy cider or, on a good day, vodka. They'd got to know a few other regular rough sleepers and the group would get together and share whatever alcohol they had managed to get hold of. This was good, although it brought back memories of the days before her girls were taken away from her, when she would meet her drinking friends in Princess Park and lose herself for days on end in the shadowy world of the alcoholic.

There were still times when she returned to the shelter. There was always hot food and usually a pile of donated clothes to choose from. With the changing of the season she needed to replace some of her winter clothes. One afternoon, after she and George had decided to visit the shelter, Sam was collared by Sydney.

'Could you come into the office, Sam? I have some good news for you.'

Samantha followed her across the large floor area to the little room on the other side. Sydney indicated for her to sit down on the opposite side of her desk.

'I have had some information from Shelter that there are two bedsits available just off the town centre. Would you like to have a look?'

Samantha was stunned into silence. Her life had become the street life. She hadn't considered that it would end. She stared blankly at Sydney, who smiled at her.

'I can see you weren't expecting news like that. It's a short-term tenancy which is only meant to give you time to find somewhere permanent. Do you want time to think about it? You won't have long, though; there are others who'll jump at it, believe me.'

Samantha was trying to envisage what it would be like to have a place to live again; somewhere warm where she could cook food, watch television, sleep in a bed every night and have hot water in the morning to wash herself. It sounded like bliss.

'The room is empty and you could move in tomorrow if you wanted to.'

Sydney offered to take her in her car to view the bedsit. It was a Victorian terrace with four floors, all of which were converted into bedsits. The one Samantha was looking at was on the fourth floor. It was tiny; just enough room for a single bed, a small cooking area and a wardrobe. The carpet was old, spotted with black marks, and threadbare.

'We can give you some bedding, Sam, and crockery. What do you think?'

Sam absorbed the bleakness of the room with an equally bleak heart, but this was the best she could expect. It was better than the streets.

She moved in the next day. Sydney had helped her sort out her benefits and it was now left to her. She was told she had to search for employment, and in order to keep her benefits in place she had to provide proof of her efforts. But however hard she tried – and she really did try hard – she found looking for a job beyond her capability. She needed help to complete application forms as she had never learnt to write properly. She managed to get some insecure work on zero-hours contracts but this made things worse rather than better. When she didn't have work she had no money and the rent didn't get paid. After six months of struggling she found herself back on the streets.

She and George had stayed together so at least she wasn't alone this time. By the time winter arrived again some of their street friends had been given hostel rooms or bedsits, and Samantha and George would sometimes get to sleep on settees or somebody's floor. Those arrangements never lasted for long, though.

One evening they were sitting on the pavement with a group of people, sharing some alcohol, when a man from the council told them they had to move on. An argument developed which resulted in George being arrested for assault and placed on remand.

The following evening, as the daylight began to fade, Samantha started to worry. She had become dependent on George. She was wondering whether to go to the shelter, although this would mean putting up with harassment from the men there. She was still contemplating the idea when she noticed someone she recognised heading in her direction. She remembered him being part of the group they'd been with the previous night. She was sitting on her blanket with her legs underneath her, leaning back against the iron railings of a churchyard at the far end of the high street. He was striding towards her as though he had known she would be there. She looked up at him curiously.

'I'm Lenny. Don't you remember me? We were together the other night. One of the other fellas told me you were on your own now; your bloke punched a copper, didn't he? You don't want to be on your own, love. It's not safe.'

Lenny was tall and skinny with a sickly yellow pallor. His matted light brown hair hung in wisps over his neck. He looked about forty but Sam had come to realise that street people often looked older than their age. Before she could answer, he sat down next to her, his shoulder pressed against hers and one hand on her knee. There was a pungent odour of stale sweat from his clothes and body as he pushed himself closer.

'My real name isn't Lenny. It's Nigel, but they call me Lenny for short.' His lips spread into a broad grin at his joke, revealing large gaps in his teeth. 'I don't usually tell anyone that. See, you're honoured. You must be special. Old Lenny's going to look after you. What did you say your name was? I've forgotten your name; stupid fucking idiot. It's the alcohol addling my brain.' He chuckled loudly, rocking back and forward, clearly amused again by his ingenious wit. 'What the fuck are you doin' sitting 'ere anyway? You ain't gonna get much down 'ere. You need to be in the main bit where everyone's shoppin'. Why are you sittin' 'ere?'

'I don't like it in town. I hate the way people look at me. I was going to go back to the shelter tonight.'

'No, you don't wanna do that. We'll go into town and get some money, buy booze and get pissed. Much better idea, don't you think?'

Sam did like the idea of getting pissed. It was unbelievably depressing living this life. Her life hadn't been great before but at least she'd had the kids and a flat, slum that it was. She'd had something to keep her going. Now there was nothing; only alcohol to live for. Getting some money, getting pissed, getting through one day to the next, and staying alive. 'OK.'

She followed Lenny into the busy town centre. He found them a spot right on the corner of the bustling high street. It didn't feel as bad, being with someone else. During the time she had been homeless she had become familiar with other regular rough sleepers who also hung around the town, hoping to get some money for sustenance, booze or drugs; whatever their priorities were.

The two of them had only been in their spot for a short time when a young woman approached them. Sam thought she recognised her but wasn't sure. The woman knelt down to talk to them before settling herself down and making herself one of the group.

'I've been looking for Luke. Haven't seen him since the other night when your bloke got arrested.' She nodded towards Samantha. 'Have you seen him?'

Samantha couldn't remember her or anyone called Luke.

Lenny gave another of his habitual chuckles. 'Don't worry, love, he'll be all right. He's smashed somewhere. I saw 'im shootin' up behind the old boat shed. That's what 'e does. Does it all the time.'

The woman turned to Samantha and started chatting as though she was an old friend. 'How come you're here then, Sam? Is it Sam? I'm Amy, if you remember.'

'Yes, it's Sam. Lenny said to come up here where there's more people.'

'No, I meant how come you're on the streets, girl; I didn't mean how did you get *here*.' She jabbed her finger at the pavement.

'Oh, sorry. I got in arrears with my rent and got kicked out. Couldn't catch up. What about you?' Sam had no intention of telling this woman about Lily Grace and Tayla.

'Domestic violence. My bloke used to beat the crap out of me. Put me in hospital a few times. He wouldn't leave, so I had to.'

'Wouldn't the council get you another place? They should have done if you were being beaten up.'

'No. I was told I was intentionally homeless.'

'Me too. As if anyone would want to be "*intentionally* homeless". Haven't you got any family who would put you up?'

'My mum, but she's got my kids, so I'm not allowed to go there.'

At the mention of kids, Samantha wanted to know more. 'Why do they live with your mum?'

''Cause he was beating me up. They said it was harming the kids. It wasn't harming them at all, it was all a great big lie, 'cause they were in bed. He never did it when they were there.'

Before she could help herself, Samantha found herself opening up about her girls. 'I've been through all that. Social workers will tell you anything to get your kids off you. Mine were really well cared for but they still got took off me. Adopted now. They should be with their mum. Don't you ever see yours?'

'I should see them once a month but last time it was due, my mum told me to piss off. She kept saying I was high on something.'

'Were you?'

Amy just shrugged.

Samantha was appalled that she could have taken drugs before going to see her kids. She gave no verbal response to this, only a disbelieving glare. 'I wish I could see my two. I'd give anything to see them. I was supposed to get letters from them every year, but if you haven't got anywhere to live there's nowhere to send them to, is there?'

Once on this subject she couldn't resist telling Amy about her two little girls. She talked about how Tayla was such a cheeky madam, how she used to try to look after Lily Grace. She told her the story about Tayla making a chocolate spread sandwich in the middle of the kitchen floor. 'She used to love school. Hated being late. If I ever slept in she used to come and wake me up, beg me to take her to school. She was so clever.'

Even after all the time that had passed and all the things that had happened, this was the one thing that could cause her excruciating pain, and she could feel her insides twisting and knotting as she spoke. She sometimes felt almost as though her heart had been ripped from her chest, but it was worse than just the loss in itself. It was the knowledge that she had failed them. She had been too weak to give up the booze.

'How much have you got?' Amy was looking at the cap on the pavement which held a number of coins and a few blue notes.

'Not enough yet,' Lenny answered.

'We need a bit more if we're going to eat and party.'

They all laughed with a distinct lack of true jollity.

By around 9pm, the town was quiet with just a few stray people wandering around; although there was still quite a bit of traffic, skirting the pedestrianised area close to where the three sat. They shared some chips before going to the supermarket and stocking up on cider and wine, and then finding a grassy bank in the park to drink it. As usual there was jollity and humorous chatter. They passed the bottles round, and the more they swigged, the quieter they became. Through her drunken haze, Samantha was vaguely aware of another male joining them, and before long he and Amy went off together.

She was sitting on the bank next to the river, holding a can of cider between her legs, when she felt a hand going up the back of her top. Everything was a bit hazy but she realised that Lenny was taking the cider from her hand and placing his body where the can had been. Before she could stop him he had pushed her down, his hands tearing frantically at her underclothes; moving roughly all over her body so quickly that she could hardly tell where they were. She fought with all her strength to stop him but he was strong and determined. Before she could even begin to scream his lips were on her mouth, pressing, licking, sucking. She wanted to plead with him to stop but the only sounds that escaped her were groans and a whimper. By the time he had climbed on top of her, thrashing up and down, she had surrendered to the inevitable.

When it was all over, Lenny became the exact same person he had been prior to the rape, just as though nothing had happened. He stood up, buttoned his trousers and sat back down beside Sam, his eyes shining happily and a friendly smile on his face. 'Here's another blanket; you can use it as a pillow if you like.'

She stared at him, trying to conceptualise what had just happened. She lay on her red tartan blanket with her head on the makeshift pillow, her eyes wide open, blood rushing around her body and heart beating like a train racing along the tracks. She wanted to get away from this man who had just violated her, but was too scared to move. The night air was bitterly cold against her cheeks and the hard, uneven ground that she lay on made her body ache in every crevice.

She could feel a painful swelling developing behind her shoulders where she had been pinned violently to the ground, and sharp pains sprang from her groin. As she watched Lenny's eyes finally close and his breathing become steady, vivid thoughts of violent revenge filled her brain. These were followed by distinct feelings of emptiness and shame, and silent tears trickled slowly down her cheeks.

Any residue of the effects of alcohol had diminished completely but she wouldn't be able to go to the shelter because they would smell it on her breath. She decided she would go and look for Amy; the only person she could think of. The closest person in her life at this time.

27

NO HOPE

Kerry waited in the school playground for Tyler to come out of his class. She stood with Tamara in the pushchair, feeling lonely and awkward as all the other mothers were standing in little groups, chatting. They had probably all known each other since their children were in nursery, if not before, whereas she was a stranger. Occasionally someone would say good morning to her but she wasn't very good at getting to know new people. She had never had to do it before, having been brought up in the same area where she'd been living with her children before the eviction.

She overheard the mum of a child in Tyler's class talking about his birthday party at the weekend. They were going to be making pizzas before playing on the trampoline in the garden. Tyler clearly wasn't invited. Although it was painful for Kerry to realise that her child had been left out, at the same time she knew deep down that it was her own behaviour that had caused this. She was fundamentally shy and socially inept, and she was petrified that someone would ask her where she lived and why she had moved to the area. She didn't want the humiliation and shame of having to admit what had happened.

To her relief, it wasn't long before the doors were opened and children came streaming out. Whether it was a consequence of her general low mood or it was true, she perceived for the first time that Tyler appeared isolated too. The other children came away from their classrooms skipping, swinging their book bags and chatting to each other. It was hardly what you would call engaging in conversation but there was a togetherness of which her son was not part. His pace was notably slower than his peers' and his solemn expression spoke loudly of loneliness and solitude.

Tyler took hold of the pushchair with his left hand and the three slowly made their way back towards Kennedy House.

'Did you have a nice day today?' Kerry asked her son.

'OK.'

'What did you do?'

'Nothing.'

Kerry was quiet for a while. She wanted to ask him if he was happy but couldn't work out the best way to do it. She knew that his answer would be yes, but she also knew that this didn't mean anything. She felt desperate to know how he really felt. 'What did you do at playtime?'

'I can't remember.'

'Do you like school?'

'Yes.'

Kerry wasn't convinced. There was a lack of enthusiasm in his answers and no sense of joy. She decided to leave it at that because there was no use pushing it, which could make him feel there was something wrong, even if there wasn't.

It was a long trek from the school back to Kennedy House and the rest of the journey was made in silence. She was sure now that her son was unhappy, and this was heart-wrenching. She hadn't thought too much about it until now because she'd expected him to take a bit of time to settle in and make friends… or was it because she had been too wrapped up in self-pity to notice? The belated recognition of her son's unhappiness added weight to the heavy burden of guilt and failure that dominated her everyday thoughts.

She lifted Tamara out of the pushchair and stood her on the

ground before unlocking the shed door and wheeling the pushchair inside. As she ascended the stairs, the familiar shadow cast itself over her. Once she was inside her room and the door was shut behind her, that was her world for what was left of the afternoon, the evening (which seemed endless), and all through the night. No one to talk to, nothing to do. Life without joy, or even hope. The small space which was her home, with its overwhelming amount of clutter and distinct lack of homeliness, always felt intolerable, but this was intensified by the mood she was in.

It was still warm outside and there was a small garden where she could take the kids to play, but she didn't want to do that on her own. She desperately needed a chat with someone; adult company, which she rarely had the opportunity to enjoy. When she reached the top of the stairs, instead of turning right in the direction of her own room, she went left towards Briony's room. She could hear movement inside, so knocked, hoping that she wasn't intruding. Briony opened the door with one hand, a tea towel in the other. Her face brightened at the sight of a visitor. Her baby, Angel, was propped up in her pushchair just in front of the door.

'Your room always looks so neat and tidy. How do you do it?' Kerry asked with genuine awe.

'I just like things tidy. I can't bear living in a mess. I suppose I'm lucky because my mum lets me keep a lot of my stuff at hers until I get a proper place. Couldn't you put some of your stuff in your mum's house?'

'She hasn't got the room. She's only got a small flat and that's chocka with stuff.'

Tyler had found himself a corner of the room where he occupied himself with a game on his mother's phone. Tamara was tickling Angel and trying to feed her with a bottle that had been lying on the side. Briony made some tea and the two women sat down on the small armchairs which took up the only available space in the room, between the television and the beds. They chatted away about all sorts of things and were soon onto the subject of their ex-partners.

Briony told Kerry that Angel's father had disappeared, never to be seen again, once he found out she was pregnant.

'Good riddance to him, that's what I thought. I wouldn't want someone like that in my kid's life anyway. Better off without him. He was a smackhead. What happened with yours? Have they got the same dad?'

'No. Tamara's dad comes in fits and starts, when there's not some tart on the scene. Haven't seen him for months now but I expect he'll come back before long, like he always does. The kids don't give a shit if he comes or not; they've forgotten who he is by the time he decides to come back anyway.'

They both laughed hysterically at this. Kerry's mood was starting to lift.

The two women chatted for some time before Tyler made his presence known by pulling at his mother's sleeve. 'Can we go home now, Mummy? I'm hungry.'

'I won't be long, love,' Kerry told him. 'Just play for a bit longer.'

He walked solemnly back to his spot at the back of the room and sat down with the phone again, where he stayed for about half an hour before giving it another try. This time he pushed his mum from behind, trying to get her to move. 'Can we go home now? I'm really, *really* hungry.' He was rubbing his tummy.

Briony went over to her kitchen area and, opening one of the high cupboards, found a packet of biscuits. She took a handful and shared them between Tyler and Tamara before handing one to Angel, who was still propped up in her pushchair, clearly not wanting – or, rather, expecting – any attention.

'Cheek of it, though,' Kerry continued. 'He makes a point of checking I haven't got someone else. Thinks I'm just gonna wait around in case he decides to come back.'

'Bloody cheek. Why don't you find yourself someone else?'

'I don't go anywhere to meet anyone, do I? I want someone with loads of money. Don't know where I would find one but that's my dream: get me out of this shithole; someone with a car to take us places.'

'I'm going to college in September,' Briony said. 'I'm going to do a childcare course. If you pass that you can train to be a social worker.'

'You're joking. Why do you want to be a social worker?'

'They earn pots of money. Haven't you seen the cars they drive? My social worker went to Thailand in December. Imagine going to Thailand! I've seen it on the telly; it's awesome. I can just see myself stretching out on a sunbed, drinking pina coladas and watching all those hot Rastafarians walking by in their Speedos.'

'Don't you need GCSEs to go to college?'

'I haven't got any but apparently they let you do maths and English while you do the other course at the same time, if you know what I mean.'

Kerry was starting to like the sound of this. She would have to look for work soon and some of the jobs she had seen that she could do were not very nice. She had heard that you had to work long hours in restaurants and didn't get paid much. She was also very worried about zero-hours contracts. Before she'd moved to this place she'd had a friend who had worked on a zero-hours contract as a waitress and she was always without money. She would sometimes work a full week but then have no work at all the next. Then she wouldn't get any money from anyone because she had to wait until the end of the month to get her benefits. She had kids to feed, too. Kerry was petrified of being in that position. Deep down, though, she knew she would never have the confidence to do GCSEs. She didn't think she could pass them anyway. She had never taken any exams. She hadn't gone to school much when she was young because she'd often had to look after her mum.

Another hour passed and Tamara was starting to grizzle. She was standing beside her mother's chair, nestling her head in her lap, clearly ready for sleep. Kerry stroked her hair absent-mindedly as she carried on chatting with Briony.

'Why don't you put the kids to bed and come back when they're asleep?' Briony suggested.

Kerry was quick to say no. She wouldn't do that again.

'You could put them to bed here, then carry them back later.'

Kerry thought about this and for a moment was tempted, but then, looking down at her little girl's curly head resting in her lap, she decided against it. They needed to be in their own beds – or mattresses, such as they were. Then she had an idea. 'Why don't you bring Angel round to mine? She can sleep in the pushchair.'

Kerry took the children home. She made them some toast followed by a bowl of tinned custard and a Fruit Shoot before washing their faces, putting Tamara into her pyjamas and settling her down on her mattress. Tyler had already climbed into bed and was almost asleep.

Briony arrived soon after with Angel fast asleep in her pushchair. She'd bought some weed.

28

UNCONDITIONAL LOVE

The traffic en route to work was heavier than normal this morning. April had left a bit later than usual, having had another restless night. It wasn't Demelza who'd kept her awake this time; it was the thought of all the work she had to do and the stress of wondering how she was going to fit it all in. The multi-agency meetings for Tamara and Tyler had been consistently negative about the children's emotional, physical and educational development, which were poor and seemed to be getting worse. Tyler was attending school regularly but was frequently late, causing him to be unsettled for most of the morning and unable to engage in the classroom. He often wore clothes that were shabby and not appropriate for school, and other children had commented on this. His teacher reported that she had been bringing in a banana for him most days because he often turned up with no snacks for break. It was really sad to hear that he had stolen food from other children's bags a couple of times, and his teacher wondered whether he had been given a proper breakfast.

Katy was still meeting regularly with Tyler and she was really worried about his general demeanour. Overall he presented as a sad little boy who didn't make friends easily and was below average in all areas of his development. Tamara was also behind her peers developmentally. April had arranged a meeting with the Local Authority solicitors to seek advice on whether they had the grounds to apply to court for Care Orders, which could mean the children being taken into care.

The legal meeting was the main issue of the day and needed to be prioritised, but April was still very worried about Isobel. Denise had reported that she had become much more secretive recently and was acting furtively. She had heard her talking to someone from her room a couple of times, but when Denise asked her about it, Isobel was adamant that she hadn't been talking to anyone. She wasn't allowed to have her phone in her room at night; therefore she must have another one. Denise had once seen Isobel push something under her duvet as she walked in the door, and was sure it was the phone she had been using.

The traffic seemed to have come to a standstill and there was no way of telling what was going on ahead. All April could do was sit and wait, take deep breaths and hope it wouldn't be for too long. Soon there was some movement; an edging forward of a couple of feet before everything ground to a standstill again. There was a left turn coming up which she could take as an alternative route to the office, but although it was tantalisingly close she just couldn't get the traffic to push up far enough to turn into it. Then all of a sudden, the traffic started to flow. She never found out why or what had happened but it was a big relief to be on her way at last.

She parked in her usual little car park and grabbed her bag from the passenger seat before heading off at full speed towards the office, in too much of a hurry to stop to sort out the thick strands of hair that the strong wind was blowing into her eyes. She pressed the code on the keypad and opened the door ready to rush through, but unfortunately two social work assistants were on their way down, one carrying a child's car seat and another, behind, struggling with a carrycot which was too wide for the narrow staircase. April tried to hide her frustration at being held up once more, and managed to greet them with a friendly smile.

As soon as she stepped inside the door, she was collared by Miles. It would normally have been a lovely surprise because she hadn't seen much of him lately, but on this occasion she really could have done without having to stop for a chat.

'April, I have been hoping to see you. We need to catch up.'

'Yes, we do, Miles, but I'm sorry; today I haven't got time for anything. I was hoping to be here an hour ago; I've got so much to do.'

'Oh, OK, I know what you mean. I haven't really got time either, I must admit. Can we arrange a time when we can meet and just have a chat?'

'Yes, of course, that will be good. I'll just find my diary.'

Their diaries were both quite full but they managed to find some space, although it wasn't for a few weeks.

April sat at her desk, set up her laptop, and as always the first thing she did was open her emails. Her heart sank when she saw one from Out of Hours. This always meant that something had happened that needed to be dealt with urgently. It was a shock to realise that it was Lawrence who had contacted OOHs. April's pulse speeded up rapidly on reading the heading, which named Florian and Leo as the subjects.

Reading through the detail, she saw that Florian had apparently become out of control during the night. He had woken up screaming and couldn't be consoled. Lawrence and Matthew realised quite quickly that he had wet his bed and tried to encourage him to let them change his sheets, but he became increasingly upset. By the time they managed to get him out of his wet pyjamas he was hysterical. They tried to comfort him with warm milk, cuddles, all the usual things, but nothing seemed to work. The more they tried to calm him, the more hysterical he became, throwing his toys around the room and against the wall, banging his head on the floor, screaming. At a complete loss for what to do or how to manage it, they'd rung Out of Hours for advice. April was horrified to read this. She was fully aware that Florian had his problems, but things had been going so well. Who could tell what experiences the poor child had suffered in the past to have caused him such trauma? She worried that Matthew and Lawrence would change their minds about adopting the boys. The application had been submitted to court and they were just waiting for a date for it to be finalised, which was expected to be within the next couple of weeks.

April made her way up the stairs and along the narrow corridor to the little meeting room where Maria and Katy were waiting with William Bennet, the Local Authority solicitor. Luckily, the meeting didn't take too long. William had read the reports from the child protection meetings and been kept up to date about how things were going, and he agreed that the concerns were enough to convince the court that the children were at risk of suffering significant harm; the criterion for taking legal action.

When April returned to her desk there was a message waiting for her on her answerphone. It was from Alison, asking April to phone her. April was a bit frustrated to have yet another distraction but decided to do it straight away before settling into the next things on her agenda, one of those being to organise a new foster placement for Isobel.

The phone rang for quite some time, and just as April was about to give up she heard Alison's voice.

'Hello, April, do you think you would be able to drop in and see me today? There's something I need to talk to you about.'

April tried hard not to sigh out loud. 'I'm not sure I will be able to today, Alison, I'm afraid. Do you want to give me an idea of what it's about?'

'It's difficult on the phone. I really need to speak to you. Could you come tomorrow, then?'

'Yes, OK, I will come tomorrow. It'll probably be early afternoon, about twoish. Is that OK?'

'Yes, thanks, April; see you tomorrow then.'

April put the phone down and slumped back in her chair. This was turning into one of those dreadful days where everything happened at once. The trouble with families was that you couldn't predict their behaviour and they had a terrible habit of all disrupting at the same time. Alongside the frustration and stress, April had a deep sense of curiosity. She really couldn't begin to imagine what Alison wanted to speak to her about so urgently. Was it possible that she had changed her mind and was going to stand by Isobel after all? April really hoped that would be the case, but at the same time she doubted it.

She reached into her bag, looking for her cheese and lettuce sandwich. It was way past lunchtime and she was starving. After clearing her desk and closing down her laptop, she gathered her things and made her way back to her car, sandwich in hand, ready to eat at the earliest opportunity. Matthew and Lawrence had asked to see her urgently.

Her heart was heavy for the whole of the journey, convinced that they were going to say they couldn't adopt the boys after all. Who could blame them after what had happened? She found herself questioning her own judgement. Had she been right to recommend adoption for the boys? The foster carer had been very worried about it, knowing how difficult Florian could be at times. Perhaps she hadn't warned Matthew and Lawrence as much as she should have about the potential for this kind of behaviour. It was always difficult to know what behaviour might emerge or when in these situations, but as the boys' social worker, she should have made doubly sure that their new parents understood how difficult things could get.

She pulled up against the pavement outside their house and looked up the short path and the neatly cut lawn on either side towards the coloured glass panel on the front door. Everything looked calm and peaceful; a haven of domestic tranquillity. Wallflowers and tulips adorned the front of the house and their perfume filled the air. She took long, deep breaths, trying to calm herself before facing what was to come. Adoption breakdown was heart-wrenching for everyone concerned: the adopters, who would feel a huge sense of failure and guilt; the social workers; and not least the children, who had been led to believe they would be with their new family for the rest of their lives.

There was a serious expression on Lawrence's face as he opened the door. 'Do come in. I've just put the kettle on, ready for you.' He held the door open and stepped aside to make way for her to enter.

'Lovely, thank you.' April just wanted to know what the damage was so that she could think about what she needed to do to help Florian and Leo.

'Matthew has taken the boys out because we thought that would be best. Is that OK?'

Oh dear, April thought, even more convinced that this was going to be bad news. 'Are we going in here?' she said, gesturing towards the lounge.

'Yes, you sit down and make yourself comfortable. I will make the coffee.'

She did as she was told: walked into the lounge and sat down on the comfortable settee. As she waited, she looked around the room as social workers do, observing the environment and its suitability for children. The furnishings were tasteful, but chosen for comfort as well as style. A pale grey two-seater sofa with thick, highly sprung cushions sat under the wide front window. The floor was natural wood, partly covered by a pale green rug with grey specks. The long, heavy curtains matched the settee. On the tiled mantlepiece was a glass photo frame in the shape of a dolphin. The photo inside was of Matthew holding Leo in his arms, both smiling broadly at the camera, and Lawrence next to them with both hands on the shoulders of Florian, from whose wide-open mouth a long pink tongue was protruding. The bottom of the frame was engraved with 'Windsor Safari Park'. On one side of the room there were plastic containers set neatly against the wall, each with various toys inside. Although the room itself was bright and orderly, there were obvious signs of children being allowed to play happily and freely; for example, April noticed little blue and yellow blobs stuck to the wooden floor in one corner which she was sure were playdough.

It wasn't long before Lawrence swept in with a mug of coffee in each hand, and placed one of them next to the pot of primroses on the little table beside where April sat. 'So, you know about what happened last night?' He leant forward on the edge of the armchair, facing April, with his hands joined and his elbows resting on his knees.

'Yes, I do. I read the report from Out of Hours. I can imagine that it must have been alarming for you both.'

'We just couldn't work out what was upsetting him. Everything we did to try to comfort him seemed to make it worse. I won't deny there's been a few times when he's kicked off a bit but we managed it all right, mostly. This time, though, we just didn't know how to handle it. He wouldn't let us near him. It was as though he was terrified of us. Leo woke up when he started throwing things, as you would expect. Of course *he* was upset then. He didn't know what was going on. Come upstairs, I'll show you the damage.'

With a heavy heart, April followed him up the stairs and into Florian and Leo's bedroom.

'Look.' With a circular wave of his arm, Lawrence indicated the bits of broken toys and a lamp which had clearly been knocked off its table but picked up and placed back again, albeit without its shade, which was buckled and twisted in the corner of the room. There was a gouge in the wooden door where Florian had thrown a toy fire engine, and long streaks of purple scrawled across the white wall. 'We left it like this so that you could see.'

They walked downstairs and back into the lounge, where April sat down in the same place on the settee.

'So what do you want to happen now?' Her eyes shut involuntarily, dreading the answer.

'Well, it's more a case of what can you do for us?'

She was a bit confused. 'I was wondering if you are having second thoughts about adopting the boys now?' She held her breath.

There was a painful silence. After a short period of high anxiety she looked at Lawrence, who was staring back at her blankly.

'April, how can you think that? We want the boys more than anything. They're ours now. We love them already and will cope with whatever we have to cope with. All we want to know is what you can do for Florian to help him. We can give him everything he needs at home but we can't take away the pain of his past. Does he need therapy or something? We just want him to be happy and to be able to live a normal life.'

April nearly burst into tears of relief. She let out a big sigh as the breath she had been holding was released. 'Oh thank God, Lawrence. I thought you were going to tell me they were too much for you after all.'

'Absolutely not. I can't believe you thought that for a minute.'

They were both smiling now.

'I just wanted you to see the extent of his outburst so that you can see how important it is for him to get the help he needs.'

Just as Lawrence finished talking, the front door opened and in walked Florian, with Leo toddling closely behind. Florian was carrying a bucket and a fishing net, and a smile spread across his face when he saw that April was there, ready to listen to what he had been doing. He walked straight over to her and showed her the bucket, which had a starfish in it. 'This is what I caught. Leo had one as well but it wasn't as big as mine, was it, Daddy?'

He turned to look for Matthew, who was tidying shoes in the hallway. Once he had put them all neatly on the shelf he joined them in the lounge.

'Has Lawrence told you about our plans?'

'No, I haven't told her yet.'

'Shall I tell her or do you want to?'

Lawrence didn't wait. 'We're planning a big party to celebrate the adoption and we would like you to come, April, if you would. The adoption should be approved in court in early July so we thought we would do a barbecue in the garden for all our friends and family the following weekend, probably Sunday.'

'That would be lovely. I will make sure I keep it free. Thank you for inviting me.'

'And your husband too, and I believe you have a little girl?'

April left feeling a huge sense of relief and joy. She wasn't such a bad social worker after all. She clearly had made the right choice of parents for Florian and Leo. They had demonstrated that they were well prepared for some difficult times ahead with Florian and their only focus was how they could help him. Another urgent task was added to her list of things to do: have Florian assessed to see if therapy would help him to deal with the traumas of his past.

29

CHANGE OF HEART

Isobel scraped her chair back before stuffing papers into her school bag and pushing back the thick hair that had fallen over her eyes. She turned to Gina, who was still bent over her desk, writing. 'Come on, let's go. Why are you still doing that?'

Gina carried on writing and, without looking up, mumbled that she had to finish the piece of comprehension otherwise she would have to do detention.

'I'm off, then. I want to get my phone to see if my mum's texted me. We used to have contact on a Tuesday but she's been really busy lately.'

Gina answered, again without looking up from her work, 'OK, I will probably see you at the bus station.'

They were no longer provided with a taxi to take them to school because they both now had bus passes, James hadn't been to school for a few weeks and nobody seemed to know why. Both Gina and Isobel had sent messages but had received no reply. Gina had asked Greta once when he had been absent for about a week but she didn't explain, although they both thought she must know why.

Isobel set off down the long, rough track that led to the main road, her huge bag slung over her shoulder, the collar of her navy blazer tucked in at the front and her long hair tumbling down her back. The lane was always quiet as the only traffic went to and from the PRU, and as there were only around fifteen students in total, and most of them caught the bus, it was generally only the teachers who drove up the track.

The wide mud track ran between two unharvested fields, and all she could hear was the squalling of the crows as they swooped and foraged. She hardly noticed them. She was still trying to come to terms with the fact that, once again, she'd had no message from April or Janey to say that her mum wanted to see her. Her mind had been totally absorbed with this for the whole day. It had been nearly a month since she had seen or heard from her mum, and she couldn't work out what was happening. She felt an aching loneliness which sometimes overwhelmed her. Denise and Harry tried their best to be kind but their home wasn't her home, and they weren't her family. There was a persistent ache in her stomach, caused by a mixture of longing for her mum and burning anger towards her. It absorbed her in every way, and the longer it went on, the deeper and more intense it became. She was starting to hate everyone and everything, including being alive.

She had almost come to the end of the track when a black car turned off the main road and drove slowly and cautiously up the track, trying to avoid the bumps and dips, until it was parallel to her, then, slowing down, pulled up beside her. She was shocked to see Damian sitting in the driver's seat, and next to him another man of about twenty. Both looked out and smiled at her.

Damian rested his elbow on the open window. 'Well, this is a surprise; fancy seeing you here, Isobel,' he said. There was a hint of sarcasm in his expression but at the same time he smiled broadly at her. 'Do you want a lift home?'

She felt quite shaken up by this sudden appearance. He had phoned her a few times since the party but had made no mention of them meeting again. When she had tried to phone him she'd always got a recorded message. She didn't know what to make of him. The relationship he wanted with her was not what she had imagined a relationship would be like. But he told her she was beautiful and bought her nice things. Why would he do that if he didn't care about her?

There were a few things that she hadn't liked, one being that he made her feel obliged to have sex with him even though she wasn't sure that was what she wanted. She had been scared but he persisted. He reminded her about the things he had bought her and made her feel guilty. He gave her cocaine and alcohol, which she enjoyed, but it didn't take away the shame, guilt and worry and the fact that, although she wasn't clear about what was going on, she still felt used. She still wasn't entirely sure about the other men whom she believed had had sex with her; the memories were vague. When she questioned Damian about them he just laughed and told her to chill out.

'Come on, Isobel, what are you waiting for? Get in the car.' Damian had opened the door and was standing in front of her, holding the door open, waiting impatiently for her to get in.

April left the office early. She was really happy that it was her last working day for this week, and was looking forward to spending the rest of the week with Demelza. She was due to meet her dad again for lunch on Friday, and Max and Joanna were coming to visit on Sunday. It was a shame Joanna was coming too but April would make the most of it and ignore the snooty comments she made whilst smiling sweetly. Joanna had no time for social workers or the families they tried to help. She just couldn't understand why anyone could get themselves into a situation where they couldn't look after their own children properly without the state's help. This was irksome to April, coming from someone who had sent her own children to boarding school at age eleven.

April planned to drop in to see Alison on her way home to find out what she wanted to speak to her about. She was hoping Danny wouldn't be there. He made her feel uneasy just by his presence, which was most probably linked to what she knew about him, but there was more to it than that, she sensed he was mocking her. She read his expression as *I got away with it and I will get away with it again, and you can do nothing about it.* It made her skin crawl and her blood pressure rise because he was right: she couldn't do anything about it.

As she drove towards Taylor's Yard she thought about the many times she had been involved in cases of children who had been sexually abused by an adult, had bravely and trustingly disclosed that abuse to another adult, and then found that they seemed to be the one who was punished. The police did what they could but the word of a child against the word of an adult was not a good balance for the justice system. This made April rage. When would the system change to meet the needs of those children, to protect them and to bring those who had abused them to justice? The victim's life was invariably ruined, their self-esteem at rock bottom; they struggled to form meaningful relationships and often ended up dependent on drugs or alcohol and suffering a lifetime of mental health problems. The irony was that, due to the abuse they had endured, the children often developed behavioural problems and commonly promiscuity, resulting in the Crown Prosecution Service judging them harshly and deeming them unreliable witnesses. April also shuddered at the thought of the high number of paedophiles walking the streets, befriending vulnerable women with children, highly skilled and proficient in their pursuit of victims and remaining free to abuse again.

When she arrived, Alison was in a dressing gown with a towel around her head, which April thought was a bit strange since it was late afternoon.

'Hello, Alison. I hope this isn't a bad time to visit,' she said as she followed her up the stairs.

'No, not at all. I had a day off today so I've been pampering myself. I needed to talk to you anyway.' Alison walked into the kitchen and filled the kettle. She retrieved two cups from hooks below the wall cupboard before asking April if she would like a drink.

'Yes please, if you're having one.'

Alison seemed pensive. She would usually be ranting about something she wasn't happy with before they had reached the top of the stairs. April struggled not to appear impatient but she was curious as to what Alison needed to talk about so urgently; and more importantly, she was eager to get away and pick up her daughter from nursery.

'So what is it, Alison? Has something happened?'

They walked into the lounge and sat down, Alison in the chair by the window and April on the small settee opposite. Alison placed the cup she had been holding between two hands on the coffee table beside her chair and leant forward towards April, spreading out her hands in front of her.

'Danny's gone.'

'Oh.' This took April by surprise. She had been imagining all sorts of things, but not this.

'I've told him to go. Isobel is my priority. I want her home with me.'

'When was this?' April wasn't sure what to think. 'What changed your mind, Alison? Did you fall out or something?'

'No, I told you,' Alison said earnestly. 'I just want my little girl home with me. I want Isobel back with me now. He's gone so there's no reason why she can't come back, is there?'

April had to stop and think hard for a sensitive way to respond. After a period of consideration, she broke the short silence with an answer which wasn't to Alison's liking. 'I'm afraid I can't agree to that at this stage, Alison.' She paused to give this time to sink in. 'It's not quite as simple as that. It's early days, and how can I be sure you won't let him come back? I need to understand what has happened to change your mind.'

There was a sudden rise of colour in Alison's cheeks as she clearly tried to contain her rage. 'Just because I didn't believe it at first doesn't mean I should never be able to have my daughter living with me again. I've changed my mind now. I do believe her. That's why I told him to go.'

'I'm sorry, Alison, and I hope what you're saying is true, but as I just said, it's not quite as simple as that. It will take time for you to prove you mean what you say.'

'I only said I didn't believe her because Danny got angry. I *always* believed she was telling the truth. I was just too frightened to say so. What would you do in that situation?' She was pleading with April now.

'Are you now telling me you *know* that it happened?'

'*No*,' Alison said belligerently, 'I'm telling you that I believe she was telling the truth. Can't you see what I'm saying? Shall I say it again? I said I *do* believe her.' Her voice was becoming louder and angrier, and she stood up. Still shouting, she moved towards April, increasingly confrontational.

April recognised quickly that she needed to calm the situation, and that, if she wasn't careful, it had the potential to escalate into something rather nasty. 'I can arrange for you to have contact with her for the time being. Isobel would really like that.'

'I want her home. I don't just want contact,' Alison said, her voice shaking with rage and her cheeks flaming.

April was growing increasingly nervous, recognising the vulnerable situation she was in, with this large, angry woman towering above her. The next thing she knew, Alison lost control, bending over her, shaking her fists, shouting abuse, eyes bulging and spraying streaks of saliva as she spoke.

'You don't fucking know what it's like, you fucking moron. What do you think it feels like to lose your daughter *and* your old man? I've lost everything, and you – *you* – just sit there, prim and proper, telling me I've got to prove myself. *Who the fuck do you think you are?!*'

Despite her fear, April tried to remain calm. She was acutely aware that with the high level of emotion Alison was experiencing, she could lose all sense of reason. One wrong word from April and she could easily be punched. Somewhere deep down, beneath the fear, was empathy for this woman who had suffered the most appalling sudden change in her life that anyone could imagine.

'Alison, I'm not saying Isobel can never come back to you. All I'm saying is that it will take time.' As she said this, she slowly rose from the chair, aware that she would be in a much less vulnerable position standing up. 'As you know, the court case is coming up which will decide whether Isobel should stay in foster care or come home to you. Isobel still insists she wants to come home, and court decisions always take account of the young person's wishes and feelings.'

Alison suddenly stopped gesticulating and became still, her arms still raised as though frozen in space. She seemed to visibly shake herself. 'Yes, you're right.' To April's relief, her whole demeanour transformed in that split second from a raging maniac to a calm and rational being. The angry expression fell away like a curtain tumbling to the ground.

'I'm going to go now then, Alison,' April said, slowly and cautiously heading towards the door, praying that Alison would stay calm at least until she was out of the flat. 'I will ring Denise when I get home and arrange for Isobel to see you. Is that what you would like?'

'Thank you. Yes, as soon as possible.' Alison wiped tears from her cheeks.

April stepped out of the front door and into the sunshine. She took a deep breath, relieved to have come out of that situation unharmed. The grief Alison was experiencing could have easily led her to do something irrational. Luckily for April it had been only verbal abuse which, although unpleasant, was better than the alternative. She guessed Alison was probably a volatile personality even in usual circumstances, but with all that was going on in her life at the moment she could easily have lost all rationality.

April's thoughts soon focused on picking up Demelza and the unsettling episode became a thing of the past. She made a mental note not to forget to phone Denise when she got home to arrange the contact as promised, knowing how desperate Isobel was to see her mum.

Demelza was tired by the time they got home, as she often was after nursery. The day was always full of activity and Demelza rarely slept during the day, although they made sure the little ones had a rest time. There were too many exciting things for her to do and she wasn't a child who liked to miss out on anything.

Jed arrived home soon after April. He always tried his best to get home early so that he could help put Demelza to bed. April loved to watch him with his child; the pride and delight in his eyes when he talked to her and she babbled in response. April had detected that there was a special relationship between them but this didn't concern her; she put it down to the fact that Demelza saw less of Jed, therefore his presence was more of a treat.

It was well after 6pm, and whilst Jed was bathing Demelza, April took the opportunity to phone Denise.

'Hello, Denise. I just wanted to let you know that I called in to see Alison today. She asked to see Isobel. Is it all right to speak to her, please? Is she there?'

'Oh, April, don't you know? I did leave a message at the office. She hasn't come home from school. She should have been back hours ago. The police are on to it but I haven't heard anything yet.'

April was shocked and dismayed. 'Oh, God. I wonder where she is this time?'

'She never tells me anything, April. I don't know what's going on with her most of the time. I don't know what she thinks, what she does at school – I don't know anything. I know she's got a friend, Gina, but the police have already spoken to her and she knows nothing. It seems to be completely out of the blue again.'

'OK, Denise. There's not a lot we can do at the moment. We just have to hope the police will find her, or maybe she will come home. Perhaps she's just decided to go off somewhere and will be home later.'

April had been feeling really upbeat about being at home for the rest of the week, and looking forward to the break. Now she was anxious and really worried about Isobel.

30

ISOBEL AND DAMIAN

Isobel climbed into the back seat of the BMW. She was nervous but flattered at the same time. *He's come to the PRU especially to pick me up. He must really like me.*

Damian didn't introduce the other man in the car, who sat quietly as they drove, looking directly ahead. Isobel didn't like the look of him. He didn't seem friendly at all. Damian, on the other hand, seemed really pleased to be with her. He chatted away, still watching the road but half-turning to the back to show her she had his attention. He joked about school, telling her some of the things he used to get up to. He made her laugh by telling her that he'd tried everything he could think of to get excluded, but whatever he did, they always made him come back.

'I thought when I shagged that girl over the desk they would chuck me out, but all they did was send me to counselling.'

Isobel found this hilarious. When she stopped laughing she looked at the man in the passenger seat and noticed that he had not laughed or taken any part in the conversation. She found this a bit weird and spooky. 'Where was the teacher?'

'I dunno, can't remember, but she'd gone somewhere.'

Isobel wasn't sure she believed that, or most of the other things Damian claimed to have done, but it was quite amusing.

The car was following the normal route to the foster home and Isobel wondered if Damian planned to drop her off there but arrange to see her again in the near future. She was really hoping that was his intention. But just a few minutes later, he took a different route. Instead of heading straight on towards the coast, he took a right turn from the roundabout which took them inland.

Isobel jerked forward in her seat. 'Where are we going? I thought you were taking me home,' she said with a quiver in her voice.

Damian turned towards her again, and on the side of his face that was visible, she perceived a trace of disappointment. 'I thought you hated your foster carer. I assumed you didn't want to go back there yet. We're going to my house. Got a few friends coming round later. I thought that's what you wanted. We'll have a gas, you and me. I've missed you. Haven't you missed me?'

Isobel felt a bit worried, but was also flattered. Damian really wanted to be with her. She was starting to feel the warm inner glow of being wanted and special. She spread her fingers through her thick brown hair and dropped it loosely over her shoulders. It felt soft and silky, and she was pleased with the richness of the colour and the abundant waves. She had been told that she was pretty by various people in the past. Perhaps it was true; Damian must think so, anyway.

Isobel was reported missing again and the formal procedures were instigated by April. She arranged a strategy meeting which included the police, Social Services and education. There were bits of information about where she had been the last time she'd gone missing, but not enough to find her. They could only go by the area she'd been picked up from as she had refused to give any information about whom she'd been with or exactly where she had been staying.

April was subjected to another screaming fit from Alison when she phoned to inform her of the situation. Alison thought that April should be able to somehow miraculously find Isobel and bring her back home. If only that were the case. At least April had prepared for the onslaught before she made the call. As Alison screamed down the phone at her, April squeezed her eyes closed as though this would shut out the noise. Although Alison's response was no surprise, it was still unsettling, particularly as she already felt quite helpless.

Damian's car pulled up outside the familiar little terraced house, and he climbed out quickly before opening the door for Isobel. The other man got out, walked around to the driver's seat, and before Isobel and Damian had opened the gate he was driving off. This unnerved Isobel. She wondered how she would get back to Denise's if there was no car there.

Inside, the house was just as empty as it had been the last time she was there. It still looked as though nobody lived there, but a strange smell filled the air. Not the usual household smells of food cooking or cleaning materials; something she hadn't come across before. It hung nauseatingly in the air. In the kitchen there was no sign of any cooking having taken place, or traces of food.

Almost as soon as they were inside the door, Damian took Isobel's hand and led her upstairs to the room they had shared the last time she stayed. He shut the curtains before turning on the dim little lamp by the side of the bed, which seemed strange since it was still early evening and bright outside. He then opened a drawer and took out a tin with cigarette papers and weed. They both sat on the bed, propped up against the wall by pillows as there was no headboard.

'This will make you feel better, Isobel. I'm worried about you, you know. You ain't happy, I can tell. You need cheering up.' Skilfully, he rolled a joint between his fingers as he talked. 'How's that bitch… what's her name? The one you live with. Is she still an old witch?'

'She's a fucking old cow. She only wants the money. They're all crap, the lot o' them. My mum doesn't give a shit. She can't even be bothered to come and see me anymore. I hate her guts, and Denise.'

Damian passed her the spliff, which she put to her lips before taking a long drag, holding the smoke in her lungs before exhaling slowly.

'I could make you pregnant, Isobel. Then we could live together: you, me and our baby.'

Isobel laughed nervously. 'I'm too young to have a kid. I'm only fifteen.'

They lay together, chatting and smoking, Isobel becoming increasingly relaxed. She loved the way the weight of her troubles gently and slowly evaporated when she smoked weed. Life felt good; her inhibitions dissipated. Nothing mattered any more. She had someone who really loved her. He loved her so much he wanted a baby with her. As they lay together on the bed, she waited, thinking he would expect sex, but he just lay back with his head on the pillow, looking up at the ceiling and contentedly puffing out billows of smoke.

It wasn't long before their idyll was disturbed by a commotion downstairs. Isobel heard a car pull up outside, a door slam, and talking, but the sounds didn't really register in her drug-addled brain. But when the front door of the house slammed and she heard the loud voices of what sounded like a crowd of people, she sat up quickly. 'Who's that?'

Damian pulled her back towards him. 'Relax, it's my friends. I told you they'd be here. Don't worry, it's going to be fun. You'll see.'

A few minutes later she heard footsteps on the stairs, and voices. Male voices. The bedroom door opened and two men walked in, both of them much older than Damian.

Damian sat up. 'Hey, Slim, come in. Join us if you like. Isobel's a friendly girl, aren't you, Isobel?'

Despite the drug-induced haze, Isobel was scared. She started to recall some of what had happened to her the last time she was here, and she was sure she recognised the one Damian had called Slim.

31

TEMPTATION

Katy had written a statement as evidence for the court with regard to Tamara and Tyler, and April was reading through it. She was impressed with the quality of the assessment Katy had completed considering she was newly qualified and this was her first court report. She was sitting at her desk, reading it on her laptop. The office was quiet, which was good because it made it easier to concentrate and it was so important to get this right.

She was about halfway through when Lynda came over and stood beside her desk, looking hot and bothered. She had a piece of A4 paper in her hand which she was waving in front of her face to cool herself down. 'Who's stolen all the fans? There used to be two or three scattered around. I can't work in this heat.'

April agreed it was hot but noticed that Lynda was wearing a three-quarter-length polyester top with sleeves, and long trousers. She didn't comment on this. 'Yes, it's always hot in here. How are you then, Lynda? I don't get much chance to talk to you these days.'

'I'm good. I suppose you know about Nick and his escapades?'

April was a bit taken aback. She didn't want to admit that Maria had gossiped about it to her. 'Umm... yes, I... sort of.'

'It's OK. Of course people will know about it. I haven't kept it a secret. Anyway, he's back now.'

'Oh, that's good. Isn't it?'

'It's really funny actually. He soon realised that a younger woman might be good for an ego boost but they're not much use when it comes to the nitty-gritty. I didn't ask for the details but he came crawling back with his tail between his legs and now I'm in charge. I think he was just a stupid old man, but I won't let him off the hook that easily. He's got a lot of suffering to do yet before things go back to the way they were.'

They both laughed.

'I don't blame you, Lynda.'

'By the way, how is our little Isobel? She's yours now, isn't she?'

'Yes. She's not great to be honest. She keeps going missing from her placement; she's missing at the moment, as it happens. I'm sure she's got mixed up with a group of men who sexually exploit vulnerable young girls but she won't say what's happening to her. Her mum has been chopping and changing her mind about what she wants. There's not much else to say, really. Isobel wants to go home. She doesn't like Denise and I can't say I'm that keen on her myself.'

'No, she's not the most nurturing foster carer, is she?'

April remembered that Lynda was now the social worker for Bradley Travers. 'How is Bradley? I was really worried about him before I went on maternity leave. He just seemed to have shut down.'

'I'm at a loss for what to do for him, and as for his mother, well, six kids, no partner and living on benefits. I just hope that's it now; no more kids. She can't look after the ones she's got, and poor Bradley, well, he's not going to be welcomed home in the near future, that much is clear.'

Lynda was just about to walk away when April noticed Maria heading their way.

'I've just about had enough today. That girl of yours, the one that keeps going missing. Does she realise how much work that makes for all of us? I've had to do reports for all the senior managers *again*, as though I've got time for all that. When she comes back, warn her that I'll have her locked up in a secure unit for the next ten years if she does it again.' Maria was half joking but if anyone from outside had heard her they would have thought she was a bit callous to say the least. She wasn't, of course, but it was quite common for teenagers to go missing from foster care, and though everyone was extremely concerned for their safety and well-being, the amount of extra work it created for the social work team and other agencies was huge. 'Who is the court report for?' She was peering down at April's screen.

'The Phillips children, Tamara and Tyler. Katy has written it. I'm just going through it. I'm glad you're here, actually. It would be good to talk it through with you if you've got a minute?'

'Course I have, come into the office.'

April followed Maria as she zigzagged through the desks to get to her office in the far corner. Maria sat down at her desk but swivelled her chair around to face April, who sat in the low winged chair opposite. It was hot and sweaty in the room, and although a slight breeze blew in through the open window, enough to cause the blinds at the side to flap, it only made it feel hotter.

'The statement's thorough and well written. It's a bit negative, though. From the beginning of her involvement Katy has been absolutely set in her view that these children shouldn't be at home with their mother. I'm not sure she's right. I'm not saying there aren't real concerns; of course there are, that's why we're taking it to court. But it's not one of those cases where you can go to court and be a hundred per cent sure that you're doing the right thing. I was sort of hoping that by thrashing it out in court the right conclusion would be reached.'

Maria rested her chin on her folded hands while she pondered April's words. 'We're asking for the children to be removed from Kerry on the grounds of neglect, and there's no question that they *are* suffering neglect. We need to take it to court, April. We need to get those kids in foster care before their development is impaired even more.'

One thing about Maria was that she was always decisive. She rarely pontificated over anything, even when the decisions they were making were life-changing. This was sometimes a good thing, but not always.

'I'm just wondering how she would be in other circumstances and if she could do better. Are we right to do this now?'

Maria looked sympathetically at April. 'You know as well as I do that when the signs of neglect are so visible and obvious there's going to be a lot more goes on than we will ever know. We have to go by what we see, not what we think we might see in different circumstances.'

April couldn't really argue with that. The outward and obvious signs spoke volumes about the children's overall care.

Kerry was on her way to her mum's. She had collected Tyler from school and then caught the bus to Brookside where her mum lived. She hadn't seen her for a few weeks and although she usually found visiting her mum depressing, it was marginally better than going back to that room in Kennedy House.

Janet, her mum, lived in a ground-floor flat with a door leading directly onto the street. Kerry knocked and heard her mum shout, 'Coming.' She waited, knowing it would take some time for her mum to get up off the settee and walk to the door, even though the outer door was only a few feet from where she sat. The door opened and her mum stood in front of her, leaning heavily on her walking stick whilst trying to recapture her breath. The stick appeared too flimsy for the size of the body it was there to support.

'Come in, love,' Janet said breathlessly, slowly and cautiously making her way back to the settee with full use of her stick. She hadn't acknowledged the children, who walked in quietly and sat down, Tyler on the floor with his knees up in front of him and Tamara next to Kerry on the settee. The small lounge was tidy enough but with brown curtains and carpet and hardly any space, it felt dark and dusty. The windows were shut but the back door which led to the tiny garden was open, letting in a light, warm breeze and a welcome stream of sunshine.

'I'm not very well again, love,' Janet said as her hand disappeared into the folds of her skirt and reappeared holding an inhaler. She took a few puffs from it, placed it back within the folds, then continued. 'I've been up all night again. Every joint in my body is hurting. If I sleep on one side it's my shoulder that hurts; the other side hurts my neck. I can't sleep on my back because of the pain in my spine.'

Tyler sat quietly listening to his grandmother's moans and groans, then, with an expression of serious concern, said, 'Is it 'cause you used to smoke, Grandma? Is that why you hurt everywhere?'

Kerry leant over and slapped him on the back of his shoulder. 'Shut up, Tyler; don't be rude to Grandma.'

He responded by putting his head down between his knees and remaining quiet as he'd been told to do. Tamara was so quiet they hardly noticed she was there.

Kerry had started to regret coming. She only ever heard about her mum's woes. She had problems of her own but it never seemed to occur to her mum to ask how *she* was. 'Social Services are taking me to court,' she said on impulse during a short lull in her mum's monologue of complaints. She hadn't thought it through but she longed for some recognition from her mother regarding her own plight.

'What are you talking about? Why would they do that? What have you done?'

'Nothing, Mum. I haven't done anything.' It was quite perverse but Kerry was revelling in for once having managed to catch her mother's attention. 'They're saying my kids are neglected. I mean, look at them; how are they neglected? They've got everything they need. They're fed, they've got clothes, they've got toys. I don't know what else they expect me to do. I've got no money to take them out. All my money gets spent on their food. I keep telling them, all I need is a decent place to live.'

'Does that mean you're going to have them taken off you, then?'

'The social worker told me it could happen if I don't do things better. Don't ask me how I'm supposed to, though. She says I've got to take them to the park more. As if that's important. It's getting a decent house that's important. It's horrible living in that dump. I hate being there. You've got druggies; the bloke upstairs yells at his wife and kids all the time. It's school holidays next week. What's it going to be like then? Can you imagine? I can't carry on living there for much longer; it's doing my head in.'

'When are they going to get you a house? You must be top of the list by now. Can't the social worker get you a house?'

'I've got one called Katy who comes to see me. She's been on to the council but she hasn't got me one yet.'

With that, Janet heaved herself up from the settee, walked unsteadily to the nearby sideboard and took a vape out of the drawer. Easing her body back into a sitting position, she started to blow thick clouds of steam into the air. 'I've got a new painkiller now. The doctor said it might take a few weeks to work. It hasn't started working yet. I might be able to get some sleep when it does.' She had clearly tired of their previous conversation.

It was getting on for six o'clock and Kerry decided to start making her way home. She gave her mum a peck on the cheek and told her to look after herself before putting Tamara in her pushchair and heading off, with Tyler trotting beside her, towards the bus stop. She had never felt more fed up.

When she was first housed in Kennedy House she'd thought it wasn't too bad. At least it was a roof over her head, and she believed it would only be temporary. She'd thought that it wouldn't be long before she was offered a council or Housing Association property. At that time she was confident that nobody would be expected to live like that for very long. But it was getting on for a year now. Over time, her optimism had dwindled. She was beginning to feel as though there was no way out for her. She had even wondered sometimes whether the kids would actually be better off in foster care. There wasn't much of a life for her or them and she just couldn't see how it was ever going to get any better.

It worried her a lot that Tyler was unhappy in school. At first he'd begged her not to send him. Then he'd started to say that he had a headache in the mornings. One morning he cried and clung to her coat, pleading that he didn't want to go. That had been heart-wrenching. He'd been happy in his old school. He had friends and was invited to parties. Kerry had thought his recent problems had settled down, but now she wondered if he was just resigned. In the meetings, the social worker and the teacher said it was because he wasn't clean and the other children sometimes said he smelt funny. This was upsetting for Kerry to hear but she tried to explain that the laundry facilities where she lived were expensive and she could only afford to do a couple of washes a week. She tried to wash small things in the sink but she didn't really like putting them outside on the line because of the type of people who lived in the building. They were likely to be stolen and she couldn't afford to replace them.

The thought of being parted from her children was unimaginable. The thought of someone else looking after them was more than she could bear, but on the other hand, she had no life and they could live with people who could give them all the things she couldn't: a nice garden to play in, with a trampoline and a swing. Tyler could play football; they might be taken on nice holidays. Although she loved the idea of her kids having those things, she knew that she could never agree to part with them.

On the way to the bus stop they walked past a small play park. Tyler stopped to peer through the iron railings. 'Can we go on the swings, Mummy?'

'It's too late now. You haven't had your tea yet. We'll go another time.'

'Please, Mummy, just for a few minutes.'

'Not today, love. You and Tamara need your tea.'

His little face, which had been so full of hope and excitement, dropped into a sulk.

They walked on, following the edge of the park, and just as they were about to cross the road, someone called out. 'Kerry! Hey, Kerry!'

She looked over the metal railings into the park and saw Dani, whom she'd known when she lived in this area. She was waving frantically, trying to get her attention. Kerry smiled and waved back before turning the pushchair round and heading towards her.

'Where are you off to? Have you just been to see your mum?'

The two chatted for a bit over the fence before Kerry accepted Dani's invitation to join her in the park. 'I can't stay too long, though; the kids haven't had their tea yet.'

Tyler ran off and within seconds was climbing the rope ladder to the slide, glee lighting up his face. Kerry sat on the bench next to Dani. They had a lot to catch up on as they hadn't seen each other since Kerry moved away. While the two women talked, Tamara rocked back and forward in her pushchair and, unnoticed by the adults, managed to wriggle out of her straps and clamber out. Kerry just happened to look up in time to spot her racing towards the swings just as a young boy swung headlong towards her. She was over there in a flash, just managing to snatch her out of the way in time.

'Naughty girl,' Kerry said angrily. 'Could have been knocked over by that swing.'

Tamara's bottom lip dropped as she sat down on the grass beside her mother, looking bewildered. Dani's three children were all playing on the swings and slide, and, seeing the little girl sitting there on her own, looking sad, Stanley, the eldest at eight, swung down from the rope he was climbing and walked over to her.

'Hello, Tamara. Do you want to go on the swings?' He looked at Kerry. 'Is it all right if I take her on the swings?'

'Yes, OK; only on the baby swings, though. I don't want her being kicked in the head by those hooligans over there,' she said, pointing to the boy Tamara had almost walked into.

'A few of us are going clubbing next Saturday; why don't you come?' Dani asked.

'Ooh, I wish. I've got no one to look after the kids, otherwise I'd be there like a shot.'

'What about your mum?'

Kerry sniggered. 'I'd have to be really desperate to leave them with her. She can hardly look after herself. Anyway, she wouldn't, even if I asked her. She doesn't like kids.'

'I can get you a babysitter. Marley's girl is fourteen; she's all right. Why don't I ask her?'

Kerry was getting quite excited about this idea. 'Do you think she'll do it? Would she come to my place?'

'Not sure. She might want the kids to stay at hers. That's what mine did.'

'They don't know her, or her mum.'

'They're ever so nice. They love kids. I've left mine with them loads.'

'See what she says, then.'

It was after 7.30 when they left the park. Tamara was asleep in the pushchair by the time they reached the bus stop and Tyler had moaned all the way that he was hungry.

A blast of hot air hit Kerry when she opened the door of her bedsit. She walked straight over to the window and opened it to let the air in and the unbearable heat out. There was an argument going on outside just below her window, between a couple and another man. It appeared the man had been smoking drugs outside the couple's bedsit and it was stinking the place out. They were shouting that their kids were being affected by the smoke and couldn't be woken in the mornings. The language was becoming heated and more and more colourful, and there was a real sense that it was about to become physical. There wasn't a lot Kerry could do about it, though; she had kids to get to bed. In a few more days the schools would break up for the summer holidays. Kerry wasn't looking forward to that at all. There would be kids all over this building shouting, swearing, parents yelling at them. She didn't know what she would do with her two to keep them occupied.

32

SECRETS

It was after three in the morning when Denise and Harry were woken by Suzie barking, whining and growling. Denise sat up with a start, whilst Harry groaned, turned onto his side and pulled the duvet over his head to shut out the noise. Denise shook him.

'Harry, someone's knocking on the door.'

The knocking had stopped. He turned towards her, groaning. 'Go back to sleep.'

By now the dog was running up and down the hallway, still barking but also throwing herself against the front door. The knocking became louder and more persistent. Harry, realising at last that it wasn't a dream, jumped out of bed, pulled on his dressing gown and ran down the stairs. He nearly tripped over Suzie, who ran in front of him, still jumping up and down. Then he opened the door and there, standing before him, was Isobel. Behind her a black car drove off with rapidly increasing speed and high revs.

Isobel stood on the doorstep, her head hanging sheepishly. Her hair was unbrushed and matted and her clothes bedraggled. The sight of her brought to Harry's mind Fagin's pickpockets in *Oliver Twist*. There was a childlike vulnerability about her which tugged at his heartstrings and he couldn't help himself; rather than be stern and angry at her behaviour, he pulled her towards him and squeezed her.

'Where've you been, Isobel? We've been so worried about you.'

By this time Denise had got up and was standing at the top of the stairs. As soon as she realised it was Isobel she came running down. 'What the hell…?' She stopped in her tracks. 'I'm glad you're back, Isobel. Come in now and let's get you cleaned up. You look as though you've been sleeping rough all week.'

She was trying hard to be kind but had failed to disguise the frustration she felt. Meekly, Isobel followed her into the kitchen.

'The first thing you need to do is get a shower. You can't sit at the table looking like that. Are you hungry?' Denise asked, as she took a towel from a pile of folded washing in the corner of the kitchen and handed it to Isobel.

'No,' Isobel answered quietly.

'Get a shower, then, and I'll make you a hot drink. Do you want chocolate?'

'Yes please,' Isobel said as she slowly made her way towards the stairs.

When she came down, Denise and Harry were both sitting at the kitchen table, waiting for her. She felt as though she was facing an inquisition, but had no intention of telling them anything. Before she had a chance to sit down, Denise was firing questions at her. When Isobel refused to say anything, Denise, exasperated, finally gave in and sat watching quietly as she sipped at her mug of chocolate. Denise thought she could see a slight swelling on one side of Isobel's mouth. She tried to inconspicuously get a closer look, but Isobel noticed and shifted her head to the side, away from her gaze.

The first message April saw on arrival in the office was the one from Out of Hours informing her of Isobel's return. 'Thank God,' she said, with a huge sigh of relief. After reading the full report, she started to think about reorganising her schedule for the day so that she could fit in a visit to Isobel. She didn't expect to find out anything about her escapades but would gauge what she could from the meeting and any snippet of information she could glean would be useful in the likely event that it happened again.

The initial hearing for the Phillips children was due to take place the following Wednesday, and April was busy trying to read the reports submitted by the health visitor, Tyler's teacher and the nursery Tamara had been attending. Professionals in these circumstances always tried hard to balance their reports by including some positives alongside the concerns they were raising, but each of them had clearly struggled to find any positives to include. Apart from the usual comments such as 'Tyler is a delightful little boy' and 'Tamara has an engaging smile', there was nothing within any of the reports about Kerry's parenting which would support the case for the children remaining at home. It was virtually all negative.

If the court agreed to an Interim Care Order, Tamara and Tyler could be taken from Kerry and placed in foster care as soon as the order was made. Katy's report was the most negative of all and her view was clear that the children were at risk of suffering significant harm if they remained in their mother's care. April would have discussed this with her to try to ease out anything she could point to that was positive but it seemed that Maria agreed with Katy on this. April, though, continued to feel unsure. She couldn't deny that Tamara and Tyler were suffering chronic neglect and this definitely needed to change, but she didn't feel that the family's circumstances allowed a fair assessment of Kerry's parenting abilities, and she wished there was a way of assessing them in another environment. The trouble was, the children were suffering at this moment in time and there wasn't any way they could change that apart from by taking them into care. April could empathise with Kerry when she exclaimed that all she needed was a decent place to live. It seemed entirely unfair to April, firstly that a family should be expected to thrive in those conditions, and secondly that Kerry was possibly going to lose her children because of it. On the other hand, she recognised that Kerry didn't seem to be trying very hard to make the best of things for her children.

April managed to arrange a visit to Isobel later in the afternoon. She planned to go home straight after; finish early for a change. She justified this with the thought that the adoption hearing for Florian and Leo was due to take place on Friday and she would have to be there even though she didn't usually work on a Friday. She wouldn't have missed it for the world, though, because she loved being present at adoption hearings; the hope and expectations of a happy and secure future for children who had suffered.

Before leaving the office, April phoned Alison. 'Hello, Alison. It's April here. I'm just phoning to let you know that Isobel has returned to her foster placement. She came back this morning, in the early hours.'

Alison gave a sustained sigh of relief before finally answering. 'Thank God. Where was she? Did she say where she was?'

'I haven't seen her yet. I will be calling in later so I will let you know if she tells me anything, which isn't very likely.'

'When can I see her? I have to see her as soon as possible. I've been worried sick. I've had all kinds of horrible thoughts going round in my head.'

April was pleased to hear that Alison was desperate to see her daughter, but slightly sceptical at the same time, considering that a few weeks ago, Alison had seemed quite happy to never see Isobel again. 'I will arrange a contact session for you as soon as I can. Is Danny still not with you?'

'No, I told you. I think he's with someone else now anyway. I want my daughter back with me. That's the only thing that matters to me now. I told you that,' Alison said aggressively.

April couldn't remember her saying that but it was nice to hear. She hoped it would continue, but only time would tell.

Isobel was, as usual, in her bedroom when April arrived. Denise and April had a chat in the kitchen first.

'You should have seen her, April. She looked like a little waif. I dread to think what's been happening to her. She's refused to say anything to us. She wouldn't say anything to me, anyway, but I thought she might tell Harry. She gets on better with him.'

'I'm really glad that she seems to be developing a good relationship with Harry.'

'Yes, but… I don't think I can keep her here, April. It's too stressful when she keeps going missing. I blame myself all the time. I know it's stupid but I always think I must have said something that upset her. Besides, it's all the being up in the night, waiting for her to come back, the police being here at all hours – you know what I mean. I've had all I can take. I'm just exhausted.'

'I can understand that, Denise. I know how difficult it must be. I was thinking of looking for a new placement for her but there's been some changes. I haven't had the chance to tell you yet. Her mum and dad have split up and her mum's saying now that she wants her back. I can't let her go back yet, of course, but if this continues and Alison demonstrates that she is putting Isobel first it's possible she might be able to go home before too long.'

'Oh, OK, I will hang on then. It would be so good if she could go home. The poor kid's been grieving over the loss of her family. You can almost see it eating away at her from the inside. I sometimes watch her when we are having our evening meal, and her face… the sadness, it's heart-wrenching.'

'I know exactly what you mean.' April was warming to Denise. Perhaps she wasn't as uncaring as she had appeared at first, and maybe she was starting to grow fond of Isobel.

Isobel was even more evasive than the last time. She refused to engage in any conversation regarding her whereabouts or who she'd been with. Her short answers of 'Yes', 'No' and 'Don't know' became quite frustrating for April, until the only option was to give up and try to revisit the subject another time, maybe when she started to see it as a thing of the past. April also noticed the swelling on the side of Isobel's mouth and the way in which Isobel was attempting to cover it with her hand.

When April mentioned that Isobel's mum had been asking to see her, her whole demeanour changed. She seemed to come alive, as though an electric wave had passed through her body. This brought home to April how much Alison being in her life meant to Isobel. It meant everything. Without her mother, she merely existed like a body without a soul.

33

ADOPTION

The adoption for Florian and Leo was approved in court on Friday 20th July. Present in the small courtroom were Matthew, Lawrence, April, the two children and the judge. There had been no objection to the adoption taking place and this session was just to finalise the legalities. The boys were then presented with a certificate each declaring that they had become Florian and Leo Ryan rather than Florian and Leo Bailey. They sat between their dads whilst the judge put on his wig and offered to pose with them all for photographs. With Leo sitting on his knee, Lawrence, sitting next to the judge, held up Leo's certificate for the camera. The happiness on all of their faces was a joy to see, and April, as she always did on these occasions, discreetly wiped a few tears from her eyes.

Normally she would have been involved with the birth family before the children came into care, trying her best to help the family care for them. This was different because she had been on maternity leave whilst that was happening, but she had studied their records and background history and had a good idea of the likely impact on the two boys individually. She was impressed with Lawrence and Matthew and the way they had managed to deal with Florian's challenging behaviour. There were no worries about the future for these boys.

The celebration party took place on the Sunday following the court hearing. April and Jed were getting themselves ready. Demelza was dressed in a white cotton dress with a pale green lace collar and white sandals. Her light brown curls were loose around her head, although April had put a sparkly silver hair slide at the side to keep them from flopping over her face.

'She looks delightful, April, but I must ask – do you think it's sensible to put her in white? She's going to a party, which means food, strawberry ice cream, chocolate cake—'

'I know what you're saying, Jed,' she interrupted, 'but doesn't she look gorgeous? She's only worn that dress once and she grows so quickly she might not get another chance to wear it.' She paused for a second. 'Do you think I should take something else to change her into just in case? Yes, I think I will. You're right.'

Jed glanced sideways at her with a twisted half-smile. He loved the way April came to her own solutions, then praised him for them.

Before they got in the car, Jed held up his phone and took a photo of all of them. Demelza was only fifteen months old but she already knew how to pose. She smoothed down her dress with her tiny hands before lifting her head and smiling proudly at the camera. April and Jed laughed, delighted at their little girl's precocious behaviour.

The party was in the little square back garden, and by the time Jed and April arrived it was full of family and friends. They were warmly welcomed by Lawrence, who showed them through the house before introducing them to the other people. Leo was on the knee of his grandmother, Lawrence's mum, and Florian was kicking a ball around at the back of the garden with his Uncle Steven. There were bunches of balloons pegged to the ground and streamers dangling from windows. The celebration cake was spectacular and like nothing April had ever seen. She had been to a number of adoption celebrations but had never seen a cake as impressive as this one. It had three tiers, each one smaller than the one below. Around the spaces between each tier was an abundance of tiny green leaves. At first April thought they were real, but on closer scrutiny she could see that they were made of icing. The detail was intricate, each leaf having a delicate line through its middle in a slightly darker shade to represent the stalk, and the rest of the leaves in varying shades of green from almost white to a deep olive, giving the impression of dappled sun light. On top of the cake was a luscious green lawn with a detailed replica of a garden shed, with various garden tools scattered around, made from chocolate icing. Sitting on garden chairs were marzipan images of Matthew and Lawrence with two little boys who looked just like Florian and Leo, the older boy with a head of thick yellow curls. April was intrigued by the whole creation and couldn't begin to imagine how long it must have taken to make, let alone how much Matthew and Lawrence had paid someone to do it.

She moved around the garden, meeting different people and chatting. She loved meeting the wider family members of adopted children; it helped give her an insight into the family dynamics and an idea of what family life would be like for the children in the future. The adoption social worker had completed a comprehensive assessment which covered extended family and April had read it, but that couldn't be compared to actually meeting them in the flesh.

Jed, as always, stayed seated, just watching. He had a friendly face and generally people were happy to approach him, but that was neither here nor there to him. He was content to sit and watch with a plate of food and a beer in his hand. Demelza's dress didn't stay white for long because almost as soon as they arrived Matthew took delight in showing her the sandpit and giving her a bucket and spade. April didn't worry about it. She had presented her daughter in her best attire but now she only cared that Demelza enjoyed herself. She could get as messy as she liked. Demelza was so absorbed in trying to put the sand in the bucket and tipping it out again that she could probably have been left there all day.

It was early evening when Lawrence raised a toast. The adults were handed a glass of champagne whilst the children were given fruit cocktails with all kinds of colourful fruits in decorative containers. To April's surprise, the first one to be toasted was her.

'We would like to say a big thank-you to the wonderful social worker, April, who has given us our two boys. Thank you for everything, April.'

They all clapped before raising their glasses to their lips. April's face turned scarlet. She hadn't been expecting this at all. It was almost as though they thought these two boys were a personal gift from her. There had, of course been a number of professionals involved in the adoption process but she seemed to be the only one who had been invited to the celebration.

Demelza was starting to rub her eyes and look sleepy. People were beginning to drift home, and Jed managed to catch April's eye as she turned for a second from the woman she was talking to. He pointed to his watch. It was Matthew's sister April was talking to, and she had been hearing about the plans the family had for making sure the two boys were fully integrated within the family unit. She managed to politely bring the conversation to an end and she and Jed prepared to leave. This was quite a sad moment for April because it marked the end of her involvement with Florian and Leo, and of course Matthew and Lawrence, of whom she had become very fond. Adopters sometimes kept in touch with the social workers and some sent photos of the children as they grew up, but they didn't have to, and generally they wanted to start afresh with their new family. This was likely to be the last time she would see or hear from any of them.

The parting was quite emotional, although they hadn't really known each other for very long. It was probably to do with the intense relationships an adoption generated between everyone involved.

On Monday morning April was back in the office, dealing as usual with the Monday morning emails. She was due to supervise a contact between Isobel and Alison later that afternoon, so wanted to get as much done as possible beforehand. She was just about to read an email from Katy, updating her on the Phillips children, when Paula walked out of the kitchen and spotted her.

'April, how are things?' She was carrying a cup of coffee in one hand and a bundle of papers under her arm, but somehow she managed to manoeuvre a chair from under the desk next to April and sit herself down on it.

'OK, thanks. Adoption is done for the Bailey boys.' April told Paula about the party and the amazing celebration cake.

'I love adoption celebrations; they make everything we do worthwhile. They make up for all the sadness we see.'

'I know. I'm so happy about this one. The boys are going to have a lovely life.'

'Wonderful. It's quite draining, though, isn't it? I always feel as though I need a long break when I've completed an adoption.'

'Well, I would love that, but unfortunately I've got a case going to court on Monday. I'm going to be asking for Interim Care Orders and removal to foster care; so loads to do.'

'Poor you. Well, let's hope there's not too much of a battle in court; then you can get on with other things. I hate it when they go on and on and just want more and more evidence, more reports, more assessments. You think you're finished, then they realise they forgot Charlie and his dog.'

April laughed. 'Funnily enough, I know that can be a pain in the neck, but in this case I'm hoping the guardian asks for further assessments.' She went on to explain the situation with Kerry and her children, and the awful environment in which she was trying to bring them up.

Paula placed her cup of coffee and paperwork on the desk next to April and turned her chair around to face the laptop in front of her, and April did the same, going back to the email she was about to read. She read it through with her mind still half on her conversation with Paula, but when it dawned on her what the email was saying she had to read it again to make sure. Katy had forwarded a letter from the Housing Department which Kerry had given to her on her last visit. It was offering Kerry the chance to view a two-bedroomed ground-floor Housing Association flat, not far from the area where she used to live. April gave a big sigh. This could not have been timed better. It could resolve her ambivalence about the removal of Tamara and Tyler from their mum.

It was time to pick up Isobel and take her to the contact session. April would usually have asked Norah to supervise but it seemed like a good opportunity to be on her own with Isobel in the car to see if she could get her to disclose anything more about her episodes away from Denise's. Also, observing the contact would add to her assessment of when and if there would be a possibility for Isobel to return home.

Isobel seemed quite upbeat on the journey to the Family Centre. She was far from what one might call chatty or vivacious, but there was a brightness about her which April hadn't really seen before.

Her mum was waiting in the family room and Isobel walked straight over to her. They wrapped their arms around each other and stood in that position for a few minutes. April found this quite moving. The two then walked over to the window which overlooked the little garden, and stood looking out as though they didn't know what to say to each other.

Alison soon broke the silence by asking Isobel how she was. She then produced a paper bag. 'I bought you these.'

'Oh, thanks.' Isobel took the bag from her mum and looked inside. It was a bottle of nail polish and a tube of lip gloss. 'Great. I needed some more lip gloss,' she said, taking the top off, stretching her lips and pasting it on before putting it back in the bag, which she stood on the little coffee table in front of her. Her lips sparkled.

They made general chatter until Alison brought up Isobel going missing, and although Isobel had become quite relaxed and almost garrulous, she immediately clammed up. Alison looked helplessly at April before changing the subject. As the time went on, the two became more relaxed again and were clearly enjoying just being together. April had asked Alison not to mention the situation with Danny, and thankfully she did as she'd been asked. She didn't think it was sensible for Isobel to know yet, just in case anything changed.

34

ALONE AGAIN

The shadowy streets were cold and eerie in the hour just before dawn. A low mist seemed to rise from the pavements, where the only sound came from Sam's shoe as the sole which had come loose flapped up and down rhythmically as she walked down the pedestrianised street; a lone figure, small, vulnerable and lost, carrying her duffle bag on her back which held all her worldly belongings. She had been hoping to see someone she recognised but there wasn't a soul to be seen. She wanted to get away from the narrow lanes with their dark, mysterious nooks and crannies which could be harbouring all kinds of threat.

The lanes were like a maze where one cobbled street led into another, all looking similar. Sometimes there would be a junction with two or even three little lanes to choose from; Samantha chose the least dark one each time. At last the sun rose high enough to cast some light on the streets and she began to realise that she was somewhere familiar. She walked past a few charity shops before stopping outside Bobbie's Tea Shop. The shutters were down but she recognised the name and realised with some surprise that she must be just around the corner from the Social Services office. Just to confirm that her memory served her well, she walked to the end of the street and around the corner to check, and there she saw the familiar keypad inside the recess where she had stood many times in the past, waiting for an appointment with April Gardiner. This had been a place of misery for her in the past. The place where she had been told that her children would not be coming back to her; where she was told that, because she was an alcoholic, her two little girls were going to be adopted and brought up in another family. Her heart had been torn out in this building, and by April Gardiner, who had made the decision to take her children away; and yet there was a strange reassurance in the familiarity of the place. It seemed incomprehensible that standing outside this office nearly two years later felt extraordinarily comforting.

For some strange reason she felt an overwhelming and irrational desire to see April. She couldn't work out why; perhaps she felt April was a link between her and her children, or was it because, somewhere deep down, she hoped April could help her? She had tried to help her before, after all: despite the fact that in April's eyes Sam had clearly failed as a mother, and despite the fact that she had no obligation to help her now that her children had been taken, April had written to her landlord to ask for a reprieve on paying the rent arrears, which was agreed for a short period. It could have been a bit of both, but Sam's mind was far too befuddled to even begin to make any sense of her feelings. There were many hours to go before the office would be open, but she decided to sit in the recess and wait. She sat down with her back resting against the door, facing out onto the street where she could watch the gradual changing of the night sky. Within half an hour of sitting down, her head slumped forward and, exhausted, she drifted off into a turbulent slumber.

It must have been the strangeness of inadvertently finding herself in this place that caused her to dream about her children. They were in a beautiful park. It was a bit like Princess Park near where she used to live, but far more exotic, with wild geese and pure white peacocks running over the extensive lawns. Birds of prey soared down from the treetops, sweeping the ground with their spindly legs, calling to each other before gliding gracefully upwards again. Tayla was eating an ice cream at the same time as pretending to look for Lily Grace, who she knew was hiding behind a bush. She was calling out, 'where are you, Lily Grace? I'm coming to find you.' Excited chuckling could be heard from behind the bush. Before long, Tayla peered around and shouted, 'Found you!', to which Lily Grace squealed with delight. The two girls then ran off into the distance, Tayla in front and Lily Grace trying frantically to keep up with her, whilst their mum watched them with a proud smile. Tayla had always been like a little mother to Lily Grace.

As Sam watched them running away from her, she suddenly noticed the large expanse of shimmering water which appeared in front of them, and realised with horror that the girls were running headlong towards it. She tried to run after them but found herself rooted to the spot. Her feet wouldn't budge. However hard she tried, she couldn't get her body to move. She watched in horror as Tayla fell in head first and disappeared into the water, then Lily Grace fell in behind her.

Sam was panic-stricken but helpless; she couldn't do anything to save them. After what seemed like forever she was able to shift her body, and she ran – or, rather, flew – towards the lake with her feet hardly touching the ground. Gasping for breath, she frantically scanned the water's surface. There was no trace of them. They were gone. She called out their names in despair but there was nothing apart from a few little ripples on the water, as though a stone had just been thrown in.

Sam could hear herself screaming in her sleep, which startled her out of her dream. As she woke she could hear a sorrowful moan, not realising at first that it was coming from her. It took some time to settle her mind after this but she eventually drifted off again, although other, less distinguishable dreams took their toll. Her mind was like a boiling pot which would not simmer down.

It was Janey who arrived first that morning, and in performing her usual ritual of turning into the recess with key in hand, ready to unlock the door, she almost tripped over the sleeping body of Sam, who by now had spread out over the concrete space and covered herself with her tartan blanket.

'What the hell…?'

Sam woke with a start. She sat up quickly but her brain took some time to work out where she was. The two women stared at each other until Janey broke the silence.

'You're not supposed to sleep here. Are you homeless? There's a shelter for the homeless; you should go there.' She was overwhelmed by the stench emanating from the human bundle, but tried hard to disguise her disgust.

'I'm here to see April Gardiner,' Sam found herself saying.

Janey looked at her curiously. 'Why do you want to see April?'

Sam's brain was slowly starting to engage with her current situation. 'What the fuck has that got to do with you?'

'I don't know if she's due in today. Have you got an appointment?'

'Yes. I've got an appointment. It's nine o'clock.'

'OK, so it's only eight now, so if you would like to come back at nine I'm sure she will be waiting for you.'

'Can I come in now and wait in there?' Sam said, pointing hopefully at the door.

'No, I'm sorry. I'm not allowed to let people in. I'm only the admin person; I'm not a social worker. If you come back at nine you will be able to come in and wait.' Janey tried to reach over Sam to unlock the door. 'You will need to move from here. Other people will be arriving soon and they could call the police if you're still here. I would go somewhere else if I were you and come back later.'

Sam felt so weary she didn't know where she was going to find the strength to get up, but she knew she had to. She rolled her head forward, then slowly pushed her body up with her hands. She gathered her duffle bag and blanket and slowly walked away.

Janey unlocked the main door and, before walking in, turned around to watch Sam depart. She had a feeling she had seen her before somewhere but wasn't sure where. As she walked up the stairs she began to feel sorry for her. She wished she had given her some money to buy something to eat and a coffee. It had been so unexpected that she hadn't had time to think straight. Feeling guilty, she put her bag down at the top of the stairs, took out her purse and ran back down to see if she could catch up with her. Unfortunately, by the time she reached the outside door Sam had gone.

April arrived at the office just after 8.30. She was due in court for the Phillips children and had been intending to go straight there, but there were a few things she wanted to tie up in the office and the hearing wasn't due to start until eleven. She was also hoping to have a chat with Maria before leaving because she hadn't had the chance to discuss the new situation concerning Kerry and the offer of a flat.

Katy collared April as soon as she walked in. She hadn't even had the chance to sit down. 'I went to see the flat with Kerry yesterday,' she said. 'It seems perfectly adequate. It needs a lick of paint and the garden's a bit of a mess, but it's a garden and with a bit of effort it could be made nice if someone put their mind to it.' There was a touch of sarcasm in her voice which April took as Katy thinking that effort on Kerry's part in any shape or form was unlikely. 'An elderly lady lived there before. She'd been there for years, apparently. They found her dead in the lounge.' Katy's shoulders seemed to quiver. 'I have to admit, April, that did give me the creeps. I know it sounds stupid but I felt a bit as though we were being watched; as though we were intruding in someone else's property.'

Some people might have found this amusing or even a bit silly, but not April. She was intrigued by the thought that the lady was still there, watching them walk around her home, perhaps thinking, *What the hell are they doing here in my flat?* 'Did the lady have children?'

'I don't know, why?'

'Perhaps she might be able to offer some parenting advice to Kerry.'

Katy smiled. 'Kerry needs someone to give her a kick up the backside, I would say.'

'Well, let's hope she can find some motivation from somewhere, anyway.'

'It's not going to be easy, starting from scratch. I hope she will be able to get some help to buy the essentials because she's got nothing. It will be a lot better than what she's got now, though, that's for sure.'

As Katy said this, April noticed Janey approaching with a serious look on her face.

'April, sorry to interrupt your discussion but I need to tell you that someone came to see you this morning. She said she had an appointment with you at nine o'clock.'

April was puzzled. 'I hope I haven't made an appointment for nine o'clock; I've got to get to court soon. Who was it?'

'She didn't say. I thought I might have seen her somewhere before but I wasn't really sure. She was a homeless person. She was sleeping outside by the front door.'

April immediately thought of Samantha. 'What did she look like?'

'Small, quite thin, funny-coloured hair; a bit red, a bit blonde with some black, long, straggly. Underneath the grime she was probably quite pretty.'

'Samantha Bushell,' April said breathlessly. 'I have been wondering about her. I thought she might end up homeless. Poor Sam. I feel so sorry for her. I wonder why she wanted to see me?'

'She didn't say. I have to admit I was a bit shocked, coming across someone sleeping down there. In all the years I've worked here I've never had a shock like that first thing in the morning. You just don't expect it, do you?'

'So she said she was coming back at nine?'

'Yes, I told her to because she said she had an appointment.'

'Thanks, Janey. I don't know what I can do for her but I will have a think about it.'

As Janey walked away, April began to tell the story of Sam to Katy, who was looking bemused. 'It's really sad. We always hope that all the parents we work with will be able to change and hold on to their kids in the end, don't we, but I especially wanted Sam to. She had so much love for those kids but was so damaged by her own childhood traumas that she just couldn't manage her own life, let alone the kids'. She was like a kid herself, really. She had a mum but she was just as hopeless so there really wasn't anyone she could turn to. Sometimes you come across people in this job where you think, *If only something could go right for them for once.* I hoped that she would at least be able to hang on to her home but clearly she couldn't. It wasn't even her fault that she got into rent arrears in the first place. Once it started it was a downward spiral.'

Katy went back to her own desk and April swivelled her chair round to face her computer. She should have been reading the guardian's report before the hearing later, but her mind was preoccupied with Sam. She found herself looking for homeless charities and taking down telephone numbers. She thought she would wait until Sam arrived before ringing them, just in case it wasn't what she wanted. She didn't want to make too many assumptions. After all, Sam was an adult who should be making her own decisions.

After finding a few numbers, April turned to the guardian's report, which had only been sent to her that morning. It was now ten past nine but she wasn't surprised because Sam had always struggled to remember what day it was, let alone keep track of the time. She just hoped she would come before she had to leave for court. The guardian's report was just as she had expected: supporting the removal of Tamara and Tyler from their mother. Whilst the guardian acknowledged the mitigating circumstances of unsuitable living accommodation, she felt that even so, Kerry was not able to provide adequate care for her children. April remained ambivalent about this but Maria was adamant that the Local Authority's responsibility was to ask the court for an order to remove the children. It was unusual for a social worker and manager to have different perspectives in a case that was going to court. Most cases were clear when they reached that stage. April still had misgivings but at the same time, could see Maria's point.

Just as she was thinking this, she noticed that Maria had come in and was settling herself down in her office. She quickly walked over to catch her before she became embroiled in other matters. April didn't have long before she had to leave.

'Maria, I'm so glad I've seen you. Have you got a minute?'

'Yes, of course, come and sit down. I thought you were in court today?'

'Yes, that's what I want to talk to you about. I was hoping to catch up with you before but we've been missing each other. It's about the Phillips children. I haven't got long but things have changed a bit. Kerry's been offered a flat.'

Maria swivelled her chair round to face April, who had sat down opposite.

'I know you felt it was too much of a risk to let the children remain in Kerry's care but now she has a chance to prove herself. What do you think?'

Maria creased her brow and tapped the pen she was holding against her lips. 'I'm not sure, April. I wish I had more time to think this through. It's a big decision.'

'I know. I can't say *I'm* sure. I hate these cases. It's just my gut feeling that she should be given a chance. It's a matter of whether the children should be potentially exposed to further neglect before they are removed, or removing them from their mother, maybe never to return, when there's a possibility that things may improve.'

'So the guardian is supporting removal?'

'She is, but she doesn't seem to have considered the new flat.'

'Why don't you ask for an adjournment for, say, a month?'

'That's what I was thinking, actually. It's a bit of a risk but I know I'll feel better. I won't be surprised, though, if the guardian still wants removal. She will probably say Kerry can prove herself during contact sessions if she wants to, but we'll see.'

April looked at the clock and was surprised to see it was 10.20. Sam had not turned up and she needed to be on her way. She went back to her desk to clear up her papers, picked up her bag and left the office in a hurry, later than she had planned. Katy had already left.

After stepping out of the recess onto the pavement, she stood for a minute and looked around. She could see nearly to the end of the high street and a long way down the lane opposite. There was no sign of Samantha. She suddenly had a thought, and took out her mobile.

'Hello, Janey, it's April. I was just thinking that Sam might turn up later. She's not very good at timekeeping. If she does, can you tell her to come tomorrow and I'll wait in the office for her?'

'Yes, will do.'

'Thanks, Janey.'

April then rushed off to get to court, where they would all be waiting for her.

35

THE FAMILY COURT

April was lucky to find a space in the car park fronting the court. She was stressed by now, realising how late she was. After turning quickly into the parking space, she reached over the seat into the back to get her bag, then quickly jumped out of the car, slammed the door shut and rushed towards the main entrance as fast as her legs would go without actually breaking into a run. After handing her bag to the security guards to be checked she hurried through the long, wide auditorium and up the large staircase towards the spacious quadrangular waiting area. She walked hastily around, peering through the glass panels in the doors of the little rooms that bordered the quadrangle, looking for the Local Authority barrister who she knew would be with the guardian and her barrister. She soon managed to locate them and, flustered and embarrassed that she was the last one to arrive, apologised to everyone before taking the only empty chair at the table.

Angela, the guardian, sat opposite. With her tall, heavily built frame, brightly coloured clothing and loud voice, she dominated the space as well as the conversation. 'I was just saying that if we all agree there's enough evidence to ask for removal, it could be done and dusted today.'

April hesitated. It was awkward because Angela clearly hadn't considered that the offer of a new flat could make a difference to the court decision. Kerry's own solicitor was with her in another room and they would almost certainly be asking for this. It seemed strange to April that she was here in court representing the Local Authority in the removal of two children from their mother when she wasn't really sure that this was right. She would normally have had plenty of time to consider the case and discuss it at length with Maria, but she just hadn't found the time on this occasion. So much had been going on with home, work and everything else. Being a mother was lovely but she was noticing a huge difference in her level of commitment to her work. She still wanted to do her best for her families and was every bit as concerned about the welfare of the children on her caseload as she had been before Demelza was born, but she was balancing those two things now, which both presented her with huge responsibilities, and that was much harder than she had ever imagined. Part of her felt that she hadn't given as much thought and attention to this case as she would have done before she was a mother, and that was why she was in this dilemma now. Perhaps it was something she would learn to manage better as time went on.

Whilst Angela continued her tirade of inflexible opinions, April tried to pull her thoughts together. She wanted to get it right for these children and she felt it was imperative to stand by what she believed. What she was thinking was going to be a surprise to everyone, and she hadn't even talked it through with her own solicitor.

'I'm afraid I'm going to throw a spanner in the works.' She looked around the table as all the faces turned towards her. 'I am aware that what I'm going to suggest is not without risk, but…' She took a deep breath. 'I think we could be making a mistake.' She paused again. 'I believe that if we don't give Kerry a bit longer to prove herself in the flat, we could be depriving the children of their right to be brought up in their birth family.'

There was a short silence, then Angela brushed her fingers through her mass of frizzy black hair before holding both hands out flat in front of her, her multicoloured blouse flapping around her arms as she moved them up and down. Then, in her heavy West African accent, she started to speak. 'Explain yourself, please, April. Do you mean what I think you mean?'

'I don't know what you're thinking, Angela, to be honest, but I think we should ask the court for an adjournment.'

There was complete silence in the room whilst they all waited for her to explain.

'I think you probably all know that I have always had misgivings about this case. I wonder if we are underestimating the impact living in conditions such as Kerry has had to put up with would have on parenting, on mental health, on motivation – I could go on.' April was aware that she should have had this discussion earlier with Angela on the phone, or arranged a meeting with her to talk it through. She knew this was a failure on her part and she probably looked a little bit silly now, changing her recommendation just before going in front of the judge, and asking other parties to change theirs. She watched the changing expressions around the table.

Christina, the Local Authority barrister, was the first to speak, and to April's relief she seemed to agree with her. 'We can be sure that is what the mother's solicitor will ask for. It doesn't seem that unreasonable to me under the circumstances. What does everyone else think?'

There was silence. Even Angela was quiet for once. April felt a bit sorry for Katy, who sat quietly, listening. She had carried out an assessment which she felt considered the potential for improvement and came to the conclusion that living conditions were not the major factor in Kerry's inadequate care of her children. She had been guided through the process of her assessment by Maria and by April, but now her conclusion was being challenged. April could understand why she would feel let down by this. However, April had a strong sense of duty to the children she worked with and she wanted to see justice done.

It was no surprise that Angela challenged her. 'So, we all agree that the children are at risk of suffering significant harm. We all agreed that they needed to be removed from their mother's care, and this was backed up by my own and the social worker's assessment. We all agreed that the assessment factored in the negative impact of the home environment, and that it was not the main mitigating factor in the care Kerry has provided for her children. Now you say you don't agree with any of the assessments, including the Local Authority's. How can that be?'

Everyone turned at the same time, waiting for April's response.

She had no hesitation. Now that she had spoken her mind, she was in no doubt that what she was suggesting – that they give Kerry that chance – was right. 'Had I known that Kerry would be offered a flat at this stage, I would not have applied for the Interim Care Order. I would have waited to see what happened. I understand that this means the children will spend longer with an inadequate mother, but we have to balance the trauma of them being removed from their mother and ultimately brought up outside their birth family against the potential harm of them remaining where they are. I think this can be managed. The family will be monitored closely, and if no improvement is evident within a short period of time then we'll need to revisit the plan.'

There was a moment of silence, with everyone staring at April, who glanced from one to the other with a stoical expression.

Unsurprisingly, Angela was the first to speak. 'I'm not sure I'm that happy about it, April. I will need to talk to Christina. ' She turned to her barrister, who suggested they leave the room for a private discussion.

Katy sat quietly looking on, but it was clear by her expression that she was not very happy. She had been proud of her assessment. It was the first one she had done for court, and it was good. Both Maria and April had told her it was good. Now April was saying her conclusion was wrong. She just could not see that where Kerry lived would make any difference; she was too lazy to bother to interact with her children in any shape or form, and appeared to have no idea what children needed. She only had a small bedsit to keep clean but she couldn't even manage that. How would she ever manage with a two-bedroomed flat and a garden? But as Katy was only a co-worker on the case and April was the senior social worker, she had no say in the final decision and would have to go along with it. She felt sure that it was only a matter of time before it would all go pear-shaped and she would be proved right.

Angela and Sajid soon returned and before they were called into court the professionals had all agreed to an adjournment. April felt really pleased that she had spoken out. As there was no opposition to the plan, it was virtually agreed, although a month was not considered long enough. The guardian suggested two months, with the proviso that intensive support was provided to Kerry alongside ongoing assessment. She wanted a fully updated comprehensive assessment within a month of Kerry moving in.

The hearing was finished by 4pm and, after walking back to her car, pulling on the seat belt and getting ready to drive away, April suddenly remembered Samantha. She couldn't help wondering whether she had returned to the office or not. She unhooked her seat belt and searched in her bag for her phone.

'Hi, Janey, it's April here. I was just wondering whether Samantha Bushell came back at all?'

'No, she didn't. At least, I didn't see her. Not unless someone else spoke to her. I'll just ask around.' April heard Janey shouting across the office. 'No. It doesn't seem as though she did.'

'OK, thanks, Janey. I'll see you tomorrow.'

36

FAMILY VISIT

On Saturday morning April and Jed were packing the car, getting ready to visit parents – Diana first, then Jed's parents on Sunday morning. They were setting off early to avoid the worst of the traffic. It was a sultry morning and their bags were packed in preparation for a scorching day: Factor 50, sun hats and swimming costumes for Demelza, who was going to love playing in the paddling pool her nanny had bought in readiness for their visit. April was dressed in a loose cream linen dress but her cheeks were flushed and she already felt a bit sticky from the heat.

'Have we got everything now, then?' Jed asked, after Demelza had been strapped in and April climbed into the passenger seat beside him.

'Yes. I think so.'

'Shall I wait a few minutes, just in case? You know what you're like.'

'What do you mean by that?' April said indignantly. 'It sounds as though you're suggesting I'm a bit scatty or something.'

'I wouldn't dream of suggesting such a thing.'

'What do you mean, then?'

'I just meant that sometimes you forget things.'

April tried to disguise her annoyance but couldn't help her curt reply. 'I would like to see you remember everything we need to take with us. I know what we should do: next time, you can pack everything while I get the car ready and lock the garage. I'm sure you will do a much better job than I obviously do.'

Jed took a deep breath before slowly pulling away from the pavement. He had only meant it light-heartedly but he had noticed lately that April was pricklier than usual. He wondered if the stress of trying to do her job well and wanting to be the perfect mother was getting a bit too much for her. He decided to let it go.

There was silence until they reached the motorway, and by then April had clearly forgotten that she was angry with him. 'I have made a decision,' she suddenly remarked.

'Oh, OK, what's that, then?'

'I'm going to have it out with my mum. I'm going to tell her she's acting like a child. I've been thinking a lot about this. How are we going to explain to Demelza when she is older that her nanny won't have anything to do with her grandad? On family occasions when Grandad can't come because Nanny doesn't want him there, what's she going to think? She's going to think it's a bit odd, isn't she?'

'You need to think very carefully about this, April. You really don't want to fall out with your mum.'

'I *have* thought about it. I just don't think we can let her carry on like this. He's more than willing to make amends. She had the affair, for God's sake. He just left her when he was angry, then wanted to come back. The more I think about it, the more convinced I am that she is to blame for everything. I've never been allowed to talk about it and I've always complied with that, but now I've got a little girl to think of I'm not willing to do it any more.' There was a long pause. 'Besides, what happens when Demelza asks questions – or should she be brought up the way I was: with dark secrets in the cupboard? Now I think about it, I realise that that damaged us as a family.'

'Are you sure you're not blowing it out of proportion, April?'

'No, absolutely not. I didn't realise then, but now I look back it's all clear. It was a dark shadow, ever present in the corner of the room, that threatened to engulf us if allowed to spread. It was hard. It was *really* hard. It wasn't just a matter of "We don't speak about Dad"; it was like something sinister eroding our trust in each other.'

There was a period of silence. Jed was thinking that April wouldn't actually carry this through. She wouldn't want to risk damaging her relationship with her mum. He could sort of see her point but was still of the view that it wouldn't be a good idea. Despite all this, Diana was a good person and had been a good mum. April would not want to upset her.

'Why not just leave it? I'm sure when Demelza is old enough to think for herself she'll be able to deal with it.'

'But… but… I don't know. We don't know what impact it might have on her. When you think about it, Mum was willing to ruin our chance to adopt a child by refusing to tell me about Dad. I don't think she should be allowed to get away with it any longer. Anyway, I'm fed up with having to keep our meetings secret. Why should I have to? I'm not doing anything wrong. She's the one in the wrong, not me.'

There was silence again before Jed spoke. 'April, have you really thought this through? She shut him out of her life completely and she must have loved him once. I'd say she *really* loved him, and that's why she couldn't forgive him for walking out. What if she does the same to you?'

This thought had not crossed April's mind. It gave her a bit of a start. 'Surely she wouldn't do that? I can't believe she would do that, especially now that we've got Demelza.'

'She's a proud woman, April. She has already let pride come between her and someone she loved.'

When the car pulled up outside the house, Diana was stood at the gate, smiling and waving. She came up to the car and, looking in the window, waved at Demelza, who was screeching, 'Nanny, Nanny!' whilst wrestling with the straps which were holding her in. April got out and gave her mum a hug before leaning over the back seat to release Demelza, who sprang from the car seat so quickly she almost banged her head on the seat in front of her. She was immediately picked up by Diana and smothered in kisses.

'How was your journey? It didn't seem to take too long. I've got home-made scones with jam and cream. I'll go and put the coffee pot on and we can sit in the garden. And what does Demelza want to drink?' She bent down towards Demelza. 'Does Demelza want drinkies?'

Demelza was nodding and pursing her lips whilst repeating, 'Doosh', which April interpreted as 'juice'.

Jed took the bags from the boot and carried them straight upstairs whilst April followed Diana, who was leading Demelza by the hand into the kitchen. The two women chatted as Diana put the coffee pot on to boil and arranged the scones on a coloured glass cake stand. She liked things to be done nicely.

'How has work been, April – still busy, or are they letting you have easier cases because you now have other responsibilities?'

April laughed. 'Whatever makes you think that would happen? You must think we are living in an enlightened age where child-rearing is treated with respect rather than as something you do once your proper job is done, if you can fit it in. Unfortunately we have a long way to go before society reaches that conclusion.'

'You can't be expected to do the same as people who haven't got small children, though; that's not fair. How are you supposed to do that?'

'To be honest with you, Mum, I don't believe it is possible. I didn't realise how much motherhood was going to change the way I work. I do my very best but sometimes I don't feel as though I've prepared for things as much as I should have.'

She turned around just in time to see that Demelza had stretched up her arm and was about to dip her fingers in the little pot of jam which was waiting to be put on the tray. 'No, Demelza, you mustn't eat Nanny's jam.'

She turned back to Diana. 'I'm always feeling as though I haven't done as much as I should have done. It's not like before, when if a case blew up, which they tend to do quite often, I would just work later or start earlier. I do work sometimes in the evenings but I'm usually really tired by then.'

'Why don't you be a stay-at-home mum, April?' Diana pleaded. 'Just think of the lovely times you could have with Demelza.'

April felt a bit annoyed at her mum trying once again to tell her what to do. She didn't respond verbally, but turned away so that Diana couldn't see the face she pulled. 'Hmmm. Well, I must say, the scones look delicious.'

April carried the plate of scones, Diana the jam and cream, and Jed the tray with the coffee and cups and a little plastic beaker with a curly straw for Demelza, into the garden. They laid them out on the white metal table before relaxing into the comfy garden chairs.

'This is lovely,' April said, putting both hands behind her head and leaning back in the chair.

'Jed, I think we need the umbrella up; it's far too hot,' Diana pointed out. 'You could get the paddling pool out too if you like, or shall we wait until we've had coffee?'

They spent the afternoon chatting whilst Demelza splashed happily in the pool. There was a boat-shaped water pistol which filled itself up when underwater, and Demelza discovered that if she squeezed it she could soak Mummy, Daddy and Nanny, which made her squeal with delight. By 5pm she was rubbing her eyes and yawning. As usual, Diana took over the bedtime routine: bath, story, bed. April was quite happy with this arrangement. She felt tired after a busy and stressful week, and it was lovely for once to be able to sit down with her feet up and let someone else take over. Jed tried to help when he was there but she always seemed to do the bulk of the tasks; she was always in control of the process and felt it wouldn't be done properly if she wasn't overseeing things. When her mum took over she was able to leave her to it. She didn't really have a lot of choice in the matter but that was fine by her.

Diana had cooked an Italian fish stew for the three adults and a bottle of Sancerre was on ice. It was a gorgeous evening but not quite warm enough to be outside, so they sat indoors with the windows wide open, enjoying the gentle breeze and the lovely scent of jasmine that wafted in. The only sounds were the fluting of the blackbirds and the rustling of the apple tree which hung over from next door's garden.

'Do you think the wind is coming up?' Diana asked. 'It feels a bit stormy.'

'Possibly,' Jed answered. He walked to the window to look at the sky. 'No sign of any storm yet.'

April watched her mum as she talked animatedly about her friend from her book group, who often came round. The two women often went for coffee together and chatted mostly about their grandchildren. April was pleased that her mum seemed so happy, and started to think that maybe Jed was right. Confronting her now did not seem like such a good idea. After the delicious stew had been eaten and the dishes cleared, Diana took a huge lemon tart and a pot of fromage frais from the fridge. April loved lemon tart. She took a mouthful.

'I can't believe I'm eating this; I was so full. It's absolutely delicious, though.'

Diana smiled with glee. She loved nothing more than to see the people she cared about enjoying the food she had cooked for them.

They finished the bottle of wine between them but there was another waiting in the cooler, which Diana handed to Jed to open.

'We need a bit more, don't you think?'

'I think you're right,' Jed said as he took the bottle from her.

April was starting to feel a little bit woozy. It wasn't just the alcohol she had drunk, but the tiredness and the alcohol combined. She hadn't realised how tired she was. It was only just after nine. She would have loved to go to bed, but thought that could seem a bit rude considering that her mum had gone to so much trouble to make the evening nice for them. Instead she sank into the comfy armchair and tried hard to keep herself awake.

It was later in the evening, just as they were about halfway through the second bottle, when Diana stunned them into silence. 'I've got some news for you.'

Jed and April looked up in anticipation. Diana had stood up from her chair and was standing by the open window, her back to them both.

'Well, what is it then, Diana? We're waiting.'

'I've had a conversation with your dad.'

They were dumbfounded. Jed was, again, the first to speak. April was trying to clear her muzzy head so that she could be sure that what she thought she had heard was correct.

'What sort of conversation?' Jed asked.

Diana turned to face them and, leaning back on the windowsill, explained. 'He phoned me.'

'Yes?' April was sitting on the edge of her chair with a new-found energy.

'He wanted to talk. He wanted to talk about you, Max and Demelza. He wants to meet me.'

April was slowly dragging herself out of her lethargy. Part of her wanted her mum to repeat what she had just said, just to make sure she had heard her right.

'And what did you say?' This was Jed again. April still appeared speechless.

'I said yes.' There was a long pause before Diana came and sat back in her chair. She had a large swig of her wine before carrying on. 'We both feel that we need to stop thinking about ourselves and start thinking of our grandchildren. He is broken-hearted that he has never met Alistair and Elinor, and he wants to be part of Demelza's life.'

April felt overwhelmed with emotion. Tears sprang up in her eyes. She could not believe what she was hearing. This was what she had dreamed of; yet her whole life as she had known it was being turned upside down. Suddenly, caution overcame her. It couldn't suddenly be OK after all these years. There must be something that could go wrong. She really wanted to be positive, but all her life, in the depths of her consciousness she had wanted her mum and dad to be together again, or at the very least be friends. All kinds of thoughts were rushing through her head. She was visualising her mum and dad laughing together at family get-togethers. Prominent in her thoughts was that, thank God, there would no longer be secrets between them.

'Does Max know?'

'No, he doesn't. I haven't told him yet. I hope he will be pleased.'

'You can be absolutely certain that he will be pleased.'

April decided that the first thing she was going to do when she got home was phone Max and tell him.

37

CONTACT ON THE BEACH

Things had moved on for Isobel. She and her mum had been attending counselling sessions together and apart. The feedback from the therapist was positive and this had helped to inform the future plans for regular contact with her mum which, all being well, should lead to Isobel returning home. Since it was now school holidays the two had been allowed to spend time together without being supervised. They were doing things in the community such as going to McDonald's, the cinema or shopping; much better than sitting in the family room at the contact centre, being watched over.

'You look very nice today, Isobel,' Denise commented as Isobel came out of her room wearing a pair of white shorts with a loose flowery top and her hair hanging loose but brushed and shining. Her legs were long, slim and tanned, and Denise was thinking how attractive she looked when she took the trouble to make the best of herself. Until recently it had been a struggle to get her to have regular showers and wash her hair, let alone take pride in her appearance.

'Me and Mum are getting fish and chips, then going to the beach.'

Denise was quite astonished at the change in her. She seemed to have metamorphosed into another person. No longer the grumpy silences or the hateful stares, the short sharp responses which often involved a swear word. Isobel had become nice; likeable.

'I can drop you off at the harbour if you like?'

'Yes please, if you don't mind.'

Denise was pleased. Isobel had hardly ever accepted anything from her, and if she had she'd done so grudgingly.

On the journey, Isobel chatted happily to Denise, who was beginning to enjoy her company. When they reached the harbour, Isobel jumped out of the car before turning around and saying, 'Thanks for the lift, Denise; I should be back around fourish.'

Denise smiled and waved. As she drove back home she thought about how nice it was that things were working out for Isobel. Now that she would be leaving shortly, Denise was wrapped with guilt. She had not been as understanding and accepting as befits a foster carer tasked with caring for damaged and traumatised children. The deeper the trauma, the more difficult they could be, and Denise could not deny that she should have done better for Isobel. Now that her placement was about to end, Denise wished she had been kinder and more understanding. It was too late to make up for it with Isobel, but she was determined to work hard to improve for the next child to be placed in her care.

Isobel walked along the promenade towards the bandstand where her mum had said she would wait. She couldn't see her, so found a bench to sit on. She watched people walk past; mostly families, or small groups of mums with children. She heard the chimes of an ice-cream van which pulled up close by, and watched as people gathered alongside it. She could see the fish and chip shop they planned to go to, and the pungent aroma of fat frying made her stomach rumble. The beach was crowded and the sea was full of children splashing about in the waves. She wished she had brought her swimming things because the water looked lovely. She started to watch the crowds more closely as they moved in her direction, weaving in and out of each other, looking hopefully among them for her mother.

After a bit she took out her phone, hoping for a message from her mum to explain her lateness. Just as she saw that there was no message, a hand stroked her hair, and to her relief she turned to see her mum standing behind her. They smiled at each other, hugged, then linked arms as they walked, smiling and chatting, towards the fish and chip shop.

After they had eaten their lunch, they sat on deckchairs and made plans for Isobel's return home.

'We will see if you can go back to your old school, Isobel. You're clever, you know; you always have been. You could get good GCSEs if you want to.'

'I won't get any GCSEs if I stay in that PRU. You don't learn anything there. The teachers don't know anything. They just give you books to read out of and copy all the time. It's really boring.'

'I'll get April to sort out the school for you. It would be nice if you could come home before they go back in September. You've got your old friends there.'

Isobel wasn't sure about the so-called friends, but she liked the idea.

When she got back to Denise's, Isobel began sorting out a few things in her room. She had a large holdall from when she'd first arrived, which she took from the bottom of her wardrobe. She then began to take things out of the little drawers by the side of her bed – hair bobbles, notebooks and pencils – and put them in her bag. She couldn't wait to get away from this house; although people here were generally kind to her, it would never be home.

She looked around her bright, airy bedroom at the pale cream lightshade with pastel flowers and the matching duvet and curtains. The double-glazed window opened onto a tranquil neighbourhood with interesting houses and pretty gardens. It was a stark contrast to the place she had come from, where her bedroom was dark and always cold due to the narrow space between it and the tall buildings opposite which blocked sunlight for most of the day. Opening her window would not fill the room with the natural scents of the seasons; rather, it would let in traffic fumes and the odour of stale curry from the Indian restaurant just around the corner. That was her home, though. There she could move around freely, take food from the fridge when she pleased, leave a mess in her bedroom, watch what she wanted on the television in the lounge, walk around in her pyjamas. The dark shadow of her father's predatory behaviour was pushed to the back of her mind, and when he wasn't there, her home was her haven.

38

NEW HOME

Kerry woke up early on Monday morning feeling almost happy. She had been given the keys to the flat and had a week to move in. She also had a bit of money to spend: a loan from Universal Credit to pay for the basic things she needed. There was a lot to do to make it look nice but she had a new vigour for life. Tamara had climbed in with her in the middle of the night and was still sleeping soundly. Tyler had found some small cars and was pushing them around on the grubby carpet, chattering away to himself in some imaginary world.

'Right, kids, we need to get ready now; we're off to see our new flat.'

Tamara murmured and stirred but turned over on her side to carry on sleeping. Kerry pulled on the clothes which had been lying on the floor beside her mattress where she had left them the night before, then began to pour Coco Pops into bowls.

The family were out in time to catch the ten o'clock bus, which dropped them off just around the corner from the new flat. There was a little rickety wooden gate which scraped across the concrete as it was pushed open. The front garden was small and woefully neglected. There was evidence that it had once been well cared for, with signs of herbaceous plants and shrubs which were partially hidden under brambles or smothered by bindweed and ivy. The path leading to the front door was cracking and slowly being reclaimed by creeping vegetation.

Kerry put her key in the lock and opened the door. In front of her was a narrow hallway with doors leading off from both sides. The carpet was old and patterned with autumn colours, and the walls were a dingy yellow that had probably once been magnolia or white satin. Intermittent squares of lighter paint dotted the walls where pictures that had hung for years had been taken down. The lounge was quite small but had an attractive double-aspect window overlooking the front garden which created an impression of spaciousness and light. She loved the old-fashioned brick fireplace but was eager to tear up the faded orange-and-green carpet, which was frayed at the edges. Other than the carpets the flat was void of furnishings, except for a thin grey roller blind hanging crookedly at the kitchen window. The kitchen was reasonable, having recently been refurbished by the Housing Association, as was the bathroom. Although basic, they were clean, and functional. Kerry was delighted. It was going to be an absolute luxury: a proper kitchen of her own, and a bathroom she didn't have to leave the safety of her room to access. She was eager to start cooking proper meals again and having cupboards to store things in.

She opened the kitchen door and stepped outside into the back garden. Despite the unruliness of the area, she took a deep breath, marvelling in the pleasure of having her own front door. She imagined the garden without its years of neglect. She planned to get on with fixing it up the minute she moved in; sorting out a proper lawn where Tyler could play football and Tamara could have a swing. In the meantime, Tyler had gone into one of the bedrooms and claimed it for his own. She decided not to disappoint him by telling him he was going to have to share it with Tamara.

Just as she was about to go inside, her phone started to ring. It was April. 'Morning, Kerry. I was just wondering if you were going to the flat today? I've been in touch with a charity who will give you some furniture to tide you over. When you've decided what you're going to need you can go and have a look at their warehouse. Katy can take you if you like.'

'Thanks, April, but I'd rather you took me. I don't like Katy; she's a snooty cow.' The way Kerry saw it, Katy wanted to take her children away from her and April had stopped her.

'I'm sorry, Kerry, but I really can't. Katy would be the best person to do it because she's got the time at the moment.'

'She treats me like a piece of shit, and she thinks I'm stupid. She's trying to take my kids away from me.'

April tipped her head to the side compassionately. 'That's really not true, Kerry. She was just doing her job. Sometimes social workers have different opinions about what should happen in the best interests of children. Now that the court has agreed they should stay with you for the time being, she will do all she can to help you to prove you can look after them properly.' April couldn't help feeling a stab of guilt. It was her fault Katy looked bad in Kerry's eyes. She should have discussed her plan with Katy before they went to court. It would then have been seen as a Local Authority decision rather than her against Katy. 'But, saying that, at the end of the day, it's down to you, Kerry. You need to prove you can be a good parent and meet the children's needs. The warehouse is quite a way out of town on an industrial estate so you will struggle to get there without someone to take you.'

'OK,' Kerry agreed reluctantly. 'Will they give me new carpets? I can't live with these manky things. Have you seen them? They look like vomit.'

April thought that was quite amusing, bearing in mind the urine-soaked carpets in the bedsit. 'No, I haven't, but they won't be able to give you carpet or laminate flooring. I'm afraid you will have to pay for those out of your loan. They usually have general household furniture which people have donated. They might be able to give you curtains, sheets and things like that. it depends what they've got available.'

Kerry returned to her hostel late in the afternoon. They had picked up a McDonald's on the way home. For the first time in ages, there was an absence of the sinking feeling in her stomach as she approached the building; the dread of having to go inside that she'd felt every time she'd gone back there. Knowing this awful period was coming to an end made it much easier to bear. She half-smiled as she thought to herself, *Only a few days left in this pigsty.*

Instead of going straight to her room, she decided to go and see Briony. She had already told her about the flat but was keen to tell her about her visit there and the work she planned to do to make it homely.

Briony opened the door with the baby in her arms. Kerry was quite surprised by this; she didn't think she had seen her holding Angel before.

'She won't sleep. I don't know what's wrong.'

'She looks hot; her face is all red. Is she teething?'

'Yes, I think she is; she's been awake most of the night. That bastard next door came round, banging on the door, shouting his mouth off, telling me to shut her up. I couldn't shut her up. I tried to but I couldn't. He threatened to call the police.'

'What a stupid prat. What could you do? It's not your fault the walls are so thin. Tell him to get you somewhere else to live if he doesn't like hearing a baby crying. That will shut him up.'

'I wouldn't mind but I've been kept awake by him yelling at his kids loads of times; early morning, late at night, you name it. He's a vicious pig. I'm just thankful I don't have to live with him like Stacey does. Poor thing. She hates his guts but you can tell she's petrified of him. So are the kids.'

'I'll be so glad to be away from all this,' Kerry said, unable to conceal the excitement in her voice. 'I couldn't take much more of it. I can't wait to get started on my flat. You'll have to come round when it's all done. Why don't you see if you can get a flat around there? It's time they gave you one as well, isn't it?'

'I think so. I've been waiting over a year now. I don't know why you've got one before me. Don't get me wrong, I'm glad for you, but it doesn't seem very fair, does it?'

Kerry didn't answer. She didn't understand why either, but she wasn't going to question it, even to Briony, just in case someone somewhere got wind of it, took her flat away from her and gave it to Briony instead.

'Why don't you come round here tonight? Bring the kids; we could have a drink.'

'I don't think I will tonight. I've got to be up early. Katy's coming to take me to the second-hand furniture place. I can get furniture for my flat. I don't want to sleep in. Then I want to go and do some work in the garden; try to get that straightened up. It's going to be hard work but I want the kids to be able to go out and play. I would like to have a patio table to sit out in the sunshine. I wonder if I could get one from the furniture place? I like those ones with reclining seats.'

'We need to celebrate you getting a flat, and we need to have a goodbye drink. You can't go without us having a goodbye drink.'

Kerry was tempted. The thought of a get-together and a chance to celebrate her new flat with a drink sounded great. Tamara had climbed onto her knee and was snuggling into her chest. She was ready for an afternoon nap. Kerry stroked her child's head gently as she contemplated how much better things were going to be for her and her children. 'No, I don't think I will tonight, Briony. I nearly had my kids taken away from me and I'm not taking any risks. I've been given another chance and I'm going to get it right this time. It scared the shit out of me, to be honest.'

Briony persisted. 'The social worker won't know. They don't know anything. They make out they do, but most of it's just guesswork. How would they know if you came round for a drink? They don't work at night, do they?'

'They knew things weren't right. I don't know how they knew but they did. I don't want that to happen again. Sorry, Briony.'

Briony gave up then and forced a smile. She was thinking, *It's OK for you; you're getting out. What about me?*

39

CAUTIOUS PLANNING

April was sitting at her desk, finalising the report for Isobel. She had paid her a visit the day before and felt really pleased with the way things were going. Isobel was keen to go home and Alison was just as keen to have her back. April was conscious that these things were never without risk but there were times in this job when risks needed to be managed rather than avoided. Nobody could be sure that Alison and Danny wouldn't ever get back together at some point in the future, but it wouldn't be fair to keep Isobel in foster care against her wishes on that basis. The court would be unlikely to agree to that anyway. The crucial factor was that Alison was now saying that she believed what Isobel had said and accepted that her husband had abused his daughter. April wasn't entirely convinced but on balance it seemed right to give her the benefit of the doubt. Another factor in the decision was that, since the plan had changed, Isobel hadn't gone missing again. The reason for that wasn't clear because Isobel wouldn't discuss it, but it was widely known that young people in care were far more likely to be victims of sexual exploitation, used as runners by drug traffickers, or, more often than not, both.

She had been typing frantically and, after finishing off the last sentence, sat back in her chair for a bit of a breather before reading it through in readiness to send to Legal. She'd shut her eyes and taken a few relaxing deep breaths when she heard someone approach.

'April, where've you been? I'm sure you must be avoiding me.'

April was delighted to see Miles standing beside her with his handsome, cheerful smile. She stood up and they gave each other a hug. Without communicating verbally, they walked across the office to the kitchen with a cup of coffee in mind. Miles filled the kettle whilst April searched for the cafetière in the bottom cupboard.

'So what's the progress on your mum and dad? Are they remarried yet?'

April smiled, but couldn't resist telling him about the latest events.

'There you are, what did I tell you? Now you can see why I'm considered to be an exceptional social worker. If you want any advice on relationships, I'm the man to ask. Will I be invited to the wedding?'

'Don't be stupid. They're agreeing to be civil to each other for the sake of their grandchildren, that's all. They're not getting back together as a couple. There's absolutely no chance of that, Miles. You're just a big romantic.'

'OK, that's disappointing, though. I would love to go to a wedding. Haven't been to one for years, and I look stunning in a dinner jacket.'

April laughed as they walked back to their desks, carefully carrying their cups of coffee.

Alison's suggestion for Isobel to return home before school started in September made sense to April. She still needed to persuade Isobel's old school to have her back. She also needed to talk to the guardian about Isobel's return home. She didn't envisage any disagreement there but it was good practice to do so and she didn't want to make the same mistake she had made with Kerry.

She finished the tasks she had prioritised for that morning before leaving the office to visit Alison. She needed to check that Alison was suitably prepared for Isobel's return. She stopped off at Bobbie's to buy a sandwich before heading off to Taylor's Yard.

Alison was there to open the door the second she rang the bell.

'That was quick. How did you manage to get down the stairs that quickly?'

Alison laughed. 'I wish… as it happens, I've just this second come in.'

'Good timing, then,' April said as she followed Alison up the staircase. She shivered a bit, as she always did when she walked up that dark concrete staircase with its plastered walls. She'd had a suspicion that Alison would demand Isobel's return sooner than planned, but she didn't even mention it. In fact she appeared perfectly amenable to April's plan, accepting that things had to be tied up properly and the guardian needed to be on board, although April explained that she was unlikely to disagree.

Before April had the chance to sit down, she was invited to follow Alison into the bedroom.

'I've done it all nice for her. I've bought a new duvet cover and curtains to match.'

April wasn't keen on the black-and-red colour scheme but guessed that Alison was more attuned to Isobel's taste than she was. 'I'm sure she'll be delighted when she knows you've gone to all this trouble for her, Alison.'

'I got her a beanbag. She's always wanted one. Don't mention it, though, will you? I want it to be a surprise when she comes home.' There was a beanbag in the recess, with a large black-and-white panda teddy sitting on it.

'That's lovely, Alison. She's going to need extra nurturing and spoiling. Don't believe those people who say you shouldn't spoil your kids. There are times when you should, and this is one of them.'

April followed Alison into the kitchen and stood by the open door as Alison put the kettle on.

'You will need to be prepared for some difficult times with

her, you know, Alison. She's been through a lot. She needs to be absolutely confident that you believe what she said about her dad. That's the only way she will feel completely safe. Remember, though, that you won't be left on your own. I won't be closing Isobel's case for a long time yet. I will be recommending that you both carry on with your therapy sessions, and I think that will help you get through.'

'I told you, April, I want to make it up to her; make up for not believing her. It was so hard, though. It was such a shock. I never would have believed he could do that to his own daughter. I can't understand why she didn't tell me. Why did she tell her teacher and not me? Surely I should have been the one she told; the one she came to first. I don't understand it. I must've been a crap mother when my own daughter couldn't tell me she was being abused.'

'You mustn't beat yourself up, Alison. Again, that is quite common. Try to put yourself in her shoes. Danny abused her but he's still her dad. We can't begin to imagine the emotional turmoil and confusion she was experiencing. She couldn't have known what would happen if she told someone, but she was wise enough to know that it could turn her whole world upside down, which it did.'

'I will never be able to live with the guilt of this; especially 'cause I took her dad's side to begin with. I should have known it was true; I mean, look at what he's done now: just walked out. I still can't understand why the police didn't find him guilty. Shouldn't he be in prison for what he did?'

April was a bit perturbed by this statement. She had a slight suspicion that this venting of Alison's anger had more to do with Danny leaving her than with what he'd done to Isobel. 'He wasn't found guilty or not guilty. Not at all. The case didn't even get to court, did it? It happens a lot in child abuse cases, unfortunately. The Crown Prosecution Service need to agree that there is enough evidence to prove a case that's brought forward, and there often isn't because it's only the word of the abuser against the word of the victim. If the CPS don't think there's enough evidence to get a guilty verdict it's unlikely to go to court. They and the police also take into account the effect the court process can have on the child.'

'So you're saying that there's a load of paedophiles walking around out there, getting away with it?'

'Yes, there absolutely is.'

Alison looked horrified. She placed a hand on either side of her face and shook her head slowly. 'I just can't believe that. It's scary.'

'Yes, it is scary. Most people don't become aware of it unless, like with you, it comes to their door.'

April left the house with mixed feelings. Alison seemed convincing in her change of stance but she had to be sceptical. There was no doubt in her mind that Alison loved Isobel and, from what she could gather from the evidence, had been a good mother to her. April had been lied to many times before, but liars usually tripped up in the end. It would have been so much easier and so much less harm done if only Alison had chosen to stand by Isobel in the first place.

40

JOY

On Sunday morning, Kerry woke up for the first time in her new flat. She stretched out, luxuriating in the comfort of her double bed. She could hear the noise of the television coming from the lounge and guessed it was Tyler in there. Tamara was probably still asleep as she couldn't hear her. Apart from the television noise, there was nothing. This was marvellous – no shouting from parents down the corridor, no revving of motorbikes, no kids screaming, no people walking past the door or thumping from upstairs.

She popped her head into the lounge to see Tyler with his legs under him and his eyes glued to the television. 'Morning, love.'

'Mornin',' he replied without turning his gaze from the screen.

A few steps away on the other side of the corridor was the children's room, and she looked in to see Tamara still sleeping soundly. Her body was lying on top of the duvet, apart from one leg which was covered up to the knee. Damp curls framed her chubby, flushed cheeks, and her arms were spread out. It was lovely to see her sleeping so peacefully, with no disturbances from outside or next door. There were people in the flat above but Kerry didn't know who they were or hear a sound from them.

She left Tamara sleeping, went into the kitchen and opened all the cupboard doors one after the other, marvelling at the space she had. She then took out some matching cereal bowls which were cream with blue flowers and had been given to her by the charity, and filled them with cornflakes. Kerry was keen to get on with her plans. More than anything she wanted her children to be able to play outside in their own garden before the summer ended.

She opened the back door and stepped out onto the small concrete area where gaping cracks had filled with ground elder. Bordering this was dense and invasive vegetation. Kerry didn't let this dishearten her. Just being able to open her kitchen door and walk outside was a joy.

She was just turning to go back in when Tyler came running towards her. 'Can I go out and play football, Mummy?' He was really excited.

Kerry laughed, stroking his hair back from his face. 'It wouldn't be easy to play football out there now, would it, Tyler? You'd be ripped to pieces. Mummy's going to sort it out for you, though. You can help if you like.' She loved seeing his little face so full of excitement.

The morning didn't go as well as Kerry had planned. All she had to do the garden with was a garden fork, a spade, and a thin pair of gardening gloves which did nothing to prevent the sharp thorns stabbing her fingers. After a few hours she had managed to clear an area of a few feet but the ground was hard and dry and the roots wouldn't budge. Disheartened, she took a chair from the kitchen and sat down outside for a cup of tea. Confronted by the reality of the task in front of her, she felt quite deflated. Weedkiller was really expensive and she didn't have much money left in her account. It was going to take a lot longer than she had thought to achieve the garden she dreamed of.

Kerry revelled in the joy of ordinary things most people take for granted, such as being able to bath her children before bed, soak in the bath herself, and go to the loo without getting dressed and going downstairs. She had been given some tins of paint by the charity and decided she would make a start on the walls in the lounge. She had already arranged for someone to give her a quote for the laminate which would be paid for with her loan. It didn't matter if she made a mess with the paint as the carpets were going anyway.

Painting the ceiling was much harder than she'd imagined and when she finished, although it was only a small room, her back and shoulders were racked with pain. She decided to leave the walls for another day.

On Monday, Katy called to see her. Kerry had been sitting outside on the bit of concrete she had cleared, watching the children blow bubbles. She brought out another kitchen chair for Katy and the two of them sat in the sunshine.

Tyler, seeing Katy, immediately came over to her. 'Look at the big bubbles I can make. Look, watch!' He held the plastic circle to his mouth and slowly emitted air from his pursed lips. As his bubbles formed, he waved the wand up and down until he almost disappeared behind his creations. When he appeared again, his eyes were shining with pride as he waited for her praise.

'That's so clever, Tyler. How did you do that?'

'I'll show you.' He then went on to demonstrate his skills, assuring Katy that she could do it as well if she tried.

It wasn't long before Tyler was bored with the bubbles. 'I'm hungry.' He rubbed his tummy as he walked towards his mum. 'Is it lunchtime yet?'

'No, it's only eleven o'clock. I'll get you a drink of milk.' Kerry disappeared into the kitchen and returned with two drinks: a beaker for Tamara and a plastic cup for Tyler. 'There you are,' she said, handing it to him. 'Be careful not to spill it.'

Katy was impressed. She had not seen Kerry be so responsive to her children before. She seemed to have been taken over by a new spirit; the body was the same but the person inside was different. She couldn't get over Kerry's transformation, or that of her children, who looked lovely with their shiny skin, rosy cheeks and clean hair.

'You've got a lot of work to do here, Kerry. Have you got anyone who could help you?'

'No, not really, but I can manage. It's going to take some time but I'll get there.' Kerry shrugged her shoulders.

When Katy returned to the office she spotted April, who had seen her come in. She swept over to her. 'I've just been to see Kerry. You wouldn't believe the difference in her. You'd hardly recognise her or the kids. I've only ever seen Tyler sitting like a statue, staring at a phone, or looking down into his milkshake. I sometimes used to wonder if he could talk at all, to be honest.'

'That's really good to hear. Remember, though, it's still early days; you know, honeymoon period and all that. We hope it lasts but we need to keep on our guard.'

'Oh… I don't like to think it will go wrong now. I think you were absolutely right, April; what you said about the impact of inadequate housing on parenting. This is proof. What a difference it's made.'

'Let's hope so.'

Katy was a bit disappointed by April's negativity. She was the one, after all, who'd thought Kerry might do better in a proper home, but now she seemed to be questioning her own judgement.

41

FAMILY TIES

April left the office at five on the dot to collect Demelza. It was her last working day this week and she felt the familiar mixed emotions of pleasure to be going home and spending some free time with Demelza, but at the same time feeling on edge because she seemed to have a number of unfinished tasks. That was the nature of the job, though; there was always more one could do if only one had the time. She would have liked to have given more time to some of her other cases but Tamara, Tyler and Isobel seemed to be all-consuming at the moment. She also had Samantha Bushell on her mind a lot of the time, even though she had no responsibility for her. She hated the idea of her living on the streets. The streets were a dangerous place for any young woman, but Samantha was particularly vulnerable. If only she had come back to the office, April might have been able to help her.

The next day she took Demelza to have lunch with her father. As usual he made a fuss of Demelza before giving April an affectionate squeeze, then the three of them made their way through the house and into the back garden. Demelza was thrilled to be looking out to sea. Although it was sunny, there was a cool sea breeze and the roaring and crashing of the waves as they hit the rocks below made conversation difficult. They decided to go inside and sit in the conservatory, where they could still look at the sea but without the wind and the noise. Anthony tipped out a huge box of colouring pencils and paper onto the little glass coffee table and Demelza got stuck in, developing creations by holding the pencils in the palm of her hand and covering the paper with streaks of colour. Anthony had laid out nibbles of cheeses, olives and garlic bread. He had also put chunky vegetables and hummus on the table, which Demelza loved.

April didn't waste much time; as soon as it was reasonable to do so, she raised the burning issue. 'Mum told us that you and she are now talking.'

He wasn't a bit surprised by this comment. 'Yes, I know. She said you were pleased. I knew you would be, of course, but what about Max? What does he say about it?'

'I will tell you what I think. This is only my opinion but I *am* a social worker and I spend a lot of time analysing people. I think he is pleased, but he didn't say that. It's his pride; he would never admit that he struggles to come to terms with the fact that you left us. He's never said so because as you know we didn't speak about you, but I am quite sure he's thought about you a lot over the years. I think he will come round, though. I just think it will take a bit of time.'

Anthony made no response. He seemed to be waiting for April to explain further.

'He's always made out he didn't care but I know that's not true. I'm going to arrange a family get-together. It's Jed's fortieth birthday at the end of September so there's a good excuse. We can all be together. I thought we should have it before the children go back to school, though, so that Alistair and Elinor can be there. What do you think?'

'I think that would be wonderful, April. I'm lost for words. It's a brilliant idea. I do hope you're right about Max, and that he'll come.'

'Of course he will.'

As April sat having lunch with her father, Isobel was having her final contact session with her mum before her return home at the end of the following week. Norah collected her and took her to meet Alison. Norah had been meeting with Isobel over the past few months to try to encourage her to talk about the episodes when she'd gone missing, and impress upon her the risks she'd taken when she'd done so.

On Monday morning, Norah filled April in on how the contact had gone. 'It's lovely to see them together. They both seem different, happier, especially Isobel.'

'That's great. I hope it all works out.'

'Oh, I really hope it does; it would be so sad for Isobel if it didn't. Do you think it might not, then?'

'We can't be sure about anything, really, in this kind of situation. All we can do is hope for the best. We will have to keep a close eye on her for a while. It would be good if you could carry on meeting with her. Even if all goes well at home, we can't be certain she won't run off again to wherever it is she goes.'

Norah returned to her desk and April swivelled her chair back to face her computer. She had a report to read for Bradley Travers from the young offenders officer. Bradley had been found in a park in possession of a knife. Things weren't improving for him; in fact, they were going rapidly downhill. He had made his girlfriend, who was only sixteen, pregnant. She was a child in care herself, with multiple problems, and the baby was more than likely going to be removed from her care at birth. This would probably be another new case for April.

42

TURMOIL

Kerry was determined to somehow improve the garden before the end of the summer, even if only by clearing enough space to put out a garden table and chairs, and so that the children could play outside. It was a slow and laborious task, though, so she alternated it with painting. She wanted to make the children's bedroom nice for them. She told Tyler that when she had painted it he could choose his own bedding. 'Would you like Spider-Man or *PAW Patrol* on your bed, Tyler?'

'*PAW Patrol*,' was his answer, although by then he had gone back to playing games on her phone and wasn't really paying attention.

Kerry had phoned Dani earlier to invite her round, and she must have left her home immediately because within twenty minutes she was at the door.

'Needs a lot of work but it will be nice when you've done it up. It's a bit like mine but your kitchen's better. I'm supposed to be getting mine done soon; so they keep saying, anyway. You're not doing all the work on your own, are you?' She had invited herself in and was walking from room to room, appraising each one.

'I have to, don't I? Haven't got anyone to help and I can't afford to pay someone. That would cost a fortune.'

Dani looked out from the kitchen window over the back garden. 'Ooh, that's going to be a killer. You can't do that all on your own. I could see if my brother will help. Do you remember Ned? He had the hots for you once, didn't he?'

Kerry's eyes lit up. 'Do you think he would help? I can't pay him anything, though. I haven't got any money for that.'

'I'll ask him. 'We're going out on Friday; why don't you come? Marley's girl Shannon will look after the kids again. They were all right last time, weren't they?'

Kerry was tempted by the idea of another night out, but she wasn't really sure about Shannon. She didn't know her or her mum, who didn't seem to be there most of the time anyway.

'Tyler told me there were other people in the house when they stayed before. Do you think she would come over here?'

'Not sure, but I could ask her.'

The thought of a night out was gathering appeal. It would be like the start of a new life. Kerry had only managed to go out a couple of times since she had been in the hostel. It was as though her life had been on hold. It was different now. She was back where she knew people, and she could get babysitters. Whilst the two women sat on kitchen chairs in the garden, Dani texted Shannon.

It wasn't long before a message came back. Shannon said she could babysit and she would come to Kerry's, although Kerry would have to pay for a taxi to get her home because she didn't want to be walking the streets late at night on her own. Kerry thought about this. She could see Shannon's point, but a taxi would probably cost about fifteen pounds. A night out was more than she could really afford, but fifteen pounds on top of that was out of the question.

'I can't afford that. I won't have any money left for food if I spend all that.'

'Why don't you let the kids stay there, then? They'll be fine. I told you before, mine have stopped there when my mum couldn't have them.'

Kerry by now desperately wanted the night out. 'OK. I'll let them stay there, but I'll tell Shannon that I don't want her having other people around. I like to know who's around my kids. You've got to be careful, haven't you? There are some nasty buggers out there.'

'Fantastic. Everyone is coming to mine first. We can have a few drinks before we go, then; cheaper than buying them in the pub. We'll go clubbing again.'

Kerry felt a surge of excitement.

Alison woke up with a bit of a headache. She turned onto her side, thinking a bit more sleep would be nice, and was momentarily startled by the presence of another body beside hers, until her memories of the previous night came flooding back.

Just as she had been thinking about getting ready for bed, the doorbell had rung. She went down the stairs and was stunned to see Danny standing there, his right shoulder lowered by the weight of a shopping bag, which she could see was full of cans of lager.

'What do you want?' The surprise in her voice was mingled with panic.

'I wanted to see you. I thought you might like a few drinks and a chat.'

Alison was flustered. She was tired and had been looking forward to going to bed. 'You shouldn't be here, Danny. I've agreed I won't see you. I've signed something… it was in court.'

'Come off it, you're not worried about that, are you? Who's going to know? April What's-'er-Name isn't going to come visiting now, is she? I just want to see you. I've missed you.'

Alison looked at his sorrowful face. 'All right, you can come in, but you can't stay.'

'I'm really sorry about those photographs. I don't know what came over me. It seemed as though you loved her more than you loved me. I don't really love Tara, and you're right, she is a slag. I'm only with her because I didn't think you loved me anymore.' He had strolled into the lounge and sat himself down as though he had never been away.

Alison was trying hard to get her thoughts together. What he was saying was clear and she knew what her options were. More than anything, she wanted Isobel back. She wouldn't be able to cope with the guilt of letting her down again.

She lay in bed, trying to work out what she should do. She had been determined not to let him stay, but… However hard she tried, she couldn't decipher her feelings. Her mind was in turmoil. She didn't want him there; she wanted him out of her life. It would have been much better if he had never returned. But he *had* come back, and he was saying he loved her, that he couldn't live without her. There was a dependency on both sides; he was vulnerable and so was she.

By the time they had finished breakfast Alison was clear about what she needed to do. She had found an inner strength. She told him she was not prepared to let Isobel down. He pleaded with her but she meant it.

He eventually left the flat, but Danny knew Alison well. He had always been in control and he had no reason to believe this had changed. It was only a matter of time.

43

DEVASTATING DISCOVERY

That evening, after Demelza had gone to bed, April and Jed were sitting together in the lounge. April was chatting away about something which somehow led to the subject of Paula and how she seemed so different since she'd met Simon.

'I don't know whether it's my imagination but she's definitely changed. She always sounds keen to meet up but then seems to avoid actually arranging something.'

'I wouldn't read too much into it, April.'

'I knew you would say that. Well, I'm going to think about it. I might speak to Miles; see what he thinks.'

'Oh, Miles. Yes, Miles will know much better than me, your husband.'

'Don't be silly, Jed. It's just that Miles knows Paula a lot better than you do.'

'Of course.'

'I don't know what's got into you. You are so touchy these days.'

'You can talk.'

'OK, I'm not going to argue.' April couldn't understand why they seemed to have so many silly tiffs these days. They never used to before they had Demelza. 'I'm going to ring my brother.'

She walked out of the room, picked up the phone from the hall and carried it into the study. Joanna answered.

'Oh, hi, Joanna, it's April here.' She felt a bit peeved because she only wanted to talk to Max, but now she had to be polite and chat to Joanna first.

'Hello, April. Lovely to hear from you.' Joanna was always gushing, but disingenuous with it. 'Is everything all right?'

'Yes, thank you. I just wanted to tell you about the family get-together I'm planning for Jed's fortieth. I was thinking end of August might be a good time. It would be nice if Alastair and Elinor could come before they go back to school. What do you think?'

'I don't see why we wouldn't. That sounds like a lovely idea. I'll get Max for you.'

Max came to the phone. 'Hello, April. This is a surprise. I don't usually get a call from you in the week.'

'Well, you're not usually there, are you? That's why.' April repeated what she had told Joanna about the family get-together.

'When you say *family* get-together, who do you mean? Are you talking about just Mum and us?'

'Well, yes… but Dad is planning to come too.'

There was an uncomfortable silence.

'Max, there's no reason why Dad shouldn't come. Mum's happy about it so why shouldn't you be?'

'I'm not sure we're going to be able to make it, April. What date were you thinking?'

'I was thinking the last Saturday in August but we can be flexible if that's not OK for you. I wasn't sure when the children go back.'

'I think we will be busy that weekend. I will have to let you know.'

'Max, don't be silly. I can tell you're being silly. Can't you make an effort to forgive and forget? Everyone else has.'

'I will let you know, April. I'm not sure what we'll be doing.'

'Jed and I will be really disappointed if you don't come, Max, but I *am* going to invite Dad. I don't think he should continue to be punished for what happened in the past, but it's not just that. What about the children? He's their grandad. I'm not prepared to deprive Demelza of her grandad who loves her and, though you might find it hard to believe, loves us as well.'

'He hasn't made a good job of showing it over the years. I can't say I'm convinced.'

'Oh, don't be pathetic. Well, I'm going to organise the party for the last week in August and I'll send you an invitation. I really hope you come but it will go ahead anyway. It's a perfect way for our family to make amends.'

When she sat back down, she and Jed were back to normal, like best friends. The rift between April and Max united them.

'I can't believe he's being so childish. If I wasn't so sensible myself I'd think it runs in the family,' she half-joked.

'I've got a lot of faith in you, April. In all seriousness, you are the one who brought them this far. But do you know what I am most impressed with? It's the way you are able to forgive. That's one of your strengths. You even forgive me for being narky with you.'

She sat next to him on the settee and kissed his cheek before snuggling into him. 'And that hasn't been easy. As you know, I never get narky, but I can understand that others are, unlike me, less than perfect.'

The next morning April woke with a heavy heart. She couldn't believe how stubborn Max was when it came to their father. Clearly, he was cursed with that excess of pride which threatened to blight their lives. As always, her spirits were lifted by Demelza calling to her whilst vigorously rattling the bars of her cot.

'All right, darling, Mummy's on her way.'

She threw her legs over the side of the bed and went straight in to Demelza, who, still holding tightly to the top of the bars, flung her head back and gave a great big smile which said, *I knew you would come as soon as I called.*

April didn't have to rush this morning because she was visiting Alison first thing to make sure she was clear about the plans for

Isobel's return on Friday. She dropped Demelza at nursery and for once stayed a little bit longer so that she could watch her child joining in with the morning songs. She watched her little rosebud lips moving in sequence with the rest of the children, although her version didn't seem to be quite in line with the others'. Halfway through the song it became clear that Demelza had forgotten about April being there, so she sneaked off and made her way to Taylor's Yard.

Being just off the pedestrianised high street, it was never easy to find a parking space. She was beginning to become quite frustrated after driving around various car parks with no success. Her stress level started to rise as she thought about the wasted time. The weather was hot and clammy and her top was beginning to stick to her body. She finally managed to get the last space in a small car park in a backstreet, which meant she came to Taylor's Yard through the back way rather than via the high street. As she turned into the narrow lane, she could see the short distance to the high street at the other end. The lane was mostly made up of small shops, some with flats above. The street was quiet except for a young man striding towards her, oblivious to everything except the music coming from his earphones.

Looking ahead, she could see two people at the far end: a man and a woman on the pavement close to Alison's flat. She stopped and watched as the man gave the woman a lingering kiss before striding off and disappearing round the corner into the high street. She was now close enough to see, to her horror, that the couple were Alison and Danny, and to confirm it she managed to catch a fleeting glimpse of Alison before she went inside and shut her door.

April stopped on the spot and, pressing her knuckles hard against her cheeks, gasped, 'Oh my God' out loud.

A passing postman, carrying a parcel, turned around. 'You OK, love?'

Unable to answer, she just nodded. He continued on his way, turning back intermittently with a curious expression on his face.

April recovered enough to think about what to do. She decided she would walk around for a while because she didn't want Alison to guess she had been seen. After fifteen minutes of wandering around she rang the doorbell of 2A Taylor's Yard.

Alison's skin looked flushed, her hair was sticking up at various angles and she had black smudges under her eyes.

'Is everything all right, Alison? You look a bit flustered.'

'No, I'm fine. I got up a bit late; completely forgot you were coming, I did.' Her lips stretched wide in a feigned smile. 'Probably signs of early dementia,' she joked.

April tried hard to suppress her rage. Alison was lying to her; treating her like a fool. She had held out the unlikely hope that she would be open about Danny's presence, and that she had nothing to hide.

April listened and watched whilst Alison spoke animatedly about Isobel and how she couldn't wait to have her home.

'I've missed her a lot. I know she could be a cow sometimes but do you know what, I don't care. She could be lovely as well. Did I tell you about my birthday?'

'No, you didn't.'

'I came home from work and she'd cooked a meal.' Alison laughed. 'It was horrible, to be honest with you, but she had tried to make it nice. After the meal she ran me a bath with some candles. I love candles. She knows I love candles – wasn't that lovely?'

It was clear that nothing was going to be said about Danny, but April waited a bit longer, just to make absolutely sure. Alison continued with her incessant babble, which April believed was to cover up her guilt. Finally she asked, 'Have you seen Danny at all since he left?'

Alison was just stretching up to reach a teabag from a high cupboard. There was a clear hesitation before she carried on with her task. 'No, I told you. He's with someone else.'

'Then can you tell me, who was the man I saw leaving here earlier? He looked very much like Danny to me,' April asked with a very heavy heart.

Alison looked stricken. She turned back to the teabags and continued to pour boiling water, but April could see her hand trembling.

'I can't begin to tell you how disappointed I am, Alison. I was really hoping you would tell me he had been here; that he'd brought something for you, just dropped it off or something like that. A reason why he might have been here other than what is now clear.'

'No… I'm not back with him. Honestly, April, I'm not. He just came around to see me. He didn't stay the night or anything like that.' Alison spread her palms out in front of her in a plea to be believed.

'I wish I could believe you, Alison, but what I can't understand is, if that's the case, why didn't you say that? The agreement we made, and you signed, was that he would not come to the house and you would have no face-to-face contact with him. You've broken that already and Isobel isn't even home yet. On top of that, you lied to me. I hate to think of what I'm going to have to do now. I am going to have to tell Isobel she won't be coming home after all. I don't know what that will do to her.'

Alison's face puffed with rage. 'You can't,' she shouted. 'You can't do that to her just because I made one mistake!' Suddenly, she softened, seeming to think better of using aggression. 'I won't do it again. If she was home I wouldn't have let him in. I need her home with me.'

Her body slumped against the cupboard behind her. She covered her face with her hands and groaned. 'Oh my God, what have I done? I've let her down, haven't I? It was just a one-off,' she pleaded. 'He's still with his slag. I won't do it again, I promise.'

April left her sobbing. She was really angry with Alison, but also with herself. She had been taken in by her. She had believed her when she'd said her daughter came first. How stupid she had been. The dread in her heart weighed heavily upon her at the prospect of telling Isobel that she wouldn't be going home. There was now a huge possibility that she would never go home.

45

END OF HOPE

April needed to brace herself to visit Isobel and tell her what had happened. She planned to speak to Denise first to alert her to what was going on and check that she was willing to let Isobel stay, just in case she had made other plans.

She called in at the office first because she desperately needed to talk this through, and was relieved to see that Maria was on her own. She was on the phone when April walked into her office, but gestured to her to sit down opposite.

April's stomach churned violently as she explained the situation. 'I just feel so bad about it. I am questioning my judgement.'

'April, that's silly. You know you didn't have a choice in the matter. The guardian was in favour of her returning home so the court would have agreed with her, especially as it was what Isobel wanted. The counsellor was very positive and felt Alison was fully committed to her daughter. You would have struggled to argue against those opinions in court. She's not safe in foster care anyway, is she, running off every five minutes? You must stop feeling bad about it. You did your very best and it's not your fault her mother is such a good and convincing liar.'

'I'm dreading having to tell Isobel. It makes me cry when I think about everything she's been through, poor kid. I would like to know if Alison planned all along to take him back, thinking we wouldn't know about it. Maybe he never ran off with someone else at all.'

'It doesn't matter now. What matters now is how the kid can be helped to come to terms with it all. It's going to be hard, as we well know. She's gonna have to be a tough cookie to get over this. Maybe in the future it could work out for her. Perhaps her mum will eventually come to her senses, but we won't hold our breath for that one.'

As April started to leave the office, Maria caught her up.

'Don't forget, we're not God, we're not omnipotent – is that the word? You know, like the Pope. We work with some extremely tricky people sometimes but we do our best. You always do your best for the kids you work with and you're a great social worker. Don't forget that.'

April had tears in her eyes. 'Thank you, Maria. I will bear that in mind.'

She left the office feeling a bit better. When she arrived at the foster home, she found Isobel out in the garden with Harry, throwing a ball for Suzie.

Denise was waiting for her, knowing she wanted to speak to her first. 'We'll go into the lounge; Harry will keep Isobel occupied out there for now.'

She shut the door behind them and they both sat down, April on the edge of her seat.

'What is it, April? What's happened?'

'It's awful, Denise. Alison is seeing Danny again. I caught them together. She's denying there's anything in it but she's not being honest.'

Denise gasped and her hands flew to her face. 'Oh, no… that's terrible. Terrible. What happens now?'

'Well, she can't go home. The case is still in proceedings and we have another hearing soon which is supposed to be the final one. I will be asking for a Care Order so that she can stay in care, and I would expect the guardian will be of the same view when I tell her what happened. I don't know how Isobel is going to take it. I don't know what this means for her future. I dread to think.'

'She can stay here… if that's what she wants. She didn't like it here, I know, but she does seem to have settled in now. It'll be hard for her to move somewhere else now, won't it?'

'Thank you, Denise. I was hoping you would say that. I don't know what she will want in the future but it will be good to be able to tell her she's welcome to stay here if she wants to.'

April stood by the open patio doors, watching Isobel throw the ball and laugh as Suzie ran full pelt to fetch it, wagging her tail vigorously. She couldn't help wondering why life had been so unfair to Isobel. What had she done to deserve all this? She almost felt sick at the thought of having to shatter her all over again with this news. It wasn't long before Isobel stopped what she was doing and looked curiously at April, as though she had picked up on her thoughts.

'We need to have a chat, Isobel.'

The two were left alone in the conservatory whilst Denise and Harry sat in the lounge.

'I've got something to tell you. I'm afraid it is going to be upsetting.'

April watched as Isobel's face drained of colour.

'Something has happened. It's changed things.' April glanced out of the window, looking for inspiration; a way of saying what she had to say in the gentlest way possible.

Isobel's eyes searched her face. 'Is it Mum? She's changed her mind?' She almost choked.

'I'm really sorry to say this but… yes, Isobel, things have changed. Your mum has been seen with your dad. She didn't tell the truth. I can't let you go home to your mum when she can't be trusted.'

Isobel stared at her. 'I'm not staying here.'

'You don't have to stay here if you really don't want to. I could find another foster placement for you, but it's probably best to stay here for the time being, don't you think?'

Isobel made no response. She just stared at the floor.

'I would like you to carry on with your counselling, though. It won't be with your mum now but I think it would be good for you to carry on.'

'OK.'

April was pleased and relieved that Isobel seemed to have taken it so well. It probably hadn't sunk in properly yet and she was sure the storm would hit later, but at least there was no violent outburst or hysterical tears. She had been prepared for both.

After their talk, Isobel went straight up to her room and April walked to the door with Denise. She told her it hadn't gone as badly as she had expected but warned her to be on her guard. 'It was almost as though she was expecting it. She didn't appear shocked at all, which is a bit of a worry. I wasn't looking forward to being shouted or sworn at but in some ways it might have been better if she had.'

'I'll keep a close eye on her, April, don't worry.'

April decided to treat herself to a lovely coffee and a fruit scone at Bobbie's before going back to the office. She needed some time to herself to recover her composure before facing the rest of the day.

46

THE SUN COMES OUT

Kerry had managed to clear a huge section of the back garden; enough space for Tyler to ride his scooter in circles around the lumpy bit of ground. She watched him from the kitchen window with a smile on her face. Tamara was playing in the lounge with a few bits from a plastic tea set Kerry had bought her for Christmas. She couldn't remember the last time she had felt so excited about everything. She had forgotten how it felt to be happy. She now had everything: her own place, her children, friends, *and* she was going out clubbing later.

Katy was due to call in again. Kerry seemed to be getting a lot of visits from social workers lately, which wasn't really appreciated. She didn't like the idea of being watched so closely. It put her on edge. It was almost five o'clock when Katy finally arrived, which was really annoying because Kerry had to get the kids ready and give them their tea before going to Shannon's.

Katy had a look around the flat before walking out into the back garden. 'You've done really well, Kerry. Perhaps you could get someone to dig it over for you before next summer, then put some grass seed down. It could look really nice.'

'Yes, that's what I'm planning to do,' Kerry replied, irritated by the perceived bossiness.

Tyler was throwing a little ball in the air and trying unsuccessfully to catch it. Katy noticed how poor his hand-eye coordination was; clear evidence of his former lack of opportunity to play.

'Hello, Tyler. Are you enjoying having a garden to play in?'

'Good, yeah. I can play on my scooter; watch me.' He ran over to his scooter, which was leaning against the wall, put one foot on it and scooted in a circle around the little space that Kerry had cleared.

'That's brilliant. And your mummy might let you eat your tea out here sometimes.'

'Not today. We've got to go to Shannon's,' he said solemnly.

Katy didn't know who Shannon was but asked, 'Don't you like going to Shannon's?'

'No. I want to stay here. I don't like staying at Shannon's house.'

Kerry had just walked out of the door as he said this, and her heart sank.

'Who is Shannon, Kerry?'

'She's a friend. She looks after the kids sometimes,' she mumbled into her chest.

Katy wanted to know how old Shannon was, how long Kerry had known her, who else would be there. She wasn't convinced by the answers she was given. 'I'm worried about this. I don't get the impression you really know her well enough to be leaving your kids with her.'

Kerry was really getting fed up with Katy now. 'I wouldn't leave them with someone I don't trust. I'm really annoyed that you would accuse me of not caring about who I leave my kids with.'

When Katy left, she gave Kerry a warning. 'You've been doing really well, Kerry. It's been lovely seeing the change in you and the kids since you moved here. Don't spoil it by doing anything stupid.'

Kerry remained on edge after Katy had left. She was annoyed with Tyler for telling her about Shannon, but deep down she couldn't deny that Katy was right. The terror she had experienced when she'd thought her children were going to be taken from her came flooding back and hit her like a tidal wave. She had noticed that Tyler's mood had changed since the mention of Shannon, and although she had been trying to shut this out of her mind, she had been perturbed by it. She looked at Tamara, who was feeding her dolly with a plastic teaspoon and pretend food, her mop of curls in disarray around her head and her cheeks aglow with all the fresh air. She was muttering to her dolly.

Suddenly it was as though Kerry was seeing her children for the first time. The dark fog which had engulfed her for so long had lifted. She could see the light at the end of the tunnel, and her precious children were in it. *I can't do it*, she thought. *I can't risk losing them. The social workers will know.* She picked up the phone. 'Dani, I've changed my mind. I'm not going out. I don't want to leave the kids. I haven't really been happy about leaving them with Shannon. Sorry to let you down.'

'What's wrong, Kerry? I don't get it. What's wrong with Shannon? Are you never going out again, then? You're just gonna sit at home on your own every night?'

'If I have to, yes. I want to be a good mother. I want the best for my kids. You don't know what it's like when you nearly lose them like I did.'

'OK, see you about, then.' Dani clearly wasn't happy.

Kerry picked up Tamara and cuddled her tightly, thinking about how close she had come to losing them both. She had been thinking quite a lot about what had happened. How she had neglected them, especially the night she had left them on their own. The guilt continued to gnaw away at her. She realised how much she had been wrapped up in her own misery. The kids had been pushed to the back of her thoughts.

'We won't go to Shannon's, then, Tyler, if you don't want to. Mummy will stay here to look after you. Will that be better?'

Tyler walked towards his mum, who hugged him tightly.

'We can play a game if you like, when Tamara is in bed. Shall we play snakes and ladders?'

Kerry felt really pleased with herself. She had completely forgotten the joy that children can bring.

47

SADNESS AND JOY

April was preparing the house for Jed's fortieth birthday party: flags, streamers, plenty of wine and food, as well as a birthday cake which was an exact replica of a pint of Guinness; Jed's favourite tipple. It was really disappointing that she hadn't heard from Max, but she was determined that it wasn't going to spoil the day. Diana was already there, busily assembling various plates of salad. Jed's parents, David and Sally, were due to arrive any time. His brother Richard was abroad. Although he was a medical doctor he seemed more interested in saving wildlife than people. He was tracking penguins in Georgia; another of his escapades which was partly funded by his doting parents.

Just after 3pm, Anthony arrived. April showed him into her house for the first time. It felt strange, and even stranger when he hugged and kissed Diana, who had come to the door behind April. Jed and Anthony shook hands. There was an awkwardness in Anthony's demeanour, but Jed, with his warm and self-assured nature was able to put him at his ease.

'Welcome to our house, Anthony. It's a real pleasure. I never thought this day would come.' He patted his shoulder as he walked in the door.

'I just can't tell you how nice it is to be here, Jed, and to meet you at last.' The two men had spoken on the phone but had never actually met.

They all sat outside in the sunshine.

'I can honestly say this is the best birthday present I could have wished for,' Jed declared. 'It means I won't have April banging on about you two all the time.'

Everybody laughed.

David and Sally turned up earlier than expected. They had brought a bottle of champagne, which Jed took from them and put in the fridge for later. Demelza was made a big fuss of and obviously there were more presents for her than there were for Jed.

They whiled away the time, talking and nibbling away at the various dishes, until early evening when the sun started to spread itself across the horizon in a golden blaze. April decided it was time to fetch the birthday cake from the kitchen. She couldn't help noticing that her parents had sat together for the whole afternoon, and were now chatting as though they were the only people present. She had tried to ignore the irritating girly giggle she'd heard a few times from her mum.

She was just about to strike a match to light the candles when the side gate burst open and in walked Max, followed by Alistair, Elinor and Joanna. April froze like a statue with her hands in the air, speechless.

'You came!' Diana exclaimed.

'He wanted to come,' Joanna said. 'All the time he wanted to come. It was just stupid pride. I told him if he wasn't coming I was going to anyway. I want my kids to know their grandad, and it's what they want too.'

April's estimation of her sister-in-law shot up. She was overwhelmed with emotion. She turned around and saw her father stand up. He was walking slowly towards Max, and she could see tears welling up in his eyes. As if in slow motion, she watched the metamorphosis of her family. The past fell away like old leaves from a tree, pushed out by the splendid glory of the new. There followed a whirl of hugging, smiling, and crying from Diana, until, exhausted by the emotion, they all flopped back into their chairs.

Anthony spoke first. 'There are no words that can say how much this means to me and how sorry I am that we have wasted all those precious years. Your mum and I have talked and talked and you will never know how much we both regret the stupidity of it all. We've been so ridiculously stupid; ridiculous.' He slapped the arm of his chair.

There was silence whilst they all tried to take in what had happened, but this was broken by a sudden gust of wind whistling across the table, scattering serviettes about the patio.

'I think we will need to go inside soon but I just want to finish,' Anthony continued. 'I know I can't make up for the lost years. I just hope we can make the most of the years to come; the years we will have together. Your mum and I will be seeing a lot more of each other from now on and we are hoping for lots more happy family occasions to make up a little bit for the time we lost.'

April couldn't explain why but she started clapping. Jed followed suit, and then they were all clapping. The champagne was brought out and shared and there was a toast to Jed's fortieth, which for a while had been quite forgotten.

On Monday morning April had a message from Out of Hours. It was horrible news. Isobel had been taken to hospital in the night and was in a coma. As soon as she could, she left the office in her haste to get to Denise, who was waiting at the door.

'What happened?' April asked as she hurried up the garden path.

'It was awful, April.' Denise was still visibly shaken. 'Come in and I'll put you in the picture.'

Once they were indoors, Denise sighed heavily. 'I went to her room at about ten to wake her up. She seemed to be sleeping soundly but I couldn't rouse her. At first I was annoyed, thinking she was just ignoring me, but then I realised something wasn't right. I'd tried everything. Then I knew: she wasn't asleep; she was unconscious. I called an ambulance. They asked me if there was any sign that she had taken pills. I said no, but then I went back into her room and pulled her duvet down, and there was an empty packet of paracetamol. And then I saw the blood. Oh, April, it was everywhere. She'd cut one of her wrists.'

April was devastated. For a moment she felt intense anger towards Alison. This was her fault. She had to check herself, though, because there were many forces involved in this. It was just that Alison was the only person who'd had the power to help her daughter, and she had chosen not to.

April was just about to leave when Denise took hold of her arm. 'There was one more thing. I'm sorry; I nearly forgot. I found a mobile under her bed. It needed charging but there were messages on there. I think you should see them.'

Every message April could see was from or to Damian, and they were sinister and alarming, confirming all of her worst fears. Her blood ran cold. This was the darkest side of social work, and if Isobel survived it would be April's job to find some way of helping her to manage her trauma and make the best of her life. It was heart-breaking to think about the long, rocky road to recovery, and April was only able to envisage a dreadfully bleak future for Isobel.

ABOUT THE AUTHOR

Teresa was brought up in a mining village and was the fourth of six children. She loved school and had great fun, but didn't take life very seriously until she decided she wanted to be a social worker. She returned to education after having her two children, acquired a degree in Social Policy at the University of Kent and qualified as a social worker two years later. She is a full member of the Health and Social Care Council and holds the advanced diploma in social work. Teresa worked in child protection for 11 years before becoming a manager. Her first novel, Broken Lives has been of interest to colleges and universities and she regularly gives presentations to social work students discussing the cases in the novel.

Teresa is an active campaigner for social justice and equality of opportunities. She uses every opportunity to advocate for fairness in society and speaks out against discrimination of any kind. She has seen for herself the hardship, deprivation and lifelong battles caused by disadvantage and poverty and this is starkly evident in her writing.